half-burnt

Peter Grandbois

SPUYTEN DUYVIL

NEW YORK CITY

Library of Congress Cataloging-in-Publication Data

Names: Grandbois, Peter, author.
Title: Half-burnt / Peter Grandbois.
Description: New York City : Spuyten Duyvil, [2019]
Identifiers: LCCN 2018053142 | ISBN 9781949966039
Subjects: LCSH: Hole-in-the-Day, Chief, 1828-1868--Fiction. | Ojibwa
    Indians--Fiction. | GSAFD: Biographical fiction.
Classification: LCC PS3607.R3626 H35 2019 | DDC 813/.6--dc23
LC record available at https://lccn.loc.gov/2018053142

Peter Grandbois writes with uncommon beauty and marvelous care about the deepest complexities of history and heart. *Half-Burnt* is filled with love and truth and pain and rage and endurance and desire. It's about false endings and true beginnings and all the jagged mysteries that attend the human journey. I'm so glad I read it.

LAIRD HUNT,

AUTHOR OF *IN THE HOUSE IN THE DARK OF THE WOODS*

This is a novel where fiction, myth, and historical reality intertwine with ponderous lyrical force. Told as a lucid dream, the story cycles from one mouth to another, from the dead to the living, unraveling like a river and piercing like an arrow. Peter Grandbois creates a splendid sense of otherworldliness echoing Rulfo's *Pedro Páramo*. We face vengeance, desire, possessing spirits, and the question of belonging to a primordial earth, a story as ancient and vivid as the touch of man. And at the end of the novel, we can do nothing but marvel at the brilliant feat and thank Grandbois for his courage.

JORGE ARMENTEROS,

AUTHOR OF *THE ROAR OF THE RIVER*

For Every Member of my tribe no matter how they spell their name: Grandbois, Grumbo, Granbois, Grumbeau, Grumbois, Grambo, Grombo. . .

To be outside the narrative is not to exist.
Paul Chaat Smith

. . . I wonder which of the 365 gods
are inside the body today
and if in the future
when the air leaves your lungs,
and, as some say, you stand at the beginning
of a tunnel,
you remember your name.
No, not that one, the real one,
The Given, the one
lost somewhere
along the way.
Linda Hogan

Dear Bishop Whipple,

We are overwhelmed with grief at the news of Chief Isaac H. Tuttle's sickness. I knew him when he was the head soldier of the celebrated Chief Hole in the Day. He was then one of the bravest warriors in the Indian country. For long years, he stood aloof from the religion of Christ, but at last the power of the Holy Spirit has brought him to us. And we should heed that call.

And so with your blessing, I would like to go to White Earth to hear his confession, to ease his passage into the next world. I know that you understand, that you harbor a deep interest for your red brothers, most important-ly for their everlasting souls. Please then tell the others what I'm going to do. Tell them that an Indian can love Jesus with all his heart. Tell them an Indian can be hap-py. I believe that. I have to believe that.

I go now to meet my old friend, to open my eyes to the darkness of the past, to the memories that grow larg-er with each passing year until they cloud my way. It is long past time for me to understand my part. If that part should be revealed, please remember me as I am now. And remember to forgive my trespasses.

Your servant in Christ,
Paul Paulson
Faribault, MN
January 10, 1874

I try to sing, brother, but can't find the words. My language of Anishinaabemowin is gone. My English words have fled, and I am left only with the shadow world, which I have come to learn is the truer one, anyway.

We smell that world in the steam rising from the hearts of bucks as they lie butchered in the snow. We smell it in the taut faces of does as they catch our scent on the crisp bite of air. And we smell it in the fear of the babies half-buried and unable to move in the frozen waste. Run with me, brother, over the hoary surface of the world. Let us hunt through the thick night until the birds mock us.

Then, let us rest.

I wake to your fetid breath upon my face, and I know you as Boy, as Gwiiwizens, neither English nor Ojibwe name conveying your spirit to me. How write a name with white man's letters?

The cry of the great gray owl through the dark wood. *Do not travel alone across the frozen lake, brother! Piichoo Manidoo waits for you there.* But you rush away. No time for my words. There is more hunting, always more hunting.

I don't need to follow to know what happens next. My mind's eye shows the great buck out on the ice, and I know it is Piichoo in another form. I cry out, but you are too far away.

I lie myself down, remembering your face as it passes from this world.

The moon grows full and wanes before I rise. Black turns to blue and blue to white and back again, until I see the river. The Kingfisher, Ogiishkimanisii, waits for me there.

The ground opens before me, a dark hole by the edge of the lake. I hesitate, until Ogiishkimanisii rests on the lip of the cave, his long, sharp bill pointing the way. I descend into the black.

Your skin stretches across the center of this womb world. Ogiishkimanisii alights on your hide, and I know what I must do.

I take your skin down from the hooks and run back through the darkness, not knowing if I'm headed in the right direction. I'm a spider in a web. Every path the same.

I emerge into a light greater than a thousand suns and look to the earth to shield my eyes. Why did I not notice your bones when I went in, brother? Were they lying there all along? I bundle them in your skin and flee.

Alone in the woods, with only Ogiishkimanisii watching from a nearby birch, I spread the bones upon your skin, lay them out in your shape. I take a deep breath and bend over them, bring my mouth close until I'm almost kissing them and release the warm air from my lungs. I do it again and again, breathing my life into those bones, wanting to crawl back myself into your shadow body. But I am only a wissakode, a half-burnt person. How can I raise the dead? I rise and curse Ogiishkimanisii for making me think I can do such a thing. I tear off my leggings, my moccasins, my shirt.

The bird flies off.

I am in human form again.

I collapse upon the ground.

At first I think it's another dream. The touch of your smooth tongue licking my naked body. I open my eyes, and there you are, your muzzle inches from my face, returning my breath to me.

I am ready.

The story I'm going to tell is not of this earth. You might think it is. At times, it might even look as if it is, but the surface of this story is a mere haunting, a shadow upon the surface of a deeper shadow. And now you must crawl in, too. Cover yourself with a new skin, my brother.

DAY ONE

I rise in the rimed air and dress in the vestments of my church, my cassock and surplice. Purple stole over my left shoulder. A black rope cincture around the waist. A priest three years now and deacon ten years before that, since the death of your four-year-old son, John. Do you remember? You told me you no longer had faith in the Mide, that you wanted to become a Christian, but you didn't dare. I took on the mantle you could not possibly have worn. I wore my cassock often beneath my blanket, then. Hid my crucifix beneath the shell that hung from my neck. Held it only when necessary. What force but my prayers do you think intervened when Commissioner Dole gave the command to shoot you?

If you were to see me now, you would not recognize me. My hair nearly gone, my face washed clean. The burnt part of me hidden. Sometimes I become "Chippewa." A check-mark in the BIA agent's census list. Not quite white. Yes, I have changed, but the reservation remains the same.

I step into the morning air, greeted by a hound's howl in the distance. The great gray owl stares down with golden eyes from a pine. Why has it strayed from the lake and not gone home to sleep?

The dank smell of rotten catfish.

The sun licks the horizon, bringing little warmth.

Cabin after wood cabin. Icicles drip down from roofs, forming a layer of ice over the crusted snow. Blankets hang from rooftops, covering windows, doors. Dogs, all ribs and broken tails, wait for scraps in entryways. Smoke curls from stone chimneys.

Everywhere, silence.

The sawmill and gristmill boarded up. Coonskins nailed to dry on walls.

Here and there a young face peering from the darkness of a doorway. An old couple standing stiff against the side of the house. A man planted in the middle of the road, wrapped in a walnut colored blanket.

Father told me about the passing of the first world. How the great wiindigoo turned the people into trees. They are still with us, I think. That's why the owl is here. Where are the other ghosts? I ask. In answer, he spreads his wings and returns to the lake.

Beaulieu stands on the front step of his two-story house, not as nice as his home in Crow Wing, but still the finest on the reservation. And where is his wife, Elizabeth? Visiting her sister in St. Paul? Or, perhaps she's left him for good this time. A black wool hat covers his fiery red hair, his white-flecked beard hiding his crooked face. Twitching hands stuffed deep in his pockets. Let's hope there is time for both of us, old man. I nod to him, but his drizzly eyes stare out at the lake. I turn my attention to the rites as they have been taught to me. Never have I performed a confession like this.

I call to Chief Tuttle through the red blanket that hangs over the door of his sod hut—the only such structure left standing on the reservation. No answer. I call again, this time whispering his Ojibwe name. It sounds strange upon my lips. I part the blanket, releasing the not unpleasant fragrance of senega root and wood cree.

"Tell my sons, my daughters who have gone before, that I will meet them soon," the old war chief says to his wife. He lies atop a buckskin robe spread upon the ground, covered by government-issue blankets to keep away the chill. A shade now of the warrior he once was. You would not recognize him, brother.

Two steel frame beds sit unused in the back. The sheets folded perfectly, a layer of dust coating the surface. No other furniture inside. Only a fire pit and cooking pot set with herbs boiling.

"Tell them yourself," his wife, Newobiik, replies, kneeling beside him. "If you are so eager to go."

He smiles, nodding his head, showing his broken, yellowed teeth. I had not seen him smile that way for nearly a quarter of a century, not since the time he returned with you, brother, from the raid of Fountain Cave, when you punished the Sioux for their massacre on Apple River.

"Does this little thing of cutting your hair trouble you?" Newobiik teases. "Is that why you wish to leave this world? So no one can see you?" She pinches his hand, holds it in her lap. "It was necessary if you truly want to become a Christian." Though she is old, her figure retains a girl's shape.

"Yes, old woman," he says. "I know. But all my bravery has left me." And with that he begins to weep.

There is nothing quite so pathetic as an old man crying.

"I miss my hair," he says between sobs. "Perhaps I will find it again on the path to the afterworld."

It is then I step forward, kneel beside Newobiik and place

9

a picture of our Lord on his chest. "You will want for nothing once you accept Christ in your life," I tell him.

Newobiik rises and retreats to the fire pit in the back. She seems to care little for my arrival. "The Mashkiigobag is ready," she tells her husband.

"Without my hair, how can I defeat the great snake who blocks the path?" he asks, his dark eyes wide like a child's.

"Not even the devil's own serpent would dare block the road to Christ," I tell him, and only then does he notice me.

"I did not see you come in," he says. "You look strange. Different from the last time, the burnt parts blurred in this wavering light."

He shifts his gaze, trying to get a fix on me. I sit upon the cold ground and wait, the Mide shell heavy about my neck. I draw it forth and set it on the blanket next to the old chief, then place the vial of blessed water beside it and pause, my hands together in prayer. I do not know what name to call him by. I have called him by the other for so long. "Isaac Tuttle," I say at last, my tongue tripping over the harsh sounds. "Dost thou renounce the devil and all his works, the vain pomp and glory of this world?"

He opens his mouth, but the words are slow in coming. "I do," he says at last.

"Dost thou believe all the articles of the Christian . . ."

"I do," he interrupts, as if now that he has started, he cannot stop the words.

And to each of my questions, he answers loud and distinct, "I do."

"You are a strange old man," Newobiik says from the darkness. "Talking that way."

It's then I take up the vial and pour the blessed water

into the shell. My only concession. I drip the water upon his forehead, slowly.

"I love Jesus, and Jesus loves me," he says. "No pain and no death can separate me from the love of my lord Jesus Christ."

"Amen."

The red blanket over the doorway sways in the chill breeze. A glimpse of gray wing beyond.

Newobiik returns to her husband's side, feeding him from her medicinal cup.

"It has begun," the great warrior says.

"I worry about you," she replies, placing a hand on his brow to check for fever. "I will go to my sister's to make you a curing broth, baaka'aakwenhwaaboo. You must sleep until the priest comes."

I wish she would shut up and leave. I know what I am. I do not need to be reminded of it. Tuttle glances at me then back at his wife. He says nothing to give me away. And then I am alone with the man who became your worst enemy, my brother.

"Help me to sit," he asks, and I take his hand. His grip is feeble, and this surprises me, though I don't know why. He is twenty-four years my senior.

"Don't tell my wife, but I feel like a man firing his gun into a flock of pheasants, hoping to hit something," he says when I sit facing him. I am happy to see he has kept his sense of humor.

"It's worth a try," is all I say.

"Yes," he says. "I have no stomach for the Mide anymore,"

The red blanket shifts. Feathers flutter in the distance.

"You sound like him," I say.

He says nothing. There are no words for the place we are now.

"Ase-anse, have you forgotten your Anishinabe name, or do you wear it under your cassock as you do your Mide shell?" *He reaches for the cup of tea Newobiik left him, but it's too far away. I do not move it closer.*

"I'm a half-breed," *I tell him.* "A wissakodewinini, a half-burnt person. A Métis. But you know this. No name fits me."

"Yes, I know this."

"When I live in the white man's world, I am Paul Paulson."

"Yes."

"And when I live in the Anishinabe world, I am Ase-anse, Little Shell, as you call me now. But what name am I to take in this world in which I walk, this world that lies between? This is the question that disturbs me most."

"I cannot answer that for you," *he says.* "Here in my home you must call me Niibiniishkang."

"He Who Treads the Earth in Summer." *The name has always suited you. Until now," I reply.* "Your body bound to this cold earth."

We speak no more. Then, slowly, he begins to weep.

I want to hit him, brother.

"You need some of Newobiik's tea," *he says, finally.* "Pour me more as well."

I rise to make my own cup. The pungent aroma clears my head. "I'm sorry for the way things have turned out."

"It no longer matters," *he replies.* "What matters is the name you carry with you. You cannot pass into the next life without it."

"I do not remember that name." *I sit and sip my tea.*

"I knew your father and mother," he says, his face a cipher.

"How can that be?" It is as if my breath has left me. "You lived in the north."

"I came to trade with your father one spring after a winter that left my people starving." Memories like shadows creep about his eyes. "He did business with Strong Ground at Sandy Lake and was known for giving a good price. He was one of the few voyageurs we trusted."

"And my mother?"

"I saw her many times." He closes his eyes. "She worked in the garden behind the trading post." He smiles. "Bi-idaaban, Coming Dawn, her name fit her well."

"Why didn't you tell me this before?"

"You lived a different life then. Had a different father, and I did not see the point in reminding you of other lives, other fathers."

"What else? What else do you remember?"

"Only what I heard."

"They were killed by the Sioux. That's all I was told."

"Not all," he replies. "The Sioux came with their white flag. And when old Bookowaabide came out to greet them, they shot him dead. They marched on the village. Your father ran to warn them of the trick and was shot in the back. Over a hundred of our people died that day."

"My mother, too."

"Yes."

"I can't remember either of them." I set my tea upon the ground. "I can't even remember a time when I could."

"Do you remember your father's name?"

"Hole in the Day, Bagone-giizhig, raised me," I say. "He

13

was my father. He took me in as one of his own."

"Yes. As one of his own." His eyes and mouth shut, as if he will say no more.

I dump my tea, and the frozen earth hisses.

Niibiniishkang lowers his head.

"Sleep well, old man," I tell him.

"And what of your own name?"

"What?" I say, though I am unsure where the voice comes from.

The shadow of my name echoes about me. I claw at dirt. Pull at roots but cannot escape. I climb the sides of my grave only to find the great, gray owl hovering over the hole, its crooked wing jailing me.

Strong Ground and the rest ride before me. Though I keep to the back with those on foot, my eight-year-old legs struggle to keep up. The women make sure I am fed, that I have a blanket to keep me warm at night. I take turns sleeping with a different family each night, and each night I cry out for my mother, my father.

Once we make camp, I am given work. They count the remaining members of Strong Ground's clan and shake their heads. There is much grieving. Women wailing from within their wigwams. Men squatting on the ground, tearing at their hair when they think no one is looking. I spend my mornings playing with the dogs. Then one day a boy appears. He stands in the distance and laughs whenever I act like an animal. I prance on all fours. I hop like a frog. Soon we are playing together, and though he is four years younger I do what he says. During the day, I rarely think of my parents.

A man watches from the distance. Shorter than many of the other men in the village and dressed plainly. Even so, as he walks through the camp, the others nod to him. Strong Ground often meets with him. Each afternoon, this man watches his boy playing with me. Each night, I go to sleep with a different family. One morning, the boy does not show up. Instead, it is the man who comes. He stares at me for a long time, his face so pained I think it will break, though I don't understand why and fear he is angry with me. When he gestures for me to come, I run away. The next day he returns. When I see him standing before me, I find I cannot move. The thought comes all at once. Like me, he grieves but does not know how to let it out. The next time he comes for me, I stay. His wives wash me. They feed me. At night I sleep beside the boy, giggling together until one of the wives silences us. Only then do I think about my parents, but already I cannot see their faces. I wake the next morning and am no longer. I am now the adopted son of the great, war chief Hole in the Day, and the people speak of how he will make the Sioux pay for their treachery.

The voice returns to me, whispering my name through the dank earth. At least I think it's my name. My real name.

"Keep it safe from both worlds."

But how can I when the words fade even as I wake to the dim light of the sod hut? My head lies in Niibiniishkang's lap, his hand stroking what remains of my hair as a woman might do. I sit up and search his face, but the deep lines betray no hint of what has passed.

"Why did you want to talk with me?" I ask, my own

voice sounds strange to me. "Why did you want me to stay?"

His hand rests on my forehead. "I want to know before I die," he replies.

"What do you want to know?" I try to sit, but his hand presses more firmly against my brow.

"Everything," he says.

The red curtain flutters in the icy breeze.

"I don't understand." Would anyone hear me if I cried out?

"I want to know why you sought the solace of the chimoo-komaan religion," he says. "I want to know why our chief failed us. I want to know who killed him. I want to know what happened to our people."

"There are those who say you killed him." I grab hold of his wrist, ready to fight.

"You didn't come to hear my confession," he says. His free hand moves to my mouth, his finger tracing the outline of my lips, calling forth the words.

"You lie! Why else would I come if not for the glory of being the confessor of Hole in the Day's war chief?"

"Perhaps you came for a confession, only it is not mine." He removes his finger from my lips.

"You know nothing of who I am or what I want." I struggle to break free, but it is as if I am bound to him.

"I know that you are here when you should not be." His words are like a poison I can't get out.

"Set me free, and I will tell you what I know."

"You will buy your freedom with a story, one that explains everything."

To struggle is useless. So I remain until my own words rise out of me, spilling from my lips onto the cold earth.

Night. The gray owl perches above, calling to me. The full moon silvers the lake. A chorus of frogs croak a feverish dream.

The little girl with eyes like agates waits for me inside the tepee. I dare not go to her. But it doesn't matter. She is there in her blood-stained smock. Screams sounding through the slit in her neck. The branches that were her hands holding her ears until her head drops away. It begins.

X was proud to ride in the hunting party with his adoptive father, Hole in the Day and Strong Ground, his uncle. He'd been out before on shorter trips with others in his clan but nothing like this, riding side by side with his brother on his first trip as a man, though at eleven winters his brother could hardly be called a man. They'd followed game along the Crow Wing River, stopping along its shores at the edge of Wah'peton territory. As the others prepared their camp, Hole in the Day stayed atop his horse, searching the woods, his war club held tight to his chest. They left him alone as they ate their dinner, the distant hammering of the woodpecker the only sound against the growing dark.

Morning came, soggy and gray. Flies beat against X's face. He opened his eyes. The forest swelled like a toad. He hit his brother, pulled him to the river. They raced through clumps of muddy snow.

"I dreamed last night I was a green heron," his brother said, arching his neck and imitating the heron before slipping on a rock and falling in the icy water. When he emerged laughing like a girl, X kicked his foot out from under him. His brother leapt from the water, hitting X in the chest with a handful of mud scooped from the river's bottom. They fell to the shore wrestling until a loud bellow startled them. It sounded like a dog with a bad cold, and it was close.

Strong Ground stood over them, a bear cub in each arm. He set the cubs down, but they didn't move. Neither did the boys, until X reached out. After sniffing, then licking his hand, the cubs waddled forward. A couple nuzzles and paws later, the boys and cubs were wrestling.

Hole in the Day stood atop the ridge backing their camp, a deer from the morning's hunt slung over his broad shoulders. He called to X to help him prepare the animal. Strong Ground went about his own business, leaving X's younger brother alone with the cubs.

X knew how to skin a deer; he'd seen it done many times. He took the knife from his belt and plunged it in at the pelvis, cutting around the anus and removing the connecting tissue. Then another long incision up the belly, careful not to cut into the intestines and spoil the meat. His father sat on a nearby stump, his eyes panning the woods beyond. He should be watching me, X thought. It's supposed to be my time. But Hole in the Day had changed since leaving home. His face turning harder with each passing day. The knife sliced too quickly, cutting through the neck and into his own leggings. The pain was sharp like a wasp. The blood took a moment to follow.

"Where are you?" his father asked.

X dropped the knife, pulled the leather away from the

wound. Not bad. It had only penetrated the surface. He scraped moss off a nearby oak and pressed it to his leg. "I was going to ask the same of you," X replied.

Hole in the Day turned to his adopted son. "You will prove a good hunter, if we can teach you to use your knife on something other than yourself." His smile duller than a crow's head.

"I have a hunter's eyes, too," X replied. "Sharp enough to see you haven't been yourself since we left on this trip."

Hole in the Day pulled out his knife, the one his father had given him. A knife that had scalped many Sioux. He ran his thumb along the blade. "We are doomed to see ourselves through the eyes of our children."

"What do I see?" X liked these moments when his father confided in him.

"Death weighs upon me."

X wiped his hands in a patch of snow that still hid in the shade of a rock, the deer's blood pooling in the dirt beside him. "Do you speak of your nephew and cousins killed in the Sioux raid three moons ago?"

"Yes," Hole in the Day replied. "And more." He threw the knife into a nearby birch. "A father never forgets," he said at last, walking to the birch, pulling out his knife, and disappearing into the woods.

X returned to his work, cutting away at the innards, scraping the hide as the day warmed him, until a scream sounded from the river. His brother. He ran toward it, passing Strong Ground on the way. His brother sat high up an oak, the bear cubs clawing and bellowing at its base.

"You are nothing but a boy," Strong Ground said, bursting into laughter.

"They turned on me," X's brother shouted. "You would have climbed the tree yourself!"

"Yes," Strong Ground replied. "So that I could rain down acorns on them from above! You think like a boy, not a warrior!" Strong Ground took the cubs and returned to camp as Hole in the Day appeared atop the rise, his war club in hand. He took one look at his son in the tree and turned away.

X sat at the base of the oak, listening to his brother's gentle sobs, waiting for him to calm down. By noon he'd stopped crying, and he was able to talk his brother from the tree. They broke camp that afternoon. In the evening, the Wah'petonwan met them where the Crow Wing splits and the prairie grows long.

The Sioux appeared happy to see them as their supplies were low and their men away hunting. While Strong Ground negotiated the trade of tobacco, powder, and sugar with the few old Wah'peton men who remained to guard the women and children, Hole in the Day stood back, a dark cloud passing over his face. Only when they offered *biindigodaadiwin* did the cloud pass. They would stay the night and smoke.

X and his brother sat squeezed between the few elder Wah'peton men and their father and uncles. No one spoke. They passed the pipe first to Hole in the Day, but instead of lighting it, he set it at his feet. His face stone. The Wah'petonwan looked to each other, fearing their hospitality was lost, until Strong Ground told the story of how two cubs treed the future chief that very morning. Strong Ground was an excellent storyteller and soon a faint trace of a smile cracked Hole in the Day's face. Even

X's brother could not contain himself now that he was hearing the tale told as if the events had happened to someone else.

The women served the elders of their clan and their guests first, then excused themselves. The deer meat was excellent. And all laughed as Hole in the Day told the story of how he became known as "Young Buck" to the white traders in his youth, how he worked as a guide for the white Governor Cass' trip through the British territories, and how he stayed loyal to them even as his own people, the northern Ojibwe, attacked their group.

"I am Hole in the Day!" he shouted to them. "And I will be your chief, the chief of all the Ojibwe!" He related how he charged out before his white comrades, shooting his gun in the air. "Remember my name," he shouted. "For some day you will answer to it!" The northern Ojibwe ran from him and never did attack the Governor on that day or any other during his trip.

"He was always an irascible character," Niibiniishkang interrupts. "His son carried some of that with him."

"Yes," I say, wondering how my life might have been different if this old man before me had been my father.

"Why do you not continue?"

His hand no longer presses down upon my head, but rests in my own, strong and warm. I see him leading me through the forest, teaching me the ways of the hunt, stepping soundlessly through fallen leaves.

"It is nothing."

"Then get on with the story."

Everyone in the Wah'peton tepee laughed at the image of the Ojibwe warriors dropping their rifles and fleeing from the man who would one day lead them. How surprised they must have been at the spectacle of their brother heading the white charge. Though X laughed with them, worry choked his throat. Did no one see the dark flash of his father's eyes, the way those same eyes moved over the Wah'petonwan, as if he would devour them, as if a wiindigoo had stolen possession of his senses. And X wondered if the Sioux had not been told this story as a warning that his chief and the whites had grown close, that their people might not take kindly to the Sioux' planned attack on Fort Snelling. His father had always been a shrewd man.

The Sioux again offered the pipe to Hole in the Day, and this time he accepted, taking a long puff of the tobacco made from the bark of the red willow. He took another puff and another, breathing out the smoke over the heads of the Wah'petonwan until Strong Ground took the pipe from him.

Then the oldest of the Sioux, perhaps encouraged by Hole in the Day's story, began to talk of how he once scalped a young Ojibwe he'd happened across in his youth. Hole in the Day did not laugh as the others had laughed at his story. And though X's uncle smiled absently at the comical description of the old man's difficulties taking his first scalp, Hole in the Day sat so still it was as if he was no longer there, as if he'd followed the smoke outside of his body and hovered above them all.

"Do you think to amuse us with your womanly antics?" Hole in the Day asked when the story was done.

No one dared answer, and Hole in the Day left the tepee followed by Strong Ground, He Who Endeavors, and his sons.

That night, X slept on his own, away from the camp. He dreamed he walked the forest blindly, bumping against one tree and then another, holding on to each, not knowing which were his parents, if any. The more he searched, the thicker the forest grew.

He woke to a smothered cry from within one of the Wah'peton tents. The shuffling of makizins against the frozen earth. Another cry. Silence. Where were his brother, his father, his uncle? Grabbing his knife, he ran to the Wah'peton tepee, stumbling over scrub brush, followed by the barking dogs. More cries. Words in Sioux he could not make out. The dogs jumped ahead of him, rushing in, snarling.

"Kill them!" Hole in the Day's voice shouted from within the Wah'peton tepee.

X stood outside, unsure what to do. A loon's call haunted the distance, measured against the nearby death march of frogs. A fly buzzed about his ear, and he swatted it, wiping the remains from his hand.

X pulled aside the blanket covering the entrance. A flash of powder. The dogs leaped at his uncles' throats. Another shot, then silence. Darkness faded to red. The two dogs whimpered on the ground, blood spilling from them. An old man and woman lay in pools of their own blood, Strong Ground and Hole in the Day standing above them. A child's cry razored the night. X searched the tepee, but could see nothing. He pressed his palms to his eyes, certain they had failed him. Gurgling breath.

The loon's call unanswered. He dropped his palms. A girl stood alone, pressed against the back of the tepee. His brother grabbed her and threw her down. He was sure of it, could see him holding her against the shadow of his body as he lay upon the ground. The two of them the same size, probably the same age. For a moment, he thought his brother meant to save her. Then, the gleam of his brother's knife at her throat. "Kill her!" Hole in the Day ordered from the darkness. "Or I'll whip you!" The girl child screamed, hands moving to her ears as if to block out the sound of her own fear. Hole in the Day barked another order, and Strong Ground ran out joined by He Who Endeavors. Still, his brother lay against the girl. X could see them both now. The black nest of her hair, the agate eyes so wide he thought they would spill out upon the ground. His brother's hand over her mouth, his lips pressed against her ear, whispering to her to shut up. Yet she kept on screaming.

"Gwiiwizens!" his father shouted. "Boy!"

X winced at the word, though it was not meant for him. His brother froze under its spell, knowing that from this moment on he would have no other name.

The girl kicked and squirmed from his brother's grasp, and yet his brother did not move. Instead, he dropped his knife, covering his ears. The girl tried to escape but ran into X, who instinctively grabbed her with one hand. His gaze locked on his brother's. X knew he should let her go, lead her into the woods if necessary, somewhere she'd be safe.

"Boy!" Hole in the Day shouted again.

X tried to let her go, but his father's shout cuffed his

hands. Boy rose, stared at the two of them, then picked up the knife and ran toward the girl, plunging it into her belly, ripping upwards. The girl slid down X's body and slumped on the dirt. X stood dumb above her. And then he fled.

The vision of what happened next followed X as he hid among the horses. His brother, now Boy, crawling over the girl in the darkness and slitting her throat from one ear to the other. His father standing above them, urging Boy to take his first scalp, his face twisted with vengeance and grief. Boy pulling her head up and cutting along the hairline, crying out even as her last breath fell hot upon his face. The drip of her red-slick blood running down Boy's arms. X waited with the horses while his chief, his uncle, and the others ran from body to body, hacking off heads, cutting out genitals. He crouched behind his own mare, whispering in her ear, stroking her, even as he listened to the gibbering in the dark beyond.

The next morning, Hole in the Day presented Boy with his first feather. "Eleven winters," Hole in the Day said, as he tied the feather to his son's head. "Too long to wait to avenge your sister's murder, and that of my first wife." Hole in the Day paused, held his son before him with both his hands. "Their spirits rest now. And those of your cousins as well." No trace of the demon from the night before remained on his face.

Boy stood dumb, as if only now comprehending the horror of the previous night. "Why have I not heard of my sister before? Why have you kept silent?"

"I had to bury her deep in my heart where it ate at me like a worm." Hole in the Day looked out over the scene of the slaughter, the slush of spring stained red, the te-pees smoldering in the orange light of morning. "But it is over now."

Boy followed his father's gaze, then turned to the assembled Ojibwe, raised his fist and screamed, daring them to joke about his manhood now.

As they packed their belongings, X wandered through the silent river of frozen bodies. Three old men. Four women. Four children. He fell before the body of the girl, knelt beside her in the snow. He told himself that no one could see clearly the night before. That no one knew what had really happened. He told himself that a wiindigoo formed of ice and snow took possession of them all.

"Come, Ase-anse, we must ride."

"I will wait here awhile," he said.

"Why stay? They are long past healing," He Who Endeavors joked, and they all laughed, knowing that X's name had been given to him because a few winters before he'd taken to wear a shell around his neck, token of the medicine man.

"Don't be too long," Strong Ground said. "With her hole carved out, she won't prove much sport. Besides the Sioux men won't be pleased when they return."

Boy sat atop his horse, his back turned to the slaughter.

X swaddled the past in his mind. If he didn't join them, he would be an orphan again. At the very least, they would make fun of him as they'd done with his brother only the day before.

The loon laughed in the distance. He saw the bodies, one after another, contorted, stiff, faces cracked by ice, as they would look a few days from now. "I will stay a while longer," he said.

Coyotes yelp. Crows circle overhead, fearing the crack of melting snow. Pines groan under the burden of wetness. Time opens slowly in the hollow of all things.

The red curtain hangs silent. Niibiniishkang reaches out, gently touches my arm. My lids flutter open.

"I do not understand this action with the Wah'petonwan," he says. "Can you explain it?"

"I cannot," I answer. And already I am drifting again.

"But, how do you account for such a strange deed?" he asks, still not satisfied.

"I can only speak of my own ghosts, Niibiniishkang," I say. Crows flock upon the snow, picking at the corpses, their cries calling me back.

"The ghosts of another are not the same." But even as I say it, I know it's another lie. One upon many.

"I still don't understand," he replies.

"Then listen further," I say. "Maybe it will yet make sense."

"You speak in riddles, Ase-anse."

"Is there another way?"

X took the girl in his arms and walked west until the sun set low in the horizon. Then he climbed the tallest oak he could find. Made a bed for her in its branches. He built his fire at the oak's base and tended it for four days to light her soul's journey to the afterworld. During that time, he did not eat. He did not sleep. His only water what he carried. If the Sioux tracked him, he did not care.

At dusk on the fifth day, as the sun broke upon the earth, the great gray owl landed and walked before him. Its golden eyes fixed on him, but it said not a word until the moon arced halfway through the sky. Then the owl spread its long wings. It returned with a white blossom in its beak. X did not know what kind of flower it was, but when he took it from the owl it stained his hand red.

The fourth world is upon us, the owl said. *You must lead them.*

"What can I do?" X replied. "I am only *wissakode,* half-burnt."

The owl took flight. X fell into a deep sleep.

In his dream, he stood atop a hill looking down at his village. A wolf bound past him, stealing a baby from one of the wigwams, swallowing it in one gulp. The wolf grabbed another child from the hands of its mother. Then another. Until the blood and mud were indistinguishable. Women, children, old people fled their homes. And the wolf returned to the forest.

X tracked the wolf to its lair. The wood thickened to shadow. Birds dropped like fire. Flames of red, green, and blue. A panting voice rose from the earth and breathed itself into being. The creature towered over him. Breath putrid with the decaying flesh of children. He stood inches from its cavernous mouth.

"The people curse you, brother," he said, even as he lay his hand upon his brother's neck. The wolf lay at X's feet.

I must eat, the wolf replied.

"I will find another way." And with that, X led the wolf to the village.

At first, the people ran in fear, cursed him as well. But he shouted to them: "He is only hungry. Set food out for him each day, and he will no longer bother you." And the people listened.

They brought forth a bounteous feast of buffalo and beaver meat, wild rice and corn. The wolf gobbled up everything they brought, then lay down to sleep at X's feet.

The people cheered. But then the tail of the wolf crackled forth, rooting down into the earth. Shoots stretched from the creature's paws, digging their way into the dirt. Its fur stiffened to bark. The wolf raised its head one last time, but instead of howling, groaned under the weight of wood. X cried out as he looked upon his brother. The people returned to their homes, having forgotten that there was ever any danger.

"What does this dream mean, Ase-anse?"

"I kept it hidden within my breast for a long time."

"What brought it forth?" Niibiniishkang takes up his waabaabiinyag and hands the string of white shells to me. "It will help," he says. "In the exorcising of the tale."

"Thank you. I lost mine somewhere along the way."

"They will help you remember."

I take the string of shells in my hand, run my fingers over them. "After my baptism, I confessed many things to Bishop Whipple," I tell him. "That night with the Wah'petonwan and this dream formed a part of that confession."

"And what did he say?"

"He said that another man had nearly the same dream. A famous man named St. Francis of Assisi. He said he became a deacon."

"I think I understand this, Ase-anse," Niibiniishkang replies. "Is that why you chose the path of the chimookomaan religion?"

But I am gone now, floating down a long river of words.

X woke to the sound of the loon. His blood quickened, and he clawed for a stone upon the ground. He opened his eyes to the swaying branches above, fighting to still his breath. Leaves rustled in the night breeze, speaking riddles. The branches of the pine twisted, and he saw his brother struggling with the girl. He shut his eyes, dug his fists into the ground, laying there like that until a tickle crept across the back of his hand. An ant wandered up his arm. He moved to slap it away and stopped.

He placed his hand flat on the ground and let the ant crawl off, then watched as it tried to crawl up the stem of a weed and across a heart shaped leaf. X broke off the leaf and brought it to his mouth, blowing gently on the ant. It changed direction. He crushed the leaf between his fingers and placed the pieces on his tongue. Bitter Nightshade. The name came to him unbidden. Not a weed but an herb, one that healed skin diseases. Boiled, the extract would relieve headaches. How did he know this? He set the ant back on the ground and waited for morning to arrive.

He cleared a space for his camp, laid out his knowledge before him. Each herb, root, or stem. He followed the raccoon through the night, collecting the berries it tasted. Boiling them in a fire pit he arranged in the center of the clearing. He ate the leaves and found they upset his stomach. Smoking them forced him to relieve himself. The juice from the stems cured his warts.

Week after week, he spent in that clearing, testing the limits of his body, never traveling far, drinking from a small creek about one hundred feet distant. The border of his world. The animals watched him, never quite accepting him as one of their own, but not moving away either. Each allowed for the strange behavior of the other. The groundhog waddled as it ran, then stopped and turned at the clearing's edge, observing X as he applied the resin from some root to a cut he'd received that morning.

Moons rose and fell until time no longer mattered. X carried his herbs about him wherever he went, so that though he was slowly expanding his world, he kept his knowledge with him. Soon, the circumference of his wandering extended a thousand feet, then a mile. He made his home on a bluff, then a coulee thick with rabbits. That was his last camp. The coyotes hunted them with abandon.

He sat in his makeshift hovel in the bank of the coulee, blocking his ears to the sickening screams of the dying rabbits. He ran out with a stick, trying to scare off the coyotes, but they ignored him, or didn't see him as a threat. He built a fire, fed the flames with wet wood to create such a smoke his eyes felt as if they were bleeding. The coyotes simply moved their hunt to the brush beyond the perimeter. He stuffed dirt in his ears, bits of leaf, anything he could find and cowered in the dark of his hovel until daybreak.

Spring, two years after the Wah'petonwan, X followed the Little Elk river home. Hole in the Day appeared much older, the lines of his face deepening to cracks, his hair streaked with white. The hand of the wiindigoo had left its mark. His father embraced him as if he'd returned from the dead. Boy stood in the distance, a foot taller if an inch. His face broad, no longer the uncertain child but a young man of thirteen winters. A scar marked his chin. X approached, but his brother turned his back to him and walked into the woods. Even X's mother, Sweet Grass, seem changed. Her normal deer's gait now burdened. Though when they sat, she showed much interest to hear what X had discovered about other uses for Bearberry roots and Bittersweet in healing.

He saw few children and fewer women. Had they left them behind? Hi uncle Strong Ground, sat in the dirt beside his wigwam, eyes closed, head nodding as he chanted. X moved to greet him, but Strong Ground opened eyes burned red with grief. The characteristic joking smile wiped clean from his face. X dared not speak.

He found his brother toward evening, working side by side with his father to build a log cabin at the center of camp. As X approached, Boy pretended to examine the daubing he'd just applied, but his father signaled for him to stop.

"What has happened?" X asked. "Why does Strong Ground grieve?"

"Why did you stay away?" Boy spat.

"I could not do anything else." It was all he could say. It would have to be enough.

Hole in the Day sat, gestured for them to join him. "It will be a strong house, a good house. We will no longer run. We make our stand here."

The forest stood thick. There had been much rain, and now the overcrowded branches sagged in the sun. Leaves curled in the heavy air.

"Why? What has happened?" X repeated.

"We've been at war so long, I don't remember a time without killing." Hole in the Day pulled a small pipe from his belt.

X offered tobacco he'd recently dried.

"I'll kill Little Crow the next time he appears," Boy said, scratching at his face as if there were stubble there to itch.

"You will do no such thing," Hole in the Day answered. He filled his pipe with the tobacco. "We must find a different way." And with that, he rose to find a fire.

X and his brother sat in silence, each chewing on the tobacco, spitting the bitter juice. "I'm sorry, brother," X said at last. "I didn't realize."

Boy pursed his lips, pulled the remains of tobacco from his mouth and tossed them upon the earth. "Strong Ground lost his wife and two boys," he said.

"How?"

"Little Crow doesn't stop. I'll hang his scalp from this cabin so all will know his cowardice."

"But the Sioux only attack because we attacked them."

"Yes," Boy replied. "And we attack them because they attack us. But that has all changed. Hole in the Day frustrates them. He is too great to kill. Last month, while the men were out hunting for food, Little Crow and three hundred warriors rode down upon our women and children. They killed seventy, shouting each time to remember the Wah'petonwan."

X pulled the tobacco from his own mouth. "It can't be."

"I was there," Boy cut him off. "I saw as Yellow Hawk

led the charge. He'd courted Star Woman once, do you remember?"

X heard only the screams of rabbits.

"She ran out of her wigwam, and he stopped before her atop his horse. He did not kill her, but touched her shoulder with his spear, marking her for death, then rode through the camp. They killed her as she defended a little girl. The daughter of Black Shawl Woman."

"I remember her." X scraped his fingernails through the dirt, squeezing the earth in his hands. "It's one more in a long history of killing," X went on. "Like the night with the Wah'petonwan. Like the massacre at Ft. Ripley before that. On and on down the line."

"You don't know what you're talking about." Boy stood, turned his back to his brother "You are only half-burnt. The Sioux murder without reason. They've killed many of my kin."

His brother had changed. He was a man for better or worse, with a man's opinions and prejudices. X picked up a stick started to sketch a figure in the sand, then scratched it out. "You forget that they also killed my parents. I know what it means to grieve." He threw the stick into the surrounding scrub.

"Then you should hate them as I do."

"Do you not think those Wah'peton women and children had kin?" X replied. He stood, walked past his brother and out toward the Little Elk River. He had no stomach for such talk.

The Sioux attacked the following night. Like phantoms culled from some ancient darkness, they emerged from the woods, so many that Strong Ground ran from hut to hut rousing the warriors, saying they would slaughter every last Ojibwe. With war club in hand and his many eagle feathers on his head, Hole in the Day went out to meet them. Strong Ground and He Who Endeavors joined him, followed by X and Boy and many others armed and shouting for battle. But even as the Sioux waited on the perimeter, Hole in the Day silenced them.

"It's for my actions alone that our enemy returns time and time again to haunt our people," he said, standing defiant before his warriors. "And so I must face them alone."

As he spoke, the Sioux streamed forth, circling the camp. Boy shouted out that he would avenge the deaths of his sister, of his cousins and friends. A few of the Ojibwe warriors raised their knives and cried out, threatening to break faith with their chief, to follow Boy into battle, or whoever would lead them.

"Do you not think, Boy, that we have had our day," Hole in the Day spoke directly to his son. The warriors about him went silent. "How much more vengeance do you need?"

Strong Ground's face strained with the desire to follow his chief. Boy gripped his spear with both hands, holding it before him like the bars of a jail.

Hole in the Day stepped forth, alone.

The Sioux ceased their circling and formed a long line, not twenty paces from the Ojibwe chief. He stood proudly before them, raised his hand in greeting but said nothing. The Sioux, some on horseback, others on foot, did not move closer, nor did they give ground. They stood like that, each side waiting for the other to make the first move, until one of the Sioux ran to Hole in the Day, hit him, then turned to face his fellow warriors, raised his fist and screamed. Hole in the Day said nothing, but Boy cried out as did many of the Ojibwe at that injustice. One by one, the Sioux took turns running up to him, bellowing their war whoops, sometimes hitting him. Still he stood, his face betraying nothing of fear or pain. Boy shook with each stroke, as if he'd endured the blows.

When the entire line of braves had their fill, Hole in the Day dropped his war club and spoke: "I am sorry for what I have done, but I was struck too hard by the deaths of those I loved. I am sorry for what happened with the Wah'petonwan, but I could not help it. Grief for my daughter clouded my mind."

The Sioux mocked him, shouting out insults and taunts as he talked. Their leader, Little Crow, a fierce warrior who sat high in the saddle, rode before him, carrying a torch and shouting: "What good are your words, Bagone-giizhig? Did you not speak kindly to the women and children who offered you their hospitality? That was not the act of a man, but of a woman. How can we trust the words of a woman?"

"You are a coward!" Boy shouted from the edge of the clearing where the Ojibwe warriors stood, his body visibly shaking now. One look from Hole in the Day silenced his son. Strong Ground paced back and forth before the Ojibwe warriors, offering words of peace, calming them and himself in the process.

Hole in the Day stood long before the Sioux. "I have no answer to this," he said, finally. "But I am ready to die for my crimes. Please kill me, but do not kill any more of my people. Do not burn once again their homes."

"No!" Boy said, almost a whisper. X held him fast. Strong Ground stopped his pacing. He clenched his war club in his fist and began chanting.

Little Crow returned to the Sioux line, talking with his warriors. For a long time it seemed that they would not come to a decision. At last, the Sioux chief nodded his head, grabbed a torch from one of his warriors, and turned back toward Hole in the Day. But as he rode up to the Ojibwe chief, the torch held high above his head, he did not so much as glance at him. He rode past and cast the torch through the open doorway of Hole in the Day's new home. The other Sioux who carried torches then rode forth, and each, one by one, set flame to another wigwam. All the while, Hole in the Day stood silent.

"Let me fight beside my father," Boy shouted, breaking free. X tried to tackle him, but Boy was too quick.

As the timbers cracked and popped, Little Crow rode before Hole in the Day and spat upon his face. Bathed in light of orange and shadow, Hole in the Day did nothing.

"You call your actions those of a man," Boy shouted as Little Crow rode away. The Sioux chief stopped and turned to see the child who dared mock him.

Boy walked proudly toward Little Crow, talking even as he walked. "You spit on a great man and call yourself a warrior," he said. "Thirteen winters ago, you and your people came to a peaceful gathering at Fort Ripley and took advantage to commit a cowardly act."

Little Crow looked down at Boy, but from X's perspective it seemed as if Boy stood over Little Crow. The Sioux chief began to speak, but Boy silenced him with a wave of his hand. "Those arrows your people shot through the open door at Fort Ripley killed my sister and my father's first wife. Do you know what it means to lose a daughter?"

Strong Ground stopped his chanting and opened his eyes. The other Ojibwe stood silent, every gaze fixed on the figure who stood defiant before the Sioux chief. Boy's face was not haughty but filled with the grace of one sure of the role he's stepped into.

"I am but a child," Boy went on. "But I've seen how grief twists the mind until we are no longer human beings. Is that why you kill, or do you have another reason?"

Little Crow sat atop his horse, speechless before this boy. Only when his own warriors called to him, did he remember himself. He pulled a spear from the man nearest to him and flung it into the burning remains of Hole in the Day's cabin, then attempted to regain the moment with a cry of triumph, and rode off.

Strong Ground, Green Feather, and the others chased after them with their war clubs held high, yelling for them to return and fight.

Hole in the Day wiped the spittle from his face, but never once turned to watch as his home slowly burned. It took most of the night before the last timber crumbled to ash, and yet he did not move from where he stood. Boy wandered behind the cabin where he thought no one could see and collapsed upon the ground, weeping.

When morning came, Hole in the Day knelt down before the embers of his home, pressed his lips to the ash, even as the sun broke upon the ground, and whispered his oath: "I will call every brave from Red Lake to the Pillagers of Leech, to our people at Sandy Lake, Gull and Mille, and I will ride upon my enemy and kill every last man, woman, and child."

The river flows, a parade of dead drowning out the thrush along the banks. Ticks scale the legs of the deer lapping at the water's edge. Bloated, they wait for the day they will recognize each other again.

"That was not the oath of a chief, Ase-anse." His hand shakes as he reaches for his tea. There is weakness in him after all.

I fight the urge to take his hand in my own, hold it to my chest. "No, it was not. And yet he was a great man, one who accomplished much for his people."

"This story you tell troubles me," he says. "It will be a difficult one to carry into the afterworld."

"Do you want me to stop?"

"No," he replies, his face set already like one of the dead. "If we cannot carry truth, we have nothing."

Little marked the passing of summer except the sound of Hole in the Day's preparations for war. Finding he no longer had the stomach for the talk of men, X kept to himself at night as the warriors smoked about the fire. Boy did not approach him nor speak to him, but shadowed always his father or uncles, often traveling on expeditions to barter with the chimookomanaag for more rifles. Though he missed his brother, X didn't mind. He passed the time at night thinking through all Sweet Grass showed him during the day, sometimes even trying out the medicine on himself, hoping for a vision that would guide him like the dream that had flown on the back of the great grey owl. He understood the path of the Mide, the medicine man, meant he would often stand alone.

Autumn arrived with its long, sallow hills of ash and birch. Bright red leaves of blueberry bushes and the gathering sweetness of apples. Then the silvered glow of barren treetops in winter's light. The dull white skull of a deer crested the rime-covered world. Smoke from countless fires curled above like a shroud. At long last, freezing rains laid bare the earth, and the seasons came full circle. The rich smoke of kinnikinnik filled the air. Coltsfoot opened. Women gathered toad root. X spent more and more time wandering the woods, gathering the herbs he would need for his medicines. Hole in the Day assembled his men, his weapons, and his supplies.

X watched the preparations of his people. The various clans assembled. He watched as the Pillagers refused to camp near the Mille Lac clan, and he watched as Boy and Strong Ground approached the chiefs of each clan in an attempt to make peace. At first they laughed at this youth who talked like an elder, but soon Boy's charm won them over. So, when Green Feather and Long Bone suggested dividing the war party into groups, each attacking a separate Sioux stronghold, the uncles allowed Boy to carry their word to the other chiefs, explaining that it was best to keep their strength in numbers. Hole in the Day watched his son's reputation rise among his people.

Soon, the uncles included Boy on their daily expeditions to patrol the perimeter. They feared that the Sioux had sent spies to determine the strength of the Ojibwe war party, and Hole in the Day made it clear that he sought to surprise the Sioux with their vast numbers.

It was on one such expedition that Green Feather stumbled upon the enemy. He'd nearly stepped on the scout, who couldn't have been much older than fifteen, as he lay hiding in the tall grass. The scout cut with his knife deep into Green Feather's thigh. Boy saw his uncle drop in the grass, then heard the scout's war cry. He ran to his uncle's aid, but Strong Ground beat him there, grabbing the scout by the hair, raising his knife, and cutting his throat even as the youth was about to plunge his own knife in Green Feather's breast. Boy watched as his uncle took the scalp, blood streaming down the scout's chest, staining the grass.

Green Feather called for his nephew's hand to help him rise, but Boy couldn't move. Strong Ground knelt beside his brother, binding his leg. When the uncles looked around, their nephew was nowhere to be seen. They spent the rest of the afternoon searching for him.

When word came to Hole in the Day that his son had not returned with the uncles, he rode out himself that night to find him. "Gwiiwizens!" he called. This time, the name was not spoken in anger.

Exhausted from the day's search, and agitated by his brother's disappearance, X slept outside their spring wigwam. He tossed and turned under the mid-May moon until the sound of the wind rushing through oak leaves woke him. The golden eye of the great gray owl stared down at him. He closed his eyes, shook his head, but when he looked again, someone moved inside him. He asked it's name, and it replied, "Free-soul." He begged it to look for his brother, and it went willingly.

The red curtain flutters. Niibiniishkang floats formless over the tall prairie grass, through the thick birch forests, swirling round and round, breathing himself out upon the world, asking only for a murmur, a voice to shatter the shape of his loneliness, requiring only the breath of another to bridge the darkness. He sees Boy before him, sitting next to X in the grass atop Lookout Hill. It is four days since Boy has eaten. He knows this. Feels Boy's hunger as his own.

His breath melts into that of the others. He walks with them to the river where they shed their clothes and slip beneath the current. With them, he sinks into the dark loam along the bottom until he is no longer sure where he begins and ends. He lies upon the bottom until he can almost imagine breaking once again into being.

"Ase-anse," Niibiniishkang shouts. "I am too old for this sort of thing. Please."

"I did not mean to take you with me," Ase-anse whispers. "But not everything is under our control. We must accept that."

"That is true, Ase-anse," Niibiniishkang replies. "Still, I would prefer to be in my own body again."

X brought a bowl of berries and wild rice to Boy as the chill night fell upon them. He lay down beside his brother, covering them both with his blanket. Though his brother's body was that of a man, the soft beating of his heart against X's chest, the moth-like flutter of his breath on X's face reminded him of the days not so long ago when they were children. He swore that if ever a time came to shield his brother with his own life he would do so willingly.

That morning, X gathered wild turnips for them, and that afternoon, they camped by the river. Neither mentioned the coming war with the Sioux nor the night of the massacre long ago. By the following morning, Boy had regained his full strength. The two brothers spent the day swimming in the river, seeing who could hold their breath the longest or who could dive from the highest cliff. Boy won each contest and not because X allowed him to win.

"I'm afraid," Boy said that night, as they lay together beneath an old oak.

"Afraid of what?"

"Of what is to come. Of what I will become."

X listened to the deep rise and fall of his brother's breathing.

"I'm not going back," Boy said at last.

The next morning, Boy spotted a trout hidden in the dappled light of the river. He reached into the water, found a large, jagged stone and threw it at the trout, hitting it along the spine. It floated to the surface, its back broken, sticking out through the skin. On all fours, he crawled after it, grasping at it with both hands, but it slipped through his fingers. He lunged forward then and caught it up, holding it aloft. But he squeezed it too hard and some of the entrails squished out, slipping down his arm and into the water, only to float away. A dark omen.

Boy returned to their camp on Lookout Hill, while X gathered turnips and berries for their midday meal. He scanned the horizon, catching sight of Strong Ground's search party long before they'd spotted him atop the hill. He thought of kicking out the fire, of running north but instead sat beneath the oak until his uncle's party arrived.

All eyes were upon them as Strong Ground and Green Feather returned, Boy riding between. Hole in the Day stepped forth, signaling his son to approach. All waited to see what Hole in the Day would do as he raised his knife before Boy. "You have proven yourself to be thoughtful," Hole in the Day said, addressing the crowd. "But you have also shown you are still impulsive." And now he dropped his gaze to his son. "The time has come for you to distinguish yourself," he said, laying the blade his own father had given him in Boy's hands. Strong Ground and Green Feather nodded their approval, and the other chiefs came forward to embrace Boy.

"My son," Hole in the Day said, raising his voice to once again address the crowd. "You will ride in the front. Your war cry will fall like sleet upon the Sioux."

The men invited X to join with them in their preparations to march on the Sioux the next morning. But he declined, preferring once again to sit with Sweet Grass and the older women as they ground bearberry and bittersweet for the coming battle. The next morning, X rode in the back much as he'd done that day when he followed Strong Ground to his new home after the Sioux killed his parents. Hole in the Day asked him to ride up front beside his uncles, but X told him he would take no part in the killing. Hole in the Day waved him away as if he wouldn't hear the words.

A wall of shells. Raging depths of silence before the shock of the gun. Bits of leaf and straw form the nest of body that crumbles beneath the thunder of hooves.

Niibiniishkang tightens his grip, but I slip through, fading to empty air.

"I'm losing you," he says. "And I want to hear."

I cling to his arms, run my fingers along the slack skin until I find the strength. "You do not know how your words help," I tell him.

"I do not care," he replies. I want you to go on with your story. This is the part where I come in." A broad smile peels across his face. It looks strange from my position below him. Turned upside down, it reminds me of this dream we call a world.

Yes, Niibiniishkang, the warrior from the north made a great name for himself that day. Not only for killing many Sioux, but for intervening when Hole in the Day's pride got the better of him.

Green Feather had scouted ahead with Long Bone and discovered that the Sioux were planning a great Medicine Feast at Battle Creek. So, the entire contingent of nearly two hundred braves lay in wait until the Sioux men were good and drunk, then they rode down upon them.

Riders brought back missives to the women. *Niibiniishkang has killed a dozen Sioux with his bare hands. Boy faced Little Crow himself and though neither was killed, they made a great show. Hole in the Day rode into the heart of the camp singing his death-song. Niibiniishkang pulled the great chief from the battle with a hundred Sioux chasing them.*

The Ojibwe lost nine that day. The Sioux ten times that number. As they rode home, Hole in the Day sang his victory song: "Surely, I will have great praise." And

Boy rode at his side. The victory had clearly established Hole in the Day as chief of all his people. If he could defeat their mortal enemy, certainly he could save them from the white encroachment. What doubts may still have lingered about Boy after he'd run off, had now been erased.

"I did not think I killed so many." Niibiniishkang looks upon me with a troubled face. "And certainly not with my bare hands. I remember I had my bow and my hunting knife. The story did not happen the way you say. The Sioux were drunk. I stood back to let the younger warriors have their day."

"What does it matter how you remember it? What matters is how the people sing of it after."

"But I thought you said I would only carry truth with me to the afterworld."

"Truth takes many forms."

Niibiniishkang sits for a long moment, nodding his head, staring at the red curtain that covers his door, as if he hopes to see through it, to see the battle as it was. "Once again, you prove yourself wise, Ase-anse," he says at last. "Still, it troubles me."

The victory never sat well with Hole in the Day, no matter how often he sang his song. When he closed his eyes, he saw only the drunken Sioux being cut down before him, felt only his own blood lust, and he did not like the taste of it. Night after night, he spent outside his wigwam, smoking his pipe until the glowing ash revealed a vision of what was to come. He foresaw the next attack by the Sioux, then his retaliation, and on and on like that until there were no more Original People left, only the chimookomaanag spreading over the land. The vision disturbed him.

That summer, Hole in the Day led a contingent of his people to Fort Snelling to make peace with the Sioux, but the Sioux ambushed him on the way, killing He Who Endeavors and Long Bone. He performed the death rites himself, refusing to let any others partake. Even Boy had to grieve his uncle from a distance. Hole in the Day sat beneath the bodies for four days, ensuring their departure to the afterlife, then called Boy to him. Asked him to prepare his spear. The same party that sought peace now hunted down the Sioux one by one.

They did not care if they killed the Sioux responsible for the ambush. Only the scalps hanging from Hole in the Day's belt mattered. No number seemed enough to sate his grief. Boy rode at the front with his father until they spotted a Sioux and his young wife on foot in the scrub brush under the light of the new moon. They ran them down like dogs, spearing them in the back before they had a chance to sing their death song. When his father asked Boy to take the man's scalp and add another eagle feather to his head, Boy refused. Hole in the Day dismounted and spit on the ground before his son. Still, Boy would not come down from his horse. "Finish it, or I'll whip you!" Hole in the Day cried.

"Do you see what we've become?" Boy met his father's gaze, saw the wiindigoo howling there. "It is the night of the Wah'petonwan once again. We cannot escape it."

Hole in the Day approached his son, pulled the knife

from his son's belt, the knife he'd given him not four moons before. He strode to the Sioux and yanked his head up by the hair even as blood bubbled forth from the man's mouth. He took the scalp and shouted his war cry. But after, he collapsed on the ground beside the body, scrubbing his hands with dirt until the others had to pull him away. They left the woman uncsalped and made camp within a stone's throw of the bodies. They returned home the following morning. That evening, Hole in the Day sent word to the white traders that he would treat with them.

Hole in the Day rode to La Pointe as chief of all the Ojibwe. He asked Boy to ride at his side, to watch and learn. Though the father was feared as a warrior, his skills in oratory were not insufficient. When White Fisher and the others tried to assume their hereditary claim as chief, Hole in the Day took off his war bonnet, displaying the many eagle feathers. None could dispute his prominence. And Hole in the Day used the respect it engendered to parley with the whites. The settlers had been afraid of Sioux and Ojibwe hostility spilling into their territory for years. Hole in the Day agreed to reign in the Ojibwe in exchange for annuity payments and land to settle along the Great River at Crow Wing. In exchange for peace, he asked for a white tutor to teach Boy and X to read and write.

The town of Crow Wing was born, but quickly became known by the Ojibwe as Neengitahwitigwayang, the Place of Separation, for nothing would ever be the same. X worked side by side with his father and brother, building wigwams for the Ojibwe who arrived each day. Hole in the Day wanted his own house in the center of town, a house with wood floors and log walls, saying he would never again move from this place of peace. After it was built, they walked through the muddy late spring streets and talked of how best to teach the people to plant seeds. X offered much advice, knowing what to look for in the soil that made it good for growing.

Hearing of the new town, many Métis left the lean-tos and hovels they'd been living in deep in the woods, hoping to find work if not the company of others. For his part, Hole in the Day welcomed them, though he did little to bring them into the community, nor to reprimand the others when they occasionally shouted out "wissakode," half-burnt, or worse. The Métis slipped away quietly after those encounters, sometimes not returning for days.

Boy and X studied each morning with their young, female tutor and learned quickly what the black marks on the paper meant and how to make those marks themselves. X, in particular, found this new study much to his liking and worked long nights as Boy went carousing with other young men. X wondered if his real father knew how to write. He'd been a trader, so he must have known, must have used the black marks to keep his records. The thought excited him, the idea that he was learning something his father would have expected him to learn.

But that same year, the territory suffered its first of many setbacks. The American Fur Trading Company collapsed, and independent traders quickly filled the void. They were the worst of men, rejects from their own people, men who would sell their mothers if given the chance, men who traded in scrip usable only at their stores for goods at inflated prices. Worst of all, they brought whiskey.

Saloons popped up until one stood on every corner. Strong Ground and Hole in the Day were often seen drinking in one or the other of them, telling stories of the plans they had for the town to the younger Ojibwe and mixed bloods who soon frequented the places.

"It surprises me Bagone-giizhig took to drink so fast," Niibiniishkang *says, stretching his legs upon the ground.*

I offer nothing.

"The chimookomaan say that we drink whiskey because we are weak," he continues, as if he could explain anything. "They don't understand the need to drown the past. The night with the Wah'petonwan must have bothered our chief deeply."

"Our chief told Father Pierz once that he did not understand the world of the long knives, but what was even worse, he'd come to believe he also no longer understood his own." The ground beneath me remains frozen. I don't understand why I cannot warm it.

"Who is this Father Pierz? I do not know him."

"You cannot rush a story, Niibiniishkang. You of all people know that."

"I did not realize there were so many parts I didn't know."

"This is only part of the one true story," I say. "And even so, its parts are without number."

The tutor gave up and returned to St. Cloud two months into her first winter. With his mornings free, X found himself venturing to the Métis encampment. He used what little authority he had as the adopted son of the chief to talk others into sharing their supplies and helping these new inhabitants build their own homes within the town. They humored him though they did not trust him.

He offered to teach them to plant seeds, but found they knew more of agriculture. From then on, he listened as often as he spoke, learning from them the best way to till the soil for turnips, the best time to plant sweet potatoes so they would grow healthy. When he thought he'd earned their trust, he again brought up the idea that they might move near the rest of the Ojibwe. They would pretend to listen, talk good-naturedly about the possibility, as they worked the soil together, then as soon as he was gone, disappear into their huts at the edge of the woods. When time came for the Sun Dance ceremony, X made the rounds, determined to invite all the Métis. He didn't know why it was so important to include them but only knew that he must. He sat by himself during the Sun Dance, lonelier than he'd ever been. Things had changed with his brother. And now he'd lost his adoptive father to drink. But it was more than that. He was a Métis who lived with the Ojibwe. They had welcomed him, made him one of them. Yet, lately, all he could think of were his real parents. What they looked like. What they did. Where he would have lived had they survived the massacre. Would he be like these Métis, slipping between worlds, not belonging to any?

For his part, Boy proved himself the son of a chief. He worked hard during the day to make sure those in need had food and blankets. He organized work groups to build huts for those without, even while his father sat drinking in one of the saloons. Evenings, he often rode out with friends, sometimes staying overnight at Gull or Otter Tail Lake. Sometimes not returning for days, as if part of him still longed for the old way. It was on one such extended stay not far north of Crow Wing that Boy spotted eight soldiers from Fort Ripley cutting down timber and carting it away with a team of oxen. At sixteen winters, Boy had heard enough to know that the recently negotiated treaty clearly stated the land to the north was theirs all the way to the British territories. He approached the soldiers unarmed and alone as his friends hid in the forest.

"Our land," he said, the chimookomaan language filling his mouth like stones.

The men appeared startled, two of them pulling their guns. But another, a red-haired youth who couldn't have been much older than Boy himself, signaled for them to hold their fire.

Boy, too, was taken aback. He'd never seen a face covered with freckles, or at least with so many. "Stop," was all he could manage to say.

The red-haired youth looked to his men before speaking. "I don't speak Chippewa," he said. "So, I hope you understand. We don't want any bloodshed. We have orders to gather timber for the Fort." He pulled a piece of paper from his jacket and waved it in front of Boy. "Here it is," he continued. "Signed by Captain John Todd." He folded the paper and put it back in his pocket.

Boy caught only a few words: *Chippewa, Fort, bloodshed,* and a name, *John Todd.* Though he couldn't make sense of what the man said, he understood the meaning. Still, he tried again. "Our land."

Another man stopped his work and approached. "Didn't you hear what the sergeant said?" He towered over the red-haired man, so that at first Boy wondered why he didn't give the orders, until he saw his narrow, badger eyes and the hand resting on the butt of his pistol.

The red-haired man signaled the others to continue working then took the badger-eyed man by the arm. "We're done here," he said, knocking the man's hand from his pistol. He gave a slant-eyed look to Boy to be sure he understood, then turned around, not bothering to check whether his subordinate followed. Boy would not humiliate himself by speaking further.

That night while the soldiers slept, Boy and his friends slipped into their camp. Silently, they stole the team of oxen, driving them through the night to the northern edge of Gull Lake. They laughed throughout their journey, recounting stories of how heavily the white soldiers slept, joking that an army of Ojibwe could have ridden their horses through that camp and still the soldiers would have snored.

They found the red-haired youth waiting for them back at Crow Wing. He'd already filed charges with the agent and was waiting to take Boy and the other youths into custody. They would serve time at Fort Ripley.

But as he attempted to lay hands on Boy, Hole in the Day stumbled from the saloon doors shouting, "Stay away from my son!" He held a green blanket in his hands, which he wrapped about himself.

Strong Ground and Green Feather fought to hold him back, but they could not shut his mouth. "Boy is a great warrior, like his father!" Hole in the Day shouted. "You cannot quell his spirit." Hole in the Day slurred his words so much the agent had a hard time translating for the red-haired youth, whose name was Brunson.

Boy went rigid as a tree, his gaze rooted in the ground.

"I was wrong to silence the warrior within my people," Hole in the Day said. "To tell them they must live in one place when their spirit must roam the land." He stumbled, falling to the mud. Strong Ground and Green Feather tried to pick him up, but he fought their attempts, dropping the green blanket.

The agent told Brunson that Hole in the Day was apologizing for the actions of his son, that he swore this would never happen again. He told the sergeant that the chief gave his word as a man loyal to the Great Father that he would make his son reveal the location of the oxen and that he personally would lead those oxen back to Fort Ripley by the end of spring.

Boy understood none of this. He saw only a figure kneeling in the mud before this red haired youth. The pain limning that figure's mouth, the bottomless ache that dulled the once bright eyes, the mud that decorated the hair where eagle feathers once hung. He did not know this man. Nor did he wish to know him.

With a little encouragement from the agent, the red-haired sergeant agreed to the terms and left. Boy stayed where he was even as Strong Ground and Green Feather carried his father home. After, he pulled the blanket from the mud, careful not to dirty himself, and walked toward the Great River.

Father Pierz arrived a week later. Word had spread that Crow Wing had opened to white influence, and the Catholic diocese acted fast, sending the priest to the newly designated town in hopes of establishing a mission there, one whose job would be to convert Ojibwe and Métis alike, perhaps even the outlying Sioux. The priest had walked all the way from Fort Snelling, a fact that impressed many, especially because he didn't appear particularly strong. Those less impressed ran frightened into the woods when they saw Father Pierz walking along the shores of the Great River, a tall, lean figure in black robe, long hair matted and tangled about his shoulders, a bushy brown beard covering his face. They shouted out that a manidoo made of sticks haunted the banks.

X could not take his eyes from the priest as he approached. The strange beard, which he'd never let himself grow for fear of being mocked. The wooden cross hanging over his chest, with the figure writhing in pain upon it. And most of all, the black robe, which hung in such a way that it hid the true size and shape of the body beneath.

Hole in the Day came down the hill to meet the new arrival, his breath sour with whiskey. "Come to my house," he offered. "Meet my son." A mistake, X feared, as Sweet Grass had moved in with her sister the month before, swearing she couldn't live with her husband any more, and Boy rarely returned home.

"Perhaps another time," X interjected, putting himself between them. "Let me take the Father to his new quarters.

"Who are you?" Hole in the Day spit, knocking X away.

"I'm your son."

Hole in the Day stared at X, trying to get a fix on him. "You are wissakode, half-burnt," he said at last, then took the priest by the arm and led him to his house. X followed behind.

The house was a shambles. Empty whiskey bottles lie scattered about the floor amongst the remains of wild rice, bread, and rat droppings. Boy was nowhere to be seen. Hole in the Day stood in the entrance as if he didn't remember the place and feared he'd brought this guest to the wrong home. Once in the door, he squatted in a corner, head lowered. Father Pierz looked to X, who gestured him inside.

"You have seen better days, ogimaa." The Father's choice of the Ojibwe word for chief was deliberate. "The Church is here to bring you to still better yet."

Hole in the Day sat as if he hadn't heard, then slowly raised his head, his hair shielding his red-rimmed eyes. "Whatever I am, I am still true to my people," he said at last. "I do not think we need your religion."

Father Pierz looked to X to bridge the silence that fell between them. "The Catholic Church is ready to build a mission here," X said, stepping toward his adopted father. "They will build the mission whether we wish it or not."

"And I will write a letter," Boy replied from behind them. He stood in the doorway wrapped in his father's green blanket.

"I don't understand." Father Pierz answered Boy in his native tongue.

"What do we get in return for allowing the church to build their mission?" Boy stepped forward into the room, standing opposite his father.

Father Pierz considered the question a moment before

answering, his fingers working through his beard as he thought. "What did you have in mind?"

"I want to write a letter," Boy replied. "I need your help. I need a tutor who will stay longer than a winter."

Yellowed teeth shone through the Father's grizzled beard. "Then I offer my services as a gesture of our good faith," he said. "I'd be happy to serve as tutor to both you and your brother."

Hole in the Day panned the room with his gaze. "I am still chief," he said to no one in particular. "I feel sure of it when I wake in the morning, though not when I fall asleep at night."

They waited for him to say more. Hole in the Day rose and made as if he would walk toward the priest, then stopped short. "I'd offer you a drink," he said at last. "But I have none left."

"That won't be necessary," the priest replied, turning to Boy even as he said it.

Supplies for the new church and rectory arrived within weeks but the problem arose as to who would build it. Hole in the Day had lost what little authority he had left, and Strong Ground lay near death, another victim of the whiskey. So, Boy took it upon himself to talk with the Ojibwe, while X invited Father Pierz to join him in attempting to enlist the Métis. The priest appeared early the following morning. Groggily, X made his way across the cold, wood floor and opened the door, inviting the priest in for breakfast and coffee.

"You're staring at me," Father Pierz said as he ate his rice. His tone and the half smile let X know he was not offended.

"You look much younger, that's all," X replied. Father Pierz had trimmed his beard and cut his hair the night before. "The beard hid your face well."

"I hope I can take that as a compliment," Father Pierz replied.

When they were done, X took their plates and carried them to the bucket by the door. "I didn't mean to offend," he said at last.

"You're not Ojibwe." Father Pierz fixed his gaze on him.

X turned away from the priest and sat on the bench by the door.

"Are you ashamed of that fact?"

"No."

"Can you read and write?" Father Pierz brought his hands to his lips as if in prayer.

"A little," X said. "I've learned some English, though my father spoke French, at least I think he did."

"You didn't know him?" Father Pierz sat beside X on the bench

"I can no longer remember him." The black robe smelled of wood smoke and musk and the dust of the road.

"I will teach you the language of God." Father Pierz took X's hands in his own. "Do you know what I mean?"

X said nothing. His fingers touched the cuffs of the priest's robe. The material was more coarse than he expected, closer to deer hide than muskrat.

"I'm talking about Latin," Father Pierz went on.

X nodded his head. The priest's breath smelled of the rice he'd just eaten, but also the sweetness of maple. The yellowed teeth that had seemed common only the day before shone like wheat.

"What is your name?" Father Pierz touched X's chin with his finger and lifted his head.

X sat silent unable to find the words. The soft eyes of the priest muddied his thoughts. "I am Ase-anse," he replied at last.

"Didn't your parents give you one?"

X said nothing more.

"I see," Father Pierz replied. "Then, I shall call you, Thomas, after the learned saint. You should have a Christian name." Father Pierz stood and walked away from X. Assuming his role as teacher, he hooked his thumbs into his robe and said, "Let this be your first lesson, Thomas. You are no longer Indian or white. You belong to the one true, holy, and apostolic Roman Catholic Church."

The words swirled in a jumble about X. He couldn't make sense of them. Even as he grabbed one from the air, it would slip from his hands like a fish. He'd always seen himself as Ojibwe. And yet he was not. But he was not white either. This man spoke of a place he could go where it didn't matter what he was.

The red curtain shifts in the wind over Niibiniishkang's door. The light of the mid-afternoon sun breaks the darkness, though it brings little warmth.

"I see now how you fell into the chimookomaan religion," Niibiniishkang says, nodding his head.

"Things are never as simple as they appear," I reply, wondering how it is that in age we inevitably fall back to the simplemindedness of childhood. "Give the story time."

Strong Ground died two weeks after the priest's arrival. They found him on the floor of his wigwam, an empty whiskey bottle in his hand. Hole in the Day refused to let the priest administer last rites but rather laid his brother's body out in the branches of an oak stretching over the Great River. He sat on the shore beneath that tree refusing to move for four days. He refused food and even drink. By the end, he couldn't stop shaking. His sons carried him back to his house even as the loon cried. After, the gray sky brought much rain. On the days when the thunder cracked and the sky shook, Hole in the Day would step out of his house and walk through the puddles where there had once been a street, looking up as if daring the sky to strike him, to make him worthy of his name.

Recruiting the Métis was a slow process, but Father Pierz was a talker, and his affable manner relaxed the mixed bloods. X studied the way the priest opened the conversation by asking what troubled them. For the first few days, they were hesitant to answer. Father Pierz would then offer a glimpse at his own troubles: the corns that bothered his feet, or the rosacea that occasionally bloomed on his face, confessing his worry that this new climate might aggravate it. Soon, he'd worked his way into their trust. X learned how Elzear Pierre, otherwise known as Strange Noise, contracted syphilis from a whore in St. Paul, how Joseph Brunelle, also called Red Bear, refused to leave his bed anymore, so that his wife now threatened to leave him. He learned how so many of the men fell to whiskey and how so many of the women watched hopelessly, then fell into their own quiet routines, cursing their husbands beneath their breath or, almost as often, turning to drink themselves. X watched and listened, wondering if the black robe gave the man this mysterious power to work his way into the lives of these people or if it came from the man himself. And each time, Father Pierz ended the conversation by placing his arm around the person saying: "Let us pray for God's guidance, so that we may live with hope."

As he promised, Father Pierz arrived at eight sharp every weekday morning to tutor the boys, spreading his books out upon the table before them as X brought him coffee. Boy demanded they work on his letter first, but Father Pierz proved equally strong in demanding he ground them in the classics. In the end, they compromised, reading *The Bible* on Mondays and Wednesdays, *The Aeneid* on Tuesdays and Thursdays, and drafting Boy's letter on Fridays. Both X and Boy liked Tuesdays and Thursdays best. At first, learning the marks on the page went slow, but the two brothers proved strong students, Boy's initial reticence overcome by the fact that the story of Aeneas captivated him. His voice would quiet to a hushed tremor as he read how Aeneas landed at Dido's home in Carthage, how he entered the temple where their defeat at Troy was recorded in pictures, and how he wept to see those sad depictions. It was there his breath would catch, and X would lean in to guide him, to point to the word or phrase that would get him going again.

X would then take over, reading of how Mercury came to Aeneas. He was glad this part came to him for he knew it would please his brother. He read how Mercury showed Aeneas the vision of Rome and his destiny as its founder. His brother leaned over his shoulder, trying to read along as X recited how once Aeneas' ambition had been incited he would dream of ways to betray Dido's love and leave Carthage.

The following Friday, they completed the letter. Boy walked it to the agent's office himself, standing tall as the agent read it over, nodding even as the agent gave him a questioning look.

"This is addressed to the President of the United States."

Boy said nothing.

"You're saying you won't return the oxen until the government pays *you* for the timber they took?" the agent asked, shaking his head.

Yes, he had done this thing. And, he would do more.

Métis and Ojibwe worked side by side, building the church and rectory in a matter of weeks. Though Boy seemed uncomfortable with this strange religion, he stood before the finished church, folded his arms across his chest, and smiled. "We've done well, brother."

"It's good to see the people working." X stepped beside his brother. "Father Pierz says that indolence is the devil's playground."

"I do not know that word, indolence," Boy said, still facing the church. "What does it mean?"

"Laziness, I think."

"The Ojibwe have never been lazy." Boy turned toward his brother. "You seem very taken with the priest. But do not forget where you come from."

"And where is that?"

"I thought you followed the Mide."

X fingered the cross he'd taken to wear beneath his shirt. A gift from Father Pierz. "We continue our lessons tomorrow. Then you'll learn many more words."

Boy said nothing. The church stood tall behind him.

Three months after Boy sent his letter, the agent's office in Crow Wing reported that they'd received a reply from none other than President Tyler himself. The White Father had not only sent letters to Captain Todd at Fort Snelling pardoning Boy and the other Ojibwe for stealing the oxen, but also promising payment for the timber taken. Word had it that Captain Todd was incensed, that he had at first refused, saying he would ride out and bring the oxen back himself, but that the powers that be in the newly forming territory calmed him, reminding him that the last thing they needed as they pushed for Minnesota to become a recognized territory and eventually a state was trouble with the Indians. Better to placate them, at least when it came to such unimportant concerns.

Boy went to his father, to tell him the news, but stopped short when he saw him hunched over the bar in one of the saloons. He never spoke of it again. He didn't have to. Word spread quickly of his prowess with the pen, and his reputation grew, so that over the next few years while his father faded from view, his people began turning to him. President Tyler proved good on his word, and they received payment for the timber. Boy used the money to buy blankets and food for his people for the coming winter, then devoted himself to learning English, imagining that if he could achieve such results with a basic command of the language what might he do for his people once he mastered it.

Hole in the Day faded from the lives of his people. When he did show up, it was most often stumbling through town, or lying in the muddy banks of the Great River, choking on his own vomit. Now only Green Feather was left to carry him home. The uncle never mentioned the many times he found their chief drunk, seemingly near death, until one day four years after Father Pierz' arrival.

The sky was a clearer blue than any autumn day they could remember. Air so still you could hear the badger rummaging roots, could see the jagged outline of ivy on the trunks of trees, feel the silence as it brushed against your skin. Hole in the Day wandered the woods outside of town, strangely present though he'd clearly been drinking. Green Feather watched his once great chief sitting high atop a boulder, crossing his legs beneath him as if he would stay awhile. When he saw the chief would not move, he told him to come home. He tried to pull him from the boulder, but Hole in the Day anchored himself well, saying he would not leave until he spoke with Boy.

"When we fight each other, we punish ourselves not the whites," he said as he sat overlooking the Great River. He swayed and shook as he spoke.

"What do I do?" Boy said as he approached. Green Feather stood silent.

"Meet with the chimookomaanag," Hole in the Day went on. "Give them what they want as long as they move the Ho-Chunk here to live between us and the Sioux."

"I don't understand. You want them as a buffer?" The flat look in his father's eyes scared him. They seemed so dark the Free Spirit must have left them.

"Lead our people," Hole in the Day said, though his eyes were closing. "Do for them what I could not. Show them how to walk in this new world."

Boy asked him many more questions after that, but his father said nothing more. In the end, his father, belly swollen with drink, fell from the rock. They carried him home, Boy staying by his side until morning.

Three days later, X brewed the coffee in anticipation of Father Pierz' arrival as the sun broke across the horizon coloring the cold that dulled the woods. He brewed the coffee over the fire, warming his hands as he did so. There are so many birds, he thought. He tried to count the different bird songs. Jays, cardinals, sparrows, the mockingbird. When he looked up, Father Pierz stood beside him.

"You care for your brother," Father Pierz said, breaking the silence.

"Yes."

"And yet there is something between you," the priest continued.

"Yes."

"Jealousy."

"No."

"What, then?"

Boy came sleepy-eyed into the room, having been up all night searching for his father once again. "I want to know what happens with this Aeneas."

Father Pierz laughed and pulled out his bible. "It's Wednesday," was all he said.

Boy slouched onto the bench and buried his head in his hands. X sat beside his brother.

"Boy, would you begin by reading Matthew 24, please?" Father Pierz asked.

"The time is coming when you will hear of wars and rumors of wars," Boy recited. "See that you are not alarmed."

It was then X's uncle, Green Feather, burst through the door with word that Hole in the Day was dead. Someone had put him in an ox-cart the night before, as he was too drunk to walk home. They'd found him by the side of the road. It seemed he'd fallen out and hit his head on a rock.

As Green Feather spoke the news, Boy kept on reading. Father Pierz rested his hand on Boy's shoulder, telling him to stop, that it was okay to express his grief. Still, Boy read on: "Such things are bound to happen: but the end is still to come. For nation will go to war against nation, kingdom against kingdom; there will be famines and earthquakes in many places. All these things are the first birth pangs of the new age." Boy stopped, rose, and went to his uncle. "Take me to him."

Boy and Green Feather went out into the cold morning air. X buried his face in Father Pierz' robe.

Maggots worry through the belly of the badger on the side of the road. Wagon tracks split the mud into a child's cry. Empty lines laid out like the hair of the dead.

The red curtain flutters in the wind. The fire is nearly extinguished. The tea cold. Niibiniishkang rubs his legs, hoping to work the blood back into them.

"Lend me your breath, brother. Breathe into me so that I can in turn breathe into you. Let our breath fill the muddy

tracks and stifle the crunching of bones that echoes through our minds."

"What do you say, Ase-anse? You are slipping outside the story."

I think I open my eyes, but I am not sure because you are staring down at me, brother. And then it is the old war chief. Back and forth until the two faces blend as one.

The night after Hole in the Day's burial, X couldn't sleep. He went for a walk outside only to lay on the banks of the Great River and stare up at the broken bowl of stars.

The next night he moved into the shed behind the rectory, sleeping on a bed of corncobs. He took his meals with Father Pierz, sometimes sat with him on the church steps as the horizon flattened to dark.

The tutoring lessons stopped. Boy moved in with his mother and aunt and did not wish to see anyone. X accompanied Father Pierz on his rounds to visit Ojibwe and Métis alike. He assisted him in administering the duties of his office and helped him prepare the services. The brief moments before sleep took him were the worst in his life. He lay alone in the shed staring at the ceiling, but it was as if he were looking down from the banks of the Great River only to see his blurred face beneath a cracked patch of drift ice.

X had heard the talk of many of the people in town. He knew what was whispered in alleyways as they passed. Father Pierz knew as well. He knew and said nothing.

"Why do you let me stay?" X asked one evening at dinner just as Father Pierz was to begin his blessing.

Father Pierz kept his hands clasped in the position of prayer. "I don't know what you mean," he replied.

"You have heard what people say," X continued. He wasn't sure what had gotten into him, only that he needed to see some aspect of his life clearly.

Father Pierz said his blessing. A candle burned between them on the table. The only light in the room.

"You have not answered my question."

"What do you want me to say?" The flame reflected in the priest's eyes made them look unsteady.

"I want you to say something that is true." X pushed his plate away.

Father Pierz laid his hands flat upon the oak table, spread his fingers.

X leaned in to him until the heat of the flame burned his eyes. "I want to know who I am," he said. "I want you to tell me."

Father Pierz studied his hands as if measuring the distance between the fingers.

"Isn't that what you do," X went on. "You tell people who they are, who they can be. All they have to do is put their faith in God. And you give them the answers."

"No!" Father Pierz said, finally looking at X. "I offer salvation for those who have faith. Nothing more." The candlelight flickered wildly in his eyes.

"What about Boy?" X asked. "Does he seek salvation? Why is he not here instead of me?"

"You know why." Sweat dotted the priest's brow. He pushed himself away from the table and moved toward X, stopping inches before him.

Misshapen silence filled the space between them. The

breath of each falling heavy upon the other. Each growing dizzy, drunk on breath.

"Ase-anse, I look through your eyes and I see Father Pierz. His eyes are wise for his age, but there is a deep sadness."

I hear the old war chief, Niibiniishkang, speaking to me, but the words hold no meaning. Sounds swirl about me, like autumn leaves. Boy stands before me. And Father Pierz. Niibiniishkang, too. I stare into them. Through them. And they shift about me, changing places as if bodies no longer matter. As if the causes could be substituted one for the other, and we would still arrive at the same result.

Father Pierz presses his lips to X's.

Niibiniishkang quivers beneath the warmth of the priest's breath. "This story is really quite strange," he says. He reaches out, almost touching Father Pierz's arm.

X returns the kiss, softly at first, then with a feverish passion. He wraps his arms about the Father.

Niibiniishkang feels the hot blood flow through his body as he has not felt for many years. The salty taste of another's skin wets his lips, and he is sure for a moment the body is his. But then Ase-anse lies before him. The other gone.

"Some people are more idea than substance," I say. "More illumination than body."

Is it Ase-anse talking? Niibiniishkang cannot be sure.

"And when you reach out for them, they disappear."

"Ase-anse, is that you?" he says.

"When you touch them, they fade until they never were."

"Am I dead, Ase-anse?" Niibiniishkang asks. "I almost feel as if I am."

"I'm no longer certain," I reply. "Where does the thin veil between life and death lie?"

When X woke the next morning, Father Pierz was gone. He'd left a note saying he was making his normal rounds to the various agencies and would return in a few weeks.

X quickly dressed and ran through the frozen mud of the village streets where he found Boy, sitting before his aunt's hut, wrapped in his father's green blanket. In his hand, he held the copy of *The Aeneid*. His face painted black in mourning.

"Where did you get that?" X demanded.

"I found it leaning against the door when I came out this morning," he said, without looking up. "He's gone, isn't he?"

"Yes."

"Why?"

X said nothing.

Boy opened the book and thumbed through the pages.

"Would you like me to read to you?" X asked, sitting now beside his brother.

"Gaawiin," Boy replied, no louder than a whisper. "I don't want to hear you. I don't want to feel you next to me. I don't want to know you. Do you understand?"

"No," X replied. "I don't." And then he opened the book to the story of how Mercury came to Aeneas, and he began to read.

Boy sobbed quietly next to him. X continued to read, putting his arm around his brother as he'd seen Father Pierz do.

An eggshell lies cracked in a corner, a broken eye staring back at me. Damp cold settles upon us. I must find another blanket for the old war chief.

"This is all too much," Niibiniishkang says.

I stand too quickly and nearly faint.

"Let me help you," he says, but I wave him away.

"The fire has long gone out." I grab a blanket from the steel frame beds in the back.

"There is more wood," he says in answer. He sits motionless in the half-light of the sod hut. A stone god.

I say nothing as I throw on more wood, work to restart the fire.

"Are you a "Two-Spirit," then?" Niibiniishkang asks.

The words hover over me. I can see them written out in English, and I reach into the air to grab them. I bring my closed hand to my mouth, peel back the fingers one by one and blow away the empty air with my hot breath. "I am not words or anything named by them," I say.

"Again you speak in riddles."

"If I am half-burnt, does it also mean I am half man?"

"No, the two are different."

"And if I am both, does each half add up to a whole, or do they cancel each other out, making me only breath?"

"I do not know the answer to that."

"Nor do I." I return to tinder the fire.

"Do you search for the answer in our Lord? Is that why you converted, Ase-anse?"

"Father Pierz told me that the first representations of Christ showed our Lord as both a man and a woman," I say, fighting off the trace of pride in the fact that I can still teach this old man something. "He spoke of depictions of Christ with a soft, round face, long flowing hair, swelling breasts and broad hips."

"I had not heard this before," Niibiniishkang replies. "Truly, this new religion is very strange."

"Yes. I myself still do not fully understand it." The fire sparks to life, and I rummage about for more tea. "Where is your wife? The day is almost over."

"Has the time flown so fast," Niibiniishkang answers. "You must not stop your story then, Ase-anse," he says. "Please continue. I can hear."

"You were present from this point on," I say. "Perhaps you should tell it." I find the tea and fix the pot, then return to kneel beside him. He looks fatigued. His eyes watery and old, the skin about them sagging.

"No," he replies as he lies back down in his bed upon the ground. "It is much better when you tell it because you remind me of things I had not remembered, and then they can become part of my own story to tell to my kin in the afterworld."

I take his hand, for I will need his strength before all is over.

A month later, Boy painted his face black, as he'd done every morning since his father had died, went to X and told him he was leaving the next day for the treaty council at Fond du lac, even though it was Green Feather who had been invited to meet with the other chiefs.

X peered through the rectory's doorway as his brother spoke, the morning sun blinding him so that he wasn't sure who it was who addressed him, if it was Father Pierz returned from his duties or the ghost of his own father. Except to scavenge food at night, he'd not left the rectory since Father Pierz's disappearance; he'd scarcely seen a human being, turning instead to whiskey. Boy's black face was a dark un-formed shadow against the day. "My brother, is that you," he asked,

"You look terrible," Boy told him.

"Yes."

"I want to take up where my father left off," Boy went on. "He told me fighting would only lead to the death of our people. That the only way was to talk with the chimookomaanag."

Through half-lidded eyes, X saw *The Aeneid* in his brother's hand. He opened the door, gestured his brother in. Boy stepped closer, smelled the whiskey sour breath, then stood in the doorway, refusing to move in or out. He told X of his plan, eyeing him to see what effect his words might have. He asked X to come with him, said he would need his help speaking to the whites at the council. But most importantly, he would need his help in reading the treaty documents, to make sure they were treated fairly.

"We should talk to Green Feather," X said at last. "He'll know what is best."

"No," Boy replied. It was with the simplicity of that declaration that Boy's face finally came into focus, and with it his words. "No," Boy repeated. "Green Feather left yesterday for Fond du lac. He is a good man, but he cannot be trusted to lead."

"Who will go with us?" X asked.

"No one," Boy replied. "We ride alone."

And in that moment, Boy's face became a bright, black sun, illuminating X so that he did not ever want to move from the warmth of this place by his brother's side.

Each night on the road to Fond du lac, the brothers read to each other from *The Aeneid,* and X could see Boy drawing strength from each page. Like a general studying the plans of his advisers the night before a battle, Boy soaked up each sentence, absorbed each word of the epic. Strangely, in those nights and for many after, X had no thought or desire for the whiskey that had nearly consumed him. He felt, in this his twenty-first year, as if reborn. And each day as he sat upon his horse, riding behind Boy under clouds that hung low like hushed willows, he thought back to the time on Lookout Hill when they'd run naked through the brush, and each night as he sat watching the lights play in the north and listening to the rush of wind as the great owl took its prey, he breathed slowly and steadily for fear he could not hold more of this strange world within him.

On the first of August, they arrived at Fond du lac. They did not skirt the town as their people were accustomed to doing but walked down the main street of the burgeoning hamlet. X had donned Father Pierz' robe, as they felt it might add authority in the negotiations, and with his black face, Boy looked like death himself marching down the street. All eyes were on them as they went. X was not afraid. Though they had no idea where they were going, he felt strangely confident walking beside his brother, dressed as he was. They continued on until they spotted the biggest house in the area. It sat just beyond the town's limits.

As Boy and X approached, two white men came out to meet them. Both tall and clean-shaven, both dressed in black suits and walking to the same inner cadence born of obedience to authority as they stepped down the porch stairs of the mansion loaned to the government agents for these treaty negotiations. Only then did the shorter of the two break stride and step out before them.

"This meeting is by invitation only," he said. "It's closed to anyone else, Indian or white."

"I did not like those chimookomaanag," Niibiniishkang says. *"They assembled us there and then wanted to dictate to us what to do. They talked as if we had already turned to trees."*

"That is how they see us," I reply.

"There is no sense in that," Niibiniishkang says. "Even at that time, I was older than both of them. It was my first encounter with the chimookomaanag, and it left a very bad taste in my mouth."

"When you don't listen to others, it's because you don't see them," I say.

"Perhaps those who don't listen don't exist themselves," he replies, smiling because he thinks he has stolen my self-pity.

"You, also, are wise, Niibiniishkang," I say. "I am glad you hear me now."

"Yes," Niibiniishkang replies. "And I would like to know who killed our chief before I die if that's possible, so please continue."

Boy walked past the short man without slowing or changing his stride. The taller of the two stepped down to block his path.

"My father negotiated the treaty you are now attempting to change," he said. "I have a right to be part of any negotiation that alters my father's wishes." He stared past the tall man as if he was of no concern.

The two men looked at each other with slanted eyes and laughed. "We're not going to be dictated to by any one," the taller one said. "Much less a painted up boy and a half-breed dressed as a priest," the shorter one added.

The government agents adjusted their hats and turned to the stairs.

"Certainly you won't mind if we observe the negotiations," X said, stepping forward. "As a gesture of good faith, I mean."

The two men looked in X's direction, their gaze lacking focus, as if they could not make him out, perhaps wondering if they had misjudged him, if he really was a man of the cloth. "He's a boy, we understand," X went on, hearing the voice of Father Pierz inside his head. "But he is also the true son of the celebrated Hole in the Day, former chief of all the Ojibwe. His silent presence will only add more authority to the proceedings, to turn him away will only hurt your position." He directed the last comment to the taller man because he'd judged him to be the more thoughtful of the two.

The taller man, whose name was Verplank, signaled the shorter to talk with him. After a moment, Verplank went inside. When he returned, he signaled for them to enter.

The house was sparsely decorated, as if it's sole purpose had been for the treaty negotiations. Inside, the chiefs White Fisher of Lake Superior, Niibiniishkang and Bad Boy of Gull Lake, Curly Head of Sandy Lake, Buffalo and Flat Mouth from Leech Lake, Eagle and First Seated Feather of Mille Lac, and, of course, Green Feather. Each chief sat straight in wood-backed chairs, having just finished smoking with the white dignitaries. Verplank and the shorter man discussed how to proceed while a large man with a dark beard, dressed in a fine, blue suit sat in a leather chair behind the others, waiting for the meeting to begin. A tapestry of a medieval stag hunt hung over the man in the armchair. A large map was spread over the only other piece of furniture in the room, a dark mahogany desk.

The chiefs welcomed Boy. They'd had great respect for his father and the bravery he'd shown often in his war with the Sioux. Green Feather even managed a sly smile, congratulating his nephew on taking such a bold step toward manhood. They did not yet realize that Boy planned on negotiating himself.

"I wasn't sitting," Niibiniishkang interrupts. "I've never been able to sit right in those chairs."

Niibiniishkang sees his brothers sitting around him quietly, the government representatives talking before him, outlining the proposed new treaty, explaining the need to redraw the lines, reasoning that the Indians had no use for the timber on the land they were requisitioning.

"I was quiet because I could not understand them," Niibiniishkang tells Ase-anse who he now sees sitting, eyes closed

before him as if in a trance. "I was waiting for Curly Head, whose English was much better than mine, to translate."

Boy stepped forward, his black face filling Niibiniish-kang's vision. The old war chief wished to take this boy aside, to tell him he was too young to take on the mantle of his father, that though he might be a great speaker, it would end badly not being tempered by the wisdom of age.

Boy removed his black frock coat, revealing his father's bagamaagan, his wooden war club, in his hand. "You have called together all the chiefs of our nation." He spoke directly to the man seated in the leather armchair in the corner, ignoring the rest. "You ask them to come here to sell to you our land west of the Great River, but they do not own the land."

Niibiniishkang stood to the side, observing, as the chiefs rose up one by one, arguing with each other, shouting at the daring young man before them.

"We will not listen to this impudence," Bad Boy said. "He does not speak for us."

The man in the leather chair pulled a cigar from his vest pocket, lit it, and puffed smoke in great plumes. "By what right do you speak," he said after.

"By the same right as you," Boy replied without hesitation. "By the right of the conqueror. My father took these lands from the Sioux, just as you try to take them from us. If you want to negotiate, you will negotiate with me alone."

The strangeness of the day echoed through the room, the light falling from the mouths of the whites. The man in the leather chair gestured for the government agents to follow him. The chiefs argued with each other: "He is tricky like his father," Bad Boy went on. "He cannot speak for all our people," Curly Head replied. White Fisher threatened to walk out, but Green Feather reminded them they came prepared to give up much. "What harm is there in seeing what this boy can accomplish?"

"The harm is that he is a boy, nothing more!" White Fisher replied.

"And were you not a brash young man once, too?" Green Feather asked. "Did you not once dream of accomplishing great things?"

"That's not the point," Curly Head joined in. "He must earn the right to speak for us."

A voice from the back spoke quietly, "Let him earn it then." Niibiniishkang stepped forward. "You know what we'd have given up. The Ho-Chunk will suffer. Let us see what the boy can do."

Ase-anse opens his eyes to the black void and wonders if he has disappeared again. He reaches out for Niibiniishkang, hoping to steady himself, to anchor himself to this world, but finds when he looks down at his own arm that he's not sure it is his at all. He turns his hand palm up and doesn't recognize the lines as his own. "Is this your hand, Niibiniishkang?" he asks.

"I do not know."

"Am I there with you at Fond du Lac or here now?"

"I do not know."

Niibiniishkang watches as the large man in the blue suit returns, flanked by the two government agents.

"Your words make a certain sense," the large man addressed Boy directly. "We would be willing to negotiate with you if the others agree."

Bad Boy and White Fisher grumbled under their breath, but Niibiniishkang silenced them with a gesture. "We are in agreement," he said, nodding to Boy.

"Very well," the man in the blue suit replied. "I am Senator Rice, and here are the terms." He gestured to Verplank who laid out several sheets of paper on the table.

Boy approached, looked over the black marks. "My brother will assist me in determining what you offer."

The white men gazed about, perplexed, as X stepped forward.

"Your brother is a priest," Senator Rice took the cigar from his mouth and snuffed it out on the table. "This should prove interesting."

Verplank pocketed his hands and pretended to look over the papers.

"They ask for much more," X said at last. "Land extending west of the Great River bounded by the Long Prairie and Crow Wing. The Ho-Chunk will have nowhere to go."

Boy stepped back from the table, raised his dark face to the Senator. "These terms are unacceptable." He spoke quietly but deliberately. "My father won these lands through his courage, and I will keep them, both for my people and for the Ho-Chunk who are not represented here."

"You speak with the audacity of a white man." Senator Rice reached for his cigar as if he meant to light it again.

"I have not finished," Boy said, his voice growing in strength with each word. "We do not wish war with the long knives. You come seeking something and so do we. Let us both go home the better for it. You may take the lumber south of the Crow Wing, but the land is ours. We require food and blankets in exchange for our lumber, money as well."

"If I'm to even discuss such terms with my colleagues," Senator Rice replied. "I need to know the name of the man with whom I speak."

The room darkens as if the moon has blocked out the sun. Niibiniishkang searches the shadows, the air thick as black moss hanging from long dead trees. He reaches out for Aseanse but finds nothing. He searches for First Seated Feather and the other chiefs but finds only shadows.

"His name is Hole in the Day," Niibiniishkang shouts at last. "He seeks to honor his father. He speaks with the same courage as his father. Let him have his father's name."

With the exception of Bad Boy and Curly Head, the other chiefs nodded their assent. Buffalo and Flat Mouth seemed pleased at what the boy had already accomplished. Green Feather smiled as he had not done in many moons.

"Very well, Hole in the Day. I am Senator Henry Rice. It is a pleasure to make your acquaintance and to know that the Chippewa people have such a man to speak for them. We'll have to discuss your compromise, and we'll get back to you once we've talked with the Great Father."

"Are you nothing but a foot solider?" Hole in the Day replied. "Are we not men? We will not leave until we know what we have." And with that, the young Hole in the Day pulled up a chair and sat at the oak table.

Senator Rice looked for a moment as if he'd inhaled the cold ash of his cigar. He cursed under his breath, then glanced at X and thought better of it. "You do not speak like an Indian," Senator Rice stammered before regaining himself. "You do not keep the company of other Chippewa, but of a priest. We will make this deal. But do not think it will be so easy the next time, Hole in the Day."

Hole in the Day. Bagone-giizhig. The name resounds in Niibiniishkang's mind. He is impressed by the youth's strong heart and hears himself swear allegiance to the new chief. He hears Bad Boy and Curly Head complaining to Green Feather and waits for Green Feather's response. He hears Green Feather, too, swear allegiance, then Bad Boy and Curly Head's curses as they storm away. First Seated Feather speaks cautiously, saying the young man has proven much this day.

"Do not lose yourself in the story, old man," I call out. "It's easy to do when stories are all we have left."

"Here I am, Ase-anse," Niibiniishkang answers. But then he is gone.

The gray swath of morning's light. The horizon bleeds like a wounded deer. The name Hole in the Day spins over the landscape of skin, climbing bark, circling close, now far until it's merely the echo of an echo.

I see the door open, see Bad Boy and Curly Head ride away in anger. I hear the name and its shadow follow them through the open door, then hover about me. I feel it move through me like a wind, stirring shadows. There is nothing left but to slip into the stillness of my own name, if only I knew what it was.

Your breath breaks upon my face like a dream, brother, and like a dream it fades. I wake and run to the water's edge. Again the Kingfisher waits, whispering what I must do.

And so I become a tree stump, my only thought to seek revenge for what Piichoo Manidoo has done to you, brother. But he is crafty, and the crow in his chest caws in warning as he approaches. He stops, sniffs at the air. Without eyes, I cannot see him, yet I feel his presence. I ask the Kingfisher to lend me one of his eyes, but he will not. I beg him to lend me his feet to better grip the bow, but he will not. I cannot help but fear that this sightless form is but a taste of the fate of my people.

With a whisper, Piichoo Manidoo calls forth the serpent. It winds about me like the early morning mist upon the lake, choking me. I wait, hoping he will not recognize me. As the coils of the serpent wrap about me, I forget who I am and drift back into the waking dream.

"Where is my mother?"

"She may have died," Kingfisher responds from atop my head. "She may be the daughter of the moon."

"You do not know?"

"I do not know. One story says your mother died when you were six, another says she lives still. I do not know."

"Which story can I tell?"

"Whichever one you choose."

"And what about my father?"

"Which story would you like to hear about him?"

"The one that is true."

"That he was a voyageur and shot in the back by the Sioux? That he left your mother before you were born?

That he lives on an island in the middle of a lake of pitch?"

"How can they all be true?"

"You think like a chimookomaan. It is better not to think at all."

"And where is my brother? Has he fallen beneath the ice?"

"Ah, good. You're learning not to trust your eyes."

"And what about the others? There must have been other people."

"The great wiindigoo turned them all to trees."

"And now I am a tree, also."

"Yes."

"I want to wake but it's as if the nightmare is inside, gnawing at me."

"Yes."

"Can't you do something?"

"From that there is no relief."

The serpent slips away, slithering through the mud along the lakeshore, until Piichoo Manidoo emerges from the turbid waters to call it back. Ice hangs from his brow, long sickles form his fingers. I draw my bow, notch my arrow and aim in the direction of the cold. But without sight, my aim is off. Without hands, I am feeble, and the arrow lodges in the shoulder above where his heart should be. He cries out and falls back into the depths of the lake. The bark of my skin softens, the roots of my feet shaping sinew and bone.

Without ballast, the day rises like dew from leaves. Gone. Each hour the same, gray upon gray. What you can't see is as real as what you can.

Day Two

I wake to the shifting wind. Branches scratching across my rooftop. I rise from my cot, the ground cold as the lakeshore's loam. I stumble toward the wood stove. Open the stove door. The cold ash flies with the draft, flakes drift down upon the floor. I shove in more wood.

Once again, I don the vestments of my office. My cassock and surplice. Moths rise from my robe, flitting half-alive in the ice-laden air. They fall to the floor, dumb. I pull the cincture tight. Today, I will find you, my brother.

I step through the snow, following my own tracks from the day before. It is as if no one moves in this place. People stare from doorways, eyes hollowed by hunger. Their bark-like faces growing hard. Their gnarled limbs stiffen and groan.

A dead dog lies frozen in the snow before me. A reddish mutt who'd cowered by a door yesterday.

The great gray owl stands waiting for me on Beaulieu's gabled roof, but Beaulieu is nowhere to be seen. Probably with one of the whores that hang about this place. He's not that old yet, and Elizabeth must have moved to St. Paul by now. I fight the urge to search his home, to see what evidence I might dig up. Somehow, he is behind your murder, my brother, or at least caught up in it. But there will be time enough for him. I have a promise to keep.

Niibiniishkang lies sleeping on the ground when I enter, the army issue blankets tossed about as if he had a restless night. His wife, Newobiik, is nowhere to be seen. She can't still be at her sister's, I think. But what do I know of time? Is it really the next day, I wonder. It looks so much like the previous.

I make a fire and put on the tea, then go to the old war chief, cover him in his blankets and sit beside him. It matters not if he is awake or sleeping, and so I begin again my story.

Father Pierz returned six months to the day after he left. X had been living in the rectory, sleeping in the priest's bed, as the shed was near freezing in the winter. He woke one morning to the priest standing above him, snow melting upon his black robe. At first, X thought he was dreaming. He reached out for the priest's robe, took the rough material in his hand. Father Pierz backed away. X saw him clearly then, as if the distance focused his vision. The priest looked older, the lines about his mouth no longer soft but cut deep. His eyes once fired by the determination to walk hundreds of miles to his new post, now seemed ashen.

"What has happened?" X asked, rising from the bed. He wore no shirt.

"No," Father Pierz replied, backing away further. "Stay where you are." He moved to the writing table in the corner of the room and sat.

"You look tired," X said, wrapping the sheet about him.

"Let me say what I came to say," Father Pierz interrupted. He leaned over the desk. "The diocese sent me back. I didn't want to come, but they made it clear my duty was here."

"I'm happy you've returned," X said, digging his clothes from the bedcovers. "I will help you. I've been ministering to your parish in your absence. They will be as happy as I."

"I am happy to be back, too." Father Pierz continued. "But we must remember, that night no longer exists. It's as if it were in a story and not real." He gazed directly at X to make sure he understood.

X nodded his head. He put on his pants, his shirt, and pulled his makazins from beneath the bed. Neither said a word until X opened the door, letting in the frigid January air. "I will find somewhere else to live," he said as he started to close the door. "But may I still assist you in the duties of your office? I would like to learn."

This time it was Father Pierz who nodded his head.

Newobiik sticks her head through the red blanket covering the door, sees her husband lying asleep and smiles. She enters the hut, carrying a chunk of flat bread. She removes the teakettle, sets the bread atop a pot on the fire to warm it, and rubs her hands against the cold.

"I have brought you a little treat," she says.

From the shadows, I watch as she sits beside the fire. I want to tell her how hard it was to work beside the priest those next two years. She would understand what it means to love someone who cannot return that love, for though her husband loves her, he is at death's door. Still, she cares for him. When the bread is warm and soft, she takes it to him. Sets it beside him.

I would tell this woman how my brother, Hole in the Day, earned the respect of his people. How his people turned from the bottle, beginning to feel hope again as they watched this young chief move from clan to clan, meeting with the leaders at Gull Lake, Leech Lake, Whitefish, and Sandy Lake, listening to them. How any trace of pride Hole in the Day exhibited at Fond du lac was gone, replaced by a patience and willingness to hear the problems of others. I would tell her how my brother rode out with the young men to hunt as they used to do, bringing back as much game as his people could eat. I would tell her how proud I was of him during those first two years, and she would understand because she'd felt the same for her husband many times.

As if she realizes she has forgotten something, Newobiik rises, moves toward the door. But as she parts the red blanket, she stops and turns back to her husband who sleeps so soundly on the ground. She goes to him, studies his face as if perhaps she is afraid he will not be here when she returns. She kneels, tears a piece of the bread from the loaf. Gently, she touches it to his lips and waits there as if she would watch him eat, then rises to go.

I am left alone with the old war chief, wondering why I am here. I no longer believe the pretence for which I came. It is clear I am the one doing the confessing. But what must I confess? My only hope is that whatever confession I give will ease his passage into the next world.

The winter of 1850 fell harsh upon the Anishinabe, as foot upon foot of snow covered the world. To make matters worse, the government of the Great Father sent spoiled provisions, moldy flour and rotten meat. Curly Head's people were the hardest hit for they had no reserves. Hole in the Day rode to Sandy Lake accompanied by X and Father Pierz to see what could be done. They arrived in time to witness the first death, a boy of three with an infectious laugh, who'd been a favorite of many for the way he ran through the camp, playing with whoever might make the time.

Hole in the Day looked on from the doorway of the wigwam as X and Father Pierz knelt beside the boy, administering last rites. Father Pierz made the sign of the cross, then stood, shaking his head. X tucked his cross back in his shirt and pulled out his Mide shell. He laid his hands on the child and murmured through the prayers Sweet Grass had taught him.

Once outside, Father Pierz stopped him with a hand on his shoulder. "You will eventually have to choose between the two," he said. "You cannot practice Catholicism in good faith if you hold to other beliefs."

X slipped the shell beneath his shirt. He did not know why he'd pulled it out, why he'd uttered the prayers of Sweet Grass, only that he felt it was necessary.

"We walk a dangerous line between worlds," Hole in the Day said, stepping between them. "We may need both the Mide and the Catholic religion before all is done."

"We will also need food," X said, happy for his brother's support.

"Yes," Hole in the Day replied. "It's time to test this treaty."

The next morning, X rode south with his brother and Green Feather to the agency storehouse at Crow Wing.

The guard took them inside, showed them the room barren of even the smallest crumb. "How can this be?" Hole in the Day asked. In answer, the guard hid his head beneath the bill of his cap. "What kind of a man is this Great Father who doesn't keep his promises?"

"We have nothing for you," the guard said at last.

"You look well fed," Green Feather replied. "Where do you get your food?"

The guard's hand moved to his sidearm, rested there. "That's not your concern," he said.

A report came from Sandy Lake that five more were dead. The next day a report of another six. And each day after, reports came of a half-dozen more deaths. They rode further south to the newly established Fort Ripley, knowing there would be a trader there to service the needs of the homesteaders.

A man met them at the door, faint of breath and lean of face, his thick mustache drooping down on each side, so that his mouth always appeared to frown. He stepped forward with a cautious hand. "The name's Fairbanks," he said in greeting.

Hole in the Day raised his hand in return, but X stopped where he was. The world before him grew dark. He fumbled for the porch railing. Caught it. Looking at the trader was like peering through a gossamer curtain. The trader stood above X, impossibly tall, then knelt before him, offering something in his hand. A stick of licorice. He took the licorice, chewed it, relishing the taste, somehow knowing he'd earned it. The trader laughed, reached out as if to hug him. "Father?" X whispered. But the man faded before him.

"I don't have much." The trader said. "The winter has been hard for all and supplies are not getting through."

X stood behind his brother, afraid to take another step.

"Your children appear healthy." Hole in the Day nodded with his head in the direction of the doorway behind the counter from which two tow-headed girls peered through the storeroom curtain. "You have money for these trinkets bought on a trip to the city no doubt." He pointed to the Christmas tree in the corner, the paper ornaments that hung from it, and the few wrapped presents that lay beneath.

The trader started various explanations, but all fell short. Hole in the Day said nothing. A young girl's questioning voice sounded from behind the curtain followed by the sound of the mother shushing her. The trader glanced nervously toward the voice, then took pencil and paper in hand and began calculating something, or pretending to.

"I can't spare but a few cans," he said, searching the face before him, trying to take the measure of this man who wore a bright pink shirt beneath a black broadcloth coat and spoke so well. "Not without any money," he said, deciding his course. "I have customers here counting on this food. Customers who can pay."

"The government agent says the same," Hole in the Day continued, hoping his words would win the day. "We wish to live in this new world, but how are we to do so without money?"

"That's a question you should take up with the Great Father," the trader replied, his hand searching for something beneath the counter. Finding it, he seemed more assured. "Now if you aren't going to buy anything, I'll have to ask you to leave."

The translucent shell of sky broke upon the people of Sandy Lake. Hunger hit the oldest and the youngest, and many died. The people scoured the earth for seeds, nuts, and twigs passed over by the deer. Curly Head was the first to curse their chief. He'd not forgotten the boy's behavior at Fond du lac and now saw a chance to strike back, to gain his footing. He said he'd failed in protecting them. The people respected Curly Head and listened to him as he talked of how they should have given the Great

Father what he wanted, that if they had, the chimoo-komaanag in turn would have honored their promises to them. Nothing was left to do but return to Crow Wing.

"We cannot live in the white world without money," Hole in the Day told his brother one evening as they sat on the steps of their father's house. Hole in the Day had taken it as his own residence since returning from Fond du lac.

"We may not be able to live in it at all," X replied. The frothy sky faded to grey then black as they talked.

"Are you not supposed to give hope," Hole in the Day replied. "Is that not what Father Pierz instructs you to do?"

The two brothers couldn't help but smile.

That night, X dreamt that the moon floated to him across a field of snow. But as the round shape grew closer, he saw it was his brother's face now painted white. The face spoke to him in a strange tongue, a language that sounded like the kind of words he used to hear Father Pierz speak during prayer. As his brother spoke, a great tower rose up behind his face, a spire so tall it looked as if it would tear a rent in the sky. X didn't understand the import of the dream, but when he woke later in the night, he walked outside his shed only to hear the call of the great gray owl, and he knew the dream spoke good tidings.

That morning, when word arrived that over two hundred of the people at Sandy Lake had already succumbed to starvation or dehydration from dysentery, Hole in the Day emerged from his home dressed in a white calico shirt and his black broadcloth coat and vest, his green blanket wrapped over all. X had been waiting for him outside since the first light of dawn. But now that he saw him, he understood what the trader had thought at seeing his brother so brightly dressed. The trader had figured this Indian was holding out on him, that he must have money stashed away. X greeted his brother even as he recalled the fact that Hole in the Day took first pick from the boxes of government issue clothes when they'd been sent. And he worried about the pride he remembered that flashed across his brother's face as he picked out those bright shirts.

"We ride to St. Paul," Hole in the Day said by way of greeting. "Prepare yourself while I gather the horses. We will ask the chimookomaan God himself for it!"

X found Father Pierz kneeling in prayer before the dim light of the altar. "I must speak with you," he whispered. "I will be leaving again. This time for a week or more."

The priest continued his prayers.

"I hope for your blessing on this journey," X said to his back. "It is one of desperation."

Father Pierz finished his prayer, made the sign of the cross and rose to face X. "I mentioned before how you must choose which world to live in," he said.

"I am devoted to the teachings of the church, but the people need more than the spirit right now," X replied, stepping toward the priest, prostrating before him. "They need food to nourish their bodies before we can provide scripture to nourish their spirit."

Father Pierz nodded his head, though he appeared unsatisfied. "I wonder if it's easier for you on these trips."

He took a cloth from a hidden drawer in the side of the altar and began cleaning the chalice.

"It gives me purpose," X replied at last. "And yes, that purpose eases my loneliness."

"Did you ever think of mine?" Father Pierz stopped his work and turned directly to X.

"Yes."

X stepped forward but stopped short of the altar, so that he was forced to look up at the priest. "I have. But on this trip we will appeal to Christians for our cause." The word sounded strange in X's mouth, perhaps, he thought, because he had not used it before in this way.

"I cannot leave my post," Father Pierz said, continuing once again to clean the chalice. "Or I would help you."

"I understand," X replied, though he knew the real reason Father Pierz would not accompany them. He could see it in the pain limning the priest's mouth even as he scrubbed at the chalice, the pain he knew that was brought on by his own presence and the fight that presence caused within the priest. It was better that he go. He crossed himself and walked to the door.

"Wait," Father Pierz spoke. "Are you serious about your desire to continue your devotion to the church?"

X turned. From this distance, the priest did not appear so tall. "Yes."

"Then I name you deacon in training," Father Pierz replied, smiling slightly. He set down the cloth and chalice and stepped to the wardrobe at the side of the altar, from which he pulled a white cassock and belt. "Here are your new clothes," he continued. "The clothes of a deacon. Wear them with the blessings of the church in hopes that they might stimulate the generosity of these city Christians."

X stepped toward the priest, not looking at the robe, but at the man who held it out to him. He took the robe in his hand.

"Wear it with my blessing as well," Father Pierz said. And it was then X understood. The robe was meant to present one image to these Christians while hiding the other even from himself.

Hole in the Day and X rode south that afternoon. As they followed the Great River out of Crow Wing, they passed the ghostly figure of an emaciated boy, no more than ten, kneeling before a birch, gnawing on the bark, the snow falling about him.

They entered the city of St. Paul, the newly formed capital of the Minnesota territory, without any idea of where they were heading. Only that they must find help. Once again, Hole in the Day headed for the tallest building he could find; in this case it was the House of Hope Presbyterian Church, the bells in its high spire calling the faithful to morning service.

Though the papers of the day often mentioned the Indians in the Minnesota territory, it was usually to announce a victory over a renegade band of Sioux or Chippewa or to fix a price on the head of any Indian scalp a white could bring in. The current bounty was fifty dollars. Still, Hole in the Day and X were in no danger. The city people saw themselves as civilized and would never shoot an Indian within the confines of the city limits. In fact, the few whites who saw them on the street that cold January morning didn't seem to notice. X's skin was light enough to pass for white, and if any still doubted, the white robe, a gold cross embroidered above his breast, led them to take him for an itinerant priest. Wrapped in his green blanket, Hole in the Day looked more like a wandering beggar than a chief. It was only as they tethered their horses and mounted the church steps that a German family arriving late to church saw them for what they were. The man had just opened the large front door of the church when he realized who climbed the steps behind him. His wife gathered their two young children in her skirts, shooing the Indians away with her hand as one would a fly while the man stood dumb, holding the door open for them. X and Hole in the Day passed into the church and walked down the center aisle as the minister read from Corinthians:

Remember this: Whoever sows sparingly will also reap sparingly, and whoever sows generously will also reap generously. Each man should give what he has decided in his heart to give, not reluctantly or under compulsion, for God loves a cheerful giver.

They could not have asked for a better introduction. Hole in the Day flung off his green blanket, revealing the bright yellow calico shirt and black vest beneath. Shouts of alarm sounded from every corner of the church as the two brothers continued down the aisle. At first, the minister, a plump, dough faced man, attempted to continue with his sermon:

And God is able to make all grace abound to you, so that in all things at all times, having all that you need, you will abound in every good work.

But then a few of the parishioners began heading toward the exits. "Please," the minister said. "Please remain seated." It was only then that he looked out at his congregation and saw what all the excitement was about. "Hello," the minister said in a hushed tone, clearly taken off guard. A few more parishioners made their way toward the exits, but a surprising number stayed.

Regaining his composure, the minister combed back his thinning, grey hair, then raised both hands toward the sky. "Remember, this is a house of God. All are welcome." Some of the parishioners who'd started for the door returned to their seats. Those already sitting began whispering amongst themselves, speculating on the strange spectacle. X and Hole in the Day stopped not ten feet before the minister on his raised dais.

"What brings you to this house of God," the minister said at last, wiping away the sweat glistening on his forehead. "Do you seek salvation?" A few of the whispers shifted in register slightly, as if already some of the parishioners understood the righteousness of what would be asked of them on that day.

Hole in the Day did not reply to the minister but instead turned to address the assembled crowd. "The salvation I seek," he said, "comes in the form of aid for my people."

"If you are looking for aid," the minister replied, looking visibly relieved. "Then you have come to the right place, for God gave his only son so that all people would . . ."

"Death is on every side," Hole in the Day continued, talking over the minister. Once again, a few parishioners cried out, but the threat of panic was quickly averted as the minister gestured for all to be calm. "And in the minds of our young men, one death is as good as another," Hole in the Day continued, his powerful voice filling the church. The minister stepped off his dais. Hole in the Day paused, letting the weight of his words sink in, the implied threat. Shuddering voices rolled through the crowd: *What does he mean? Are the Indians going to attack? Will there be an uprising?* Then, before the voices could grow to a roar, he sang out above them all. "They wish to throw themselves away. They are like some poor animal driven into a hole and condemned to die." The voices of the parishioners slowly subsided, for they pictured now in their minds, not the warring savage, but a pitiful thing that needed saving. And they began to see what they called their Christian duty. "Your government asks us to live as you do," Hole in the Day went on, the timber of his voice changing, growing soft. "But we do not know how. And when we ask for help, they promise to give it, but no help comes." It was then X understood. And he marveled at the way his brother painted the picture the whites so wanted to see. He wondered at how his brother could speak with such pride before the gathering of chiefs at Fond du lac and how he was now able to bury that pride so deep no trace of it was visible. Is this our fate? he thought. To split down the center and wander the world like traveling mendicants.

The minister stepped down into the aisle, standing beside Hole in the Day, stretching out his arms and addressing the congregation. "You have come to the right place," he said, matching Hole in the Day's cadence and tone, as if he understood the importance of capitalizing on this moment. "You have come to the home of Christians, and we will teach you what that word means."

X had seen many things he'd wanted to forget in his life. But until that day he didn't know the long list of things to forget included himself.

"My life is made up of forgettings," I say to Niibiniishkang, though he is deep in sleep. "Dream, my friend," I tell him. "For dreams are the best kind of forgetting."

Niibiniishkang's eyelids flutter, his eyes racing beneath his lids. "Sleep, my friend," I tell him again. "Sleep and dream."

Not only did the parishioners give hundreds of dollars to Hole in the Day and X, but the St. Paul paper ran a front-page article on Hole in the Day's appearance in church and his speech. The article quoted the minister as saying, "The new Hole in the Day now seems friendly to our work. If by the grace of God he should be led to Christ, none can tell what he might do for his people. I, for one, will meet with him and work to bring both he and his people back to God." The result was a flood of donations of food, clothing, and money sent to the agency at Crow Wing. The people at Sandy Lake took the food, and the elders smoked to Hole in the Day's leadership in such a trying time. Children ran laughing with the dogs through the snow. The women returned to tanning the hides, making makizins for their men as they'd already worn their old ones thin in vain attempts to hunt throughout the winter. And the men smoked and told stories of winters past when game was so plentiful the deer walked into your wigwam and gave themselves up. The disaster at Sandy Lake had been averted, and Hole in the Day was now firmly ensconced as chief of all the Ojibwe.

X took up his duties as deacon full time under Father Pierz' tutelage, spending long days working with him and even, occasionally, sitting for evening supper. They talked quietly over plates of rice and sometimes chicken or fish, each ready at the first touch of silence to shift the conversation to their shared calling. X still wore the Mide shell beneath his robe. Alone at night, he pulled his otter skin Midewayaanag bag from beneath his make-shift bed, blew into it, then poured out the many shells, arranging them on the ground. He did not ask himself what he prayed for.

They found Fairbanks' body in a ditch a mile outside of Crow Wing. He'd been stabbed and scalped. The trad-er's wife screamed Hole in the Day's name to the papers. The government of the Minnesota territory issued boun-ties. Officials came asking questions. Rumors spread that it had been the half-breeds who were responsible and not the chief. In truth, the whites didn't want to hear any news that might implicate their new Christian knight among the heathens as a possible murderer.

Two days later, a posse of whites from the city round-ed up three Métis and lynched them, half-breeds who'd been living on their own outside the agency at Crow Wing. X knew them each by name, not government issue names or the names given to them by those who dream names but the names given to them by their parents: Alexis, Louis, and Pierre. They'd been farmers, occasional hunters, making their living from the land. Two had families of their own. Pierre had been too young to wed, though he'd kissed his first girl. X had met them on Father Pierz' rounds, and now he stood before the oak tree from which they swung.

He'd arrived just after the posse of men had left, narrowly missing getting lynched himself. With the help of Green Feather, he cut the men down and laid them on the ground. Their blue faces and blood-flecked eyes made it difficult to tell who was who, much less whether they were half-breeds or not. X tried to push the engorged tongues back in their mouths but could not do it. He sat beside the bodies long after Green Feather had gone for a shovel, trying to recall Father Pierz' conversations with each. If he concentrated hard enough, he could just barely see Father Pierz standing in the doorway.

X found his brother sitting on his porch steps, smoking his pipe, wrapped in his green blanket. "Do you know what the whites have done?"

"Geget," Hole in the Day replied.

X waited a very long time before speaking again. "Did you kill the trader?" he asked at last.

"What does it matter," Hole in the Day replied. "It has been done." He worked the pipe round and round in his hands as if he could not feel its shape.

"But by whom?"

"There are those who would say he died by his own hand. That actions have consequences."

"Look at me." X stood before his brother, resting his hand on his shoulder. "And what of the consequences of his murder?"

Hole in the Day took a long puff on his pipe, blew the smoke into the air and watched it disappear. "Three wissakode," he said at last. "They have no homes. No people. Who will mourn them?" He knocked the ashes of his pipe out into the frozen earth.

X swallowed the contorted faces of the hanged men. The memory went down like a worm inside him. "How can you say that?" he replied. "I am a wissakode, a half-burnt."

"No you are not." Hole in the Day stood, took a step toward the grey horizon. "You are one of us."

"I do not understand you. I thought you would choose differently than your father." He stepped forward, leaned his face within inches of his brother's.

"I cannot change what has been done."

"I thought that the night with the Wah'petonwan would have stayed with you if it stayed with anyone."

"Don't lecture me brother," he said. "I've learned the lessons of my father. To do what I can to further our people, to move them on the only path left to us." He turned from X and said nothing more.

X walked down to the Great River and stared out over its waters. Gray clouds flattened in the distance. Ice slurred the banks. Steam rose above all, scouring the earth.

A crow caws incessantly beyond the red blanket. Has my time come? Am I not allowed to finish my tale?

"I must," Niibiniishkang shouts from his sleep. "For my children, I must." His hand jerks as if grabbing something at his side. Eyes race behind shuttered lids.

"I think I'm beginning to trust you," I whisper to the form sleeping before me. "If you killed him, you did it with a pure heart."

Niibiniishkang thrashes his teeth. "No more!" he shouts.

And I smile, for I know of what he speaks. My skin hardened to bark long ago. I know it is only a matter of time before my arms curl and twist about me. "Don't worry," I tell him. "I don't think it will be your fate."

The border between yesterday and today drifts like a flock of starlings darkening the horizon. Shadows reel and stagger at the crow's cry.

Spurred by his success in St. Paul, and perhaps also in an attempt to quell the rumors about him and regain his good name, Hole in the Day began writing letters to the editor of the St. Paul paper. He spoke out against the removal of the Wisconsin Ojibwe to Sandy Lake, reminding the whites of the starvation that had barely been averted the year before. How did they expect the area to support four thousand more? His letter writing campaign was a success, and once again Hole in the Day was seen as the savior of his people.

Then the Sioux broke the strained peace by attacking a party of Ojibwe on the banks of the Apple River. Within days, Hole in the Day raised an army of three hundred who traveled down the Great River only to lie in ambush for the Sioux at Fountain Cave. X followed his brother, counseling peace, even as they prepared for war. That night, as they sat in the firelight of the cave, he reminded his brother that he was repeating his father's mistakes. Hole in the Day would not listen. They punished the

Sioux deeply for their transgressions, winning Hole in the Day fame that traveled even beyond the Minnesota territory. It seemed he could do no wrong.

X started a letter writing campaign of his own, writing to Bishop Whipple and Governor Ramsey, urging them to work for peace between the Sioux and Ojibwe before hostilities broke out again. The governor arranged for a council at Fort Snelling, inviting the Sioux and Ojibwe leaders. At first, Hole in the Day scoffed at the idea. War had brought him more fame than his speeches and letter writing, and he would not so easily give it up. X simply asked him how he wished to be remembered. Hole in the Day nodded his head in thanks, then left without a word.

Fort Snelling was packed with women on the day of the peace council, the wives of officers and diplomats who all came to see for themselves the chief everyone was speaking about. The Sioux refused to sit in the room much less take part in negotiations with women present, but Hole in the Day said, "We would be honored if the beautiful ladies would join us on our side of the table." Two of the women fainted on the spot at being asked to join the celebrated chief. The Sioux never had a chance after that. Not only did Hole in the Day win the peace, but he managed to take more of their land in the bargain.

By 1854, word had reached Washington of the Ojibwe chief who spoke with the eloquence of a statesman. The chief who chose the pen over the sword. The chief who could woo the wives of white senators and officers. The President wished to meet this great leader and test his skill even as the white government hoped to negotiate a new treaty that sought to extinguish the title of the Mississippi, Pillager, and Winnibigoshish bands to any and all lands in the Wisconsin and Minnesota territories. An invitation arrived through Willis Gorman, the newly appointed governor of the Minnesota territory, asking Hole in the Day to lead a delegation to Washington to discuss the Ojibwe options.

"You cannot journey with me this time," Hole in the Day told his brother that January morning after he received the train tickets. It is for the chiefs alone to talk with the Great Father."

"I have been of use to you before," X replied. "I may be of use again."

"Yes, you have been of value to me, brother," Hole in the Day replied, then turned away before X could say more.

"I see you," Niibiniishkang says from his sleep. "I hear your story, but I also taste the bitterness in your mouth. Drink more tea. It will help." And with that, he cracks a smile even from the other world.

I lean my face towards his, press my ear to his lips. "Tell me," I whisper. "Be my eyes and ears and tell this part for me. I fear if I continue it will be the end of me."

I lay my head upon his chest, and I listen for the deep dream of his story. It begins as a slow rumbling:

"We were like children," Niibiniishkang says, though his lips do not move. I am not sure how I hear his voice.

We stared wide-eyed out the windows of the train at the cities of the east with their towers that blocked out the sun, the people bustling by with their big hats, their walking sticks. Horses with carriages everywhere. But our chief would not look out his window like the rest of us: Shawboshkung, Gaa-nandawaawinzo, Gwiiwizhen-zhish, and Bizhiki. The closer we came, the more agitated Bagone-giizhig became. He wanted his people to be self-sufficient, to live like the chimookomaanag. But the more wealth and wonders he saw out the window, the more he feared that was impossible. Who would share such wealth? He would have a difficult job convincing the Great Father to give up anything. We tried to offer advice, but it was as if the ears of our chief were swollen with ticks. In the end, Bagone-giizhig said he would follow his own counsel. Each of us looked one to another, wondering what lay in store, for we were starting to understand that though both fate and the chimookomaanag had made him our leader in this endeavor, we knew not how to read him.

A delegation of black clad men met us at the station in Washington. They looked like priests except instead of white at their collar they wore a tied black ribbon. Gaa-nandawaawinzo asked if they were in mourning. They ignored his question. A tall man with a broad brow and eyebrows like overgrown moss seemed to be their leader. His name was Manypenny. After a word of greeting, he ushered us into a waiting carriage.

While the other chiefs stared out the window at the statues and monuments that lined the streets, Bagone-giizhig sat opposite Manypenny, quietly observing him. The white man, who we later were to learn was commissioner of Indian affairs, ignored him until our chief broke the silence.

"If we are to live like chimookomaanag," Bagone-giizhig began, "we need money and land." He sat straight as he spoke, fixing the commissioner with his gaze, using the tone and tactics that had been successful at Fond du lac.

Manypenny raised his hand, a fist of bees. "If you want to live like the whites," he replied, "then work hard like the whites." He gestured out the carriage window as if the sight and splendor of the city would be enough to end their conversation.

Bagone-giizhig did not look away. At last, he leaned across the carriage and actually tapped Manypenny on the knee. We worried our chief had already overstepped his bounds. "Could you support your family on nothing?" he asked. "No matter how hard you worked?"

Manypenny continued staring out the window, pretending he hadn't heard our chief at all. But I could see his mind working, seeking an answer to deal with an Indian whose belligerence he'd clearly underestimated. "The Indians must turn from hunting to farming," he said at last. He ran his palm along the edge of the carriage window, still not bothering to look at our chief. I counseled Bagone-giizhig to wait, to save his argument for the Great Father, but he would not listen.

"You are right to say we need education. But re-education is a long-term solution. It must be coupled with relief of our short term needs, and that means money and land." Bagone-giizhig moved so that Manypenny could not help but see him. Still, the commissioner picked at a loose thread in the fabric of the carriage door.

"Look at me, when I speak," Bagone-giizhig demanded. "We are not simpletons."

Manypenny opened his palm, letting loose the fist of bees. "Put away your arguments," he said, then added with a wry smile: "Save them for the President. I'd like to see what he makes of them, and of you."

The next day, we were taken to the White House. Our chief dressed in his pink shirt, his finest broadcloth and leggings. He wore a headdress with many eagle feathers upon his head, one for each scalp taken in the war with the Sioux, and the green blanket that was now his trademark.

Manypenny led the delegation to meet us on the steps before that great door. Bagone-giizhig asked to meet the President immediately, but the Commissioner told him it would all occur in good time. First, they wanted to give us a tour. What they really wanted to do was show us off to the other White House guests and to impress us with more statues and pictures of their forefathers. They told us about their President's prowess as a warrior. They said he rose to the height of Brigadier General in the Mexican-American war, and we nodded our heads.

President Pierce stood waiting for us in a large room filled with paintings of more long dead spirits. His unkempt hair made me think at once he was a wind manidoo. But that impression quickly vanished. He held a near-empty whiskey glass in his hand and offered each of the chiefs a glass when we arrived, then looked us straight in the eye and assured us he would listen to all we had to say. He spoke with Bagone-giizhig last of all, speaking of how his reputation preceded him, how the great work he'd done for his people would assure him a place in history. I didn't understand all of it, only that he seemed very good at placating his enemies. This President had the look of a man who meant well, and yet in his eyes, the tight clench of the jaw, and above all, the hair that flew about his head, he seemed troubled.

Pierce. Pierz. Father. Lover. Chimookomaan. Shadow of need binding to body. Blood cooling to black hunger. Trees growing out of the dark earth. Names swirl about like leaves, like stones. They land and bite the earth.

I open my eyes, trying to see past Niibiniishkang's chest, but the swirling stones block my vision. Niibiniishkang continues with his story, but I cannot make sense of it. Leaves fall about my eyes. I cannot bear their weight. I try to rise, but cannot. Does Niibiniishkang hold me to him once again? I cannot tell. I do not feel his body nor my own.

"Our history is different," Niibiniishkang says. "Our forefathers did not teach us to till the land, to read and write."

"I hear you," I say. "But I cannot stay and listen any more.

President Pierce took our chief out to the balcony, made his offer to Bagone-giizhig alone, but our chief laughed at him, saying, "Do not joke with me."

Manypenny moved between them, ready to signal the guards.

"Stop speaking, Niibiniishkang, I beg you."

I swat away the darkness until I stand on the same balcony. My wish granted to be beside my brother. Manypenny stands before me, dismissing me like a child, as he did all the chiefs.

My brother holds his blanket like a fortress tight about him, explaining that money is needed to build schools, to buy farm equipment and hire teachers, all that would be necessary to retrain his people. I realize, then, that both men want the same thing, assimilation. They only differ in their means. Manypenny cannot see the great divide between the whites and the Ojibwe. He does not understand that you cannot so easily change a hunting society to an agricultural one. And my brother for all his good intentions, does not know what a little money and a sedentary lifestyle will do to his people. President Pierce carefully observes the calm but assured manner of the young chief before him. The President is an intelligent man, I think, one who can be reasoned with. The argument goes on with neither side giving an inch, until President Pierce says enough. We adjourn to a sitting room, and he calls for more whiskey. I wait at my brother's side. And though he does not ask for it, I tell him what the President needs to hear, and he listens.

"We cannot both be in this dream, Ase-anse," Niibiniishkang says to me.

"Then throw me from it," I tell him. "Because I cannot remove myself. I am part of it now."

"If I knew how to do that, then I would be the Mide sorcerer and you the chief."

"Then we are both stuck until our parts are played out." But already Niibiniishkang is fading from my sight or I am fading from his. It no longer matters.

The servant returned with another bottle and clean glasses. Bagone-giizhig waited until all had their whiskey. No one said a word, each thinking that the first to speak would be the first to lose. But not this time. Bagone-giizhig stood as the last member of the delegation was served. "It is seven years since I took my position as leader of my people," he began. "And I will tell you we do not want this mock show."

Manypenny set his face hard, ready to deflect any attack. He raised his fist, but it was empty of bees, our chief had taken them all inside him and was ready to spit them out upon his foes.

President Pierce set his whiskey aside, leaned forward ever so slightly.

"We do not live outside, but within your nation," Bagone-giizhig went on, crossing the room to stand directly before President Pierce. "Why do you look upon us, then, as a foreign nation? We want to cease to be Ojibwe and become Americans. We want to be citizens and have the right to vote."

"Wait, my brother," I shout. "Do not be so quick to renounce who you are. There is another way."

"What other way?" Niibiniishkang asks. "We tried to fight and that path led only to death. Others surrendered and have become trees. Of what path do you speak?"

I try to answer but cannot. Words fade as soon as they are spoken.

Manypenny stood, raising his hand to interrupt. "I believe this has gone far enough." But President Pierce waved him back, and Bagone-giizhig continued talking. "A thick veil hides us from your view," he said. "The veil of Indian Affairs. Remove that veil and see if we are not as good Americans as you. Call upon us and see if we do not know how to fight. We will stand by you in time of war. We want the right of suffrage, the right to vote, to be subject to your laws, to earn our living from the soil. We have set our hearts on it." And with that, Bagone-giizhig returned to his seat.

President Pierce took up his whiskey and sipped it slowly, deep in thought. The other chiefs and I argued once again about Bagone-giizhig's methods, many questioning the rightness of his path, others saying it was the only way. I reminded them that the chimookomaanag respected audacious speeches and acts, that the quiet with which the Ojibwe chiefs sought accord was not respected by them.

"You are a remarkable young man," President Pierce offered at last. He stood, pocketing his hands. "Come back tomorrow. We'll have Senator Rice meet with you to write up a list of proposals."

Before President Pierce could finish his speech, Bagone-giizhig raised his own hand to silence him. "I have met with Senator Rice before at Fond du lac," he said. "And I do not trust him. He promised food that shortly thereafter disappeared. Here is our list." He pulled a piece of paper from his breast pocket and laid it on the table. "You'll find everything I have said written here."

The President gave a strained smile. He pressed his finger to the paper, pinning it there. Manypenny put his hand out as if staving off a dog. Clearly, neither was prepared for this. An Indian who was an orator was one thing. There had been a few. But more rare still was one who could read and write. They'd been used to men signing treaties they couldn't understand.

Before the President or Manypenny could add anything, Hole in the Day made his final point. "We need money and land, yes. But most important, we need teachers to train our people on how to work the land. Unlike the whites, we will not use the money to hire men to work for us, or worse yet, slaves." Bagone-giizhig pulled the blanket about his shoulders, looking for a brief moment like an old man.

The room fell silent. The other chiefs looked to each other, unsure if they liked the tenor of Bagone-giizhig's words or what the consequences might be if they followed him. Manypenny eyed President Pierce for his reaction, but the President only raised the whiskey to his nose and inhaled deeply. "You are an anomaly," he said at last to our chief. "No. Stranger than that. An enigma. A chief and a citizen. A civilized man and a savage. You invoke the law and then you defy it. You say you need money, but not what it buys—the power of men to do the work for you." He walked to the door ahead of Bagone-giizhig. "You exist on the border of things it seems to me. And it is time we brought you in. Come, let us speak alone." And with that, he gestured for our chief to follow him into the antechamber. Manypenny paled, then stormed out. I turned to the other chiefs, fearful of what would come to pass, wondering at the hidden meaning in the white leader's words.

"Can you see from this side, Niibiniishkang?" I ask. "Do you understand now? Is this where things went wrong? Was it because of my advice or because I was not there at all? I place my ear again upon his breast but hear only the raspy breathing of an old man deep in sleep.

I rise and stir the fire. The embers have almost died, ash graying to white. It is late. The afternoon peels away and with it the day. I add a few twigs, a log to the fire, blow gently upon the ashes. The rising smoke stings my eyes. A flame catches. Good, I think. There will be light, warmth. Maybe we will know today. Maybe we will understand what happened to my brother, to us. And then Newobiik enters, carrying a pot. I can smell the stewed rabbit within. She sees her husband still sleeping and smiles. She puts the pot atop the fire, then comes to her husband, pulling the blanket about him. I return to Niibiniishkang's side, take his hand in mine. I will fight her for him if I must.

The new treaty established reservations at Mille Lac, Sandy Lake, Leech Lake and Gull. In return for their ceded land, much of the northern Minnesota territory, the Ojibwe were promised money with which to pay teachers, to buy farm equipment and seed. Hole in the Day himself was given six hundred and forty acres and several thousand dollars to "distribute as he pleased"—something the government had never done before, and probably would not again. He cleared one hundred acres for farming and planned to use the rest of the land and the money to create a farming community on the edge of Crow Wing for his people. He named the community New Rome and set it two miles north of Crow Wing, far enough, he said, from the "pernicious influence of that place." X was not sure what his brother meant by that. More Métis arrived in Crow Wing every week. They now outnumbered the Ojibwe. Of course, more people meant more saloons, more whiskey.

Hole in the Day used the money to begin work on a road between his community and Crow Wing, and a ferry to cross the Mississippi, so his people could have access to the agency. Because of course part of President Pierce's deal involved sending a new agent to distribute the money and goods, and to watch over the affairs of the Ojibwe. More importantly, to watch over the land. The agent's name was Lucius Walker, a tall and somewhat eccentric man prone to outbursts. He almost always complained of the cold, probably because he kept his head shaved close. By the fresh cuts along his face most days, he seemed obsessed with keeping clean of facial hair as well.

Attracted by the growing population and the promise of working with the government to supply the people of Crow Wing and New Rome, a trader from Fond du lac by the name of Clement Beaulieu set up shop soon after Walker arrived. A tall man with a bushy red beard and hair, and wild, nervous hands, he was the opposite of Walker in almost every way. He told Walker upon his arrival, "Never before has an Indian negotiated money for his people. I want to help them spend it."

Beaulieu. Dirty faced man. Jaw slack as a possum. His lips do not move when he lies from his gravel mouth. Killer. Murderer. Let me say the words now. Name him, so we can be done with this story. Say the word. Killer. Leave it for a swarm of crows.

A shrewd businessman, Beaulieu set up a contract with the government to distribute supplies to the Ojibwe and Métis alike. The first month he also gave away certain goods to the people of both towns, bags of coffee and seed, and beer and whiskey as well. He stood on the porch of his new store on the edges of Crow Wing addressing all who came for the free goods. "You can rely on the government supplies if you like, but I wouldn't advise it. In a short time, they will cease."

"But we were promised those supplies," Green Feather shouted back.

It was then Beaulieu smiled, showing his stained and broken teeth. He knew he had them. "I have worked with the white government before," Beaulieu went on, scratching at his red beard as if he had an itch that would not go away. "I know how their promises work. I don't need to remind you of Sandy Lake."

It was then Hole in the Day stepped forward from the back of the crowd. "I remember Sandy Lake well," he said. "But I also remember that we cannot trust traders."

Beaulieu's smile thinned. "You are a cautious man," he said. "I like that. And I want to earn your trust." With that, he went inside his store, returning a moment later, his arms piled high with blankets. "Take what I offer. And take more," he said. "As a show of good faith."

Hole in the Day strode forth, picked up a bottle of whiskey from the crate beside the other goods. "We accept your offer," he said. "But not your whiskey." He laid the bottle at Beaulieu's feet and took the blankets from the trader's arms.

Beaulieu scratched at the back of his neck as if he was infested with lice. "Very well," he said at last. "Let us work together." He reached out his hand, forcing Hole in the Day to set aside the blankets in order to shake it.

Beaulieu stood smoking on the porch of his store, as one by one, people came to take the supplies. He smiled and nodded to each one, proud of the fact that they knew nothing of him, that he was Métis on his mother's side, that both his mother and father had been killed by the Sioux. He was fond of cards, playing poker whenever he had the chance, and he knew it was important to keep at least one secret in dealing with anyone, white or Indian. Besides he didn't look like a half-breed, and he'd learned long ago it was best not to advertise the fact.

From that day forward, Hole in the Day took to wearing a colt revolver beneath his green blanket. A gift from President Pierce. And he began work on a large home in the center of New Rome. As soon as the living room was complete, he hung a portrait of President Pierce above the buffet that housed his fine china tea set, more gifts from his trip to Washington.

Mornings, Hole in the Day farmed his own land. Afternoons, he made the rounds with X, encouraging the Ojibwe to join him at New Rome, showing them what he'd done and offering them some of his land to farm on their own. X suggested they talk also to the Métis, invite them to the new town, but each time his brother met him with an excuse, saying "Not today."

Hole in the Day's fame grew. Journalists arrived from Little Falls and beyond to confirm the rumors of the chief who modeled his town on a white farming community. X found himself trailing his brother and the journalists, as they walked through corn fields and gardens of squash, carrots, and peas, his brother bragging all the while of how he would make this town a model for others of their kind fighting for a path that would allow them to survive.

When it came time for tea with the journalists on his brother's gleaming white porch, X found he did not have the stomach for it and returned to the church.

He was no longer sure what his brother had become. So he returned to Father Pierz, assisting in the services, bringing the communion wafers to the Father, wiping his lips of the wine after the priest took his sip. Week after week, he stood at the side of the altar, watching Father Pierz bless those who kneeled before him, taking communion, unsure what this path offered him that following his brother did not.

After the service, Father Pierz would ask him to join him in prayer or some other task, always using the name he'd given him, as in: "Thomas, let us pray." Or, "Thomas let us discuss Jeremiah 15. Tell me what it suggests of false religion." Or, "Thomas, would you read over my sermon for tomorrow? I value your input."

During this first year after the treaty, Beaulieu slowly cut off his gifts, charging the people now in furs or services, whatever he could get. Most people stayed in Crow Wing trying to survive off the combination of government supplies and what Beaulieu was willing to trade. A few joined Hole in the Day, trying their hand at farming, and some even met with success. All the while, the government agent Walker observed both the chief and the trader from afar, taking notes and sending those notes back to Washington.

The following spring, Curly Head came to visit, bringing with him his youngest daughter Agidajiwekwe. He knew what he was doing. He'd been worried about Hole in the Day's rising influence since that day at Fond du lac. And now he sought an alliance. All eyes, Ojibwe,

Métis, and white followed Curly Head's daughter as she walked, dressed in black calico, beside her father down the Main Street of Crow Wing. The men buzzed about her like flies. And yet, unlike other pretty girls, who received so much attention in a settlement starved of young women, she showed no outward signs of vanity, but kept her head low, her hands clasped together before her.

Hole in the Day was twenty-eight, and though he had been with many women, he'd never taken a wife. Hearing of the daughter's beauty, Hole in the Day invited Curly Head to his house in New Rome, along with Father Pierz. He wanted to show them the crops that had already started to grow, perhaps enlist the priest's help in converting others to this new way of life. The visit was exactly what Curly Head had hoped for.

X knew what the old chief was doing. Curly Head was a shrewd man. He'd hovered around Crow Wing, waiting to be invited, waiting until word of his daughter's beauty found its way to Hole in the Day's home. X studied Curly Head's calculated manner as he presented his daughter to them, pointing out her finer attributes, mentioning her many suitors back home at Sandy Lake. As Curly Head talked of some of his own attempts to work the land, he shepherded Hole in the Day ever closer to his daughter. All the while the father talked, the daughter sat quietly, hands crossed in her lap.

"What do you think of the white practice of taking only one wife, Agida? Of a woman taking only one husband?" Hole in the Day asked, perhaps trying to get the girl to look up so that he could judge her eyes.

Curly Head started to answer for her, but his daughter

cut him off. "I think it's also the Ojibwe practice when the man and the woman honor each other," she said, her face still bowed.

Hole in the Day smiled, his eyes gleaming. She would make a worthy wife for a chief.

It was then Curly Head nodded to his daughter. She rose from the table, grabbed a basket and went outside to gather the vegetables from the garden.

"You have done well," Hole in the Day said to Curly Head, offering him a pipe. "She will make a fine wife."

Curly Head smiled and took the pipe. "Agida is a hard worker. You'll need little help with her around. She can do the work of three wives."

"Do you worry I might form alignments with other clans?" Hole in the Day's smile was calculated

Curly Head nearly choked on his smoke. He set down the pipe. "I only meant that she is worth much."

Hole in the Day stood and walked to the window where he could see Agida working. "The white path is the only way," he said. "In everything. I will have *one* wife."

Curly Head nodded and picked up the pipe once again.

Later, as Agida tried to figure out how to use the wood stove in the kitchen, her father heaped praise on Hole in the Day for raising such a fine crop in his first year. Hole in the Day swelled with pride.

"This is nothing," he said. "Before the year is out, I will not only have enough to live on, but I'll be able to give some back to our people. Show them what they can do if they are willing to change."

"What if the cost of that change is that they forget who they once were," X spoke without thinking.

The two chiefs turned to X. He could feel Father Pierz stiffen beside him. For her part, Agida pretended not to hear as she cooked the vegetables. Curly Head passed the pipe to Hole in the Day, as if waiting for him to speak. Hole in the Day approached his brother, handed the lit pipe out to him, nodded for him to take a puff. "Have you lost so much, brother?" he asked. "We took you in. You became one of us. You assimilated."

X stared at the pipe.

It was then Father Pierz finally looked at X. "You have the best of both worlds, Thomas," he said. "Look at you now. You're on your way to becoming a deacon."

He'd meant it as a compliment. X took the pipe offered to him, turned it around and around in his hands, examining it. Hole in the Day and Curly Head nodded as if the issue had been decided. Agida stirred the pot, glancing up for the first time, catching X's eye. Only she understood.

X put the pipe in his mouth and closed his eyes, inhaling the rich scent. He breathed it into his lungs, but the fire had burned too hot, and the smoke scorched his throat.

The cold grinds flesh to flour. Ice gnaws skin until nothing remains. I heap more blankets on the old war chief, worried the chill will take him in his sleep.

"The world is made fresh every day," I tell Niibiniishkang. "While we cling to the fleeting mirage of the old." I take my cup, bring it to my lips, and realize only then I have forgotten to fill it. I rise and go to the fire. The tea is still warm. "You sleep well for an old man," I say to him. "No wonder

Newobiik stays away. She must seek other things to do, other means of entertaining herself."

I return to Niibiniishkang's side. *"You are a lucky man to have a wife who loves you so. I had that once, but I didn't know what to do with it. I hope you never forget how rare it is."*

Agida and Hole in the Day married. Not a Christian marriage as Hole in the Day wanted, but an Anishinabe one. In these matters, the woman always wins out. The ceremony was joyous, bringing people from every band. Clearly, Hole in the Day had united his people, not just by saving the band at Sandy Lake or negotiating peace with the Sioux, but now by joining with those who would speak ill of him. Curly Head even served as Hole in the Day's sponsor, giving advice on matters of family as well as governing the people. And all the while, X watched his brother, wishing he could feel the same happiness at having someone by his side. Each night he sat for dinner with Father Pierz, but the priest would not look at him, at least not in the same way he did that night long ago. The candlelight burned between them. X stared into the flickering flame even as they made small talk. *Yes, Moose Dung looks healthier now that he's left the bottle. I hadn't realized that Louis Tessier was no longer with his wife.* As the flame burned down, the priest blurred before him.

The night of Hole in the Day's wedding, X lay with his first woman, a frail young Pillager from Leech Lake named Flower. Both had drunk too much and so didn't remember how they tumbled into X's bed made of poplar branches, nor how her dress curled back over her waist,

124

or how he stuck his fingers inside her, waiting for his own sex to stiffen.

Cracked and rotten dreams swirl like leaves over a dead lake. Shadows shift over the mud-clouded surface. Sift through the smoke, looking for true north.

The red curtain flutters. Niibiniishkang watches Ase-anse attempt to enter Flower and fail. He notes the sweat dripping from Ase-anse's brow, the fierce look in his eyes, as if he is not trying to find himself at all, but destroy whatever bit still lives inside him. He sees how Flower closes her eyes and weaves her head from side to side. And he reaches out to touch them both, to tell them there are other ways to fight off the tumble fever of desire. But as he does so, he joins with them and soars out into the moonless night.

Father Pierz writhes within his narrow bed, kicking at sheets, reaching out, grasping nothing but air.

In another dream, Hole in the Day lies atop Agida in their wedding bed, thrusting into her again and again.

I bite down on the bitter paste of pine.

Niibiniishkang drifts back to his own dreams of horses upon a crimson plain.

Father Pierz buries his head in his pillow, calls out a muffled name.

Hole in the Day slows, feeling a tingle like breath upon his back, then resumes his thrusts.

In the morning, X rose quickly, dressed and went outside to sit in the dirt as the sun broke over the line of birch in front of his hut. He'd expected to find the young girl gone, had even wondered if she'd been there at all.

But he woke to his pounding skull only to feel her warm skin pressed against his. He didn't know what he would do, only that he dared not go back inside.

So, she came outside. She'd made a bowl of wild rice and carried it to him, the fair skin of her face and shoulders glowing in the rose colored sun. Her red and black calico dress hung loosely about her, hiding her taut limbs.

"You are Métis, a wissakode?" he asked.

The girl didn't say anything.

"It doesn't matter," he said.

She brought him the plate. The wild rice smelled nutty.

X studied her before taking it. "We are born half-burnt," he whispered as if talking to himself. "The sun scorches us before we ever step into this world." He sat upon the ground, scooping mouthful after mouthful from the plate with his hands. She sat beside him. Her skin smelling like the rice.

"I am not ashamed," she said.

That afternoon, X packed his things and headed to the rectory. Flower met him at the door, but kept her eyes downcast. She didn't say a word.

"You can stay if you like," X told her. He touched her shoulder, trying to make the moment right. "If you have no home, make this one yours." She turned, but he could not meet her eyes.

He found Father Pierz kneeling beside his bed in prayer. He hadn't knocked and now wished he would have. The priest looked tired, the lines about his eyes cut dark. He knew the priest heard him. Why would he not turn? He stepped closer until he could touch him.

"What do you want with me?" Father Pierz asked, his eyes shut and his hands clasped in prayer.

"It's time we talked," X replied.

Father Pierz pushed himself up as if it were an effort and turned to face X. "We already have, Thomas," he said.

"No," X replied, taking the priest's hands in his own. "We haven't. To say we cannot speak of things is not to talk. It is silence. It is death."

Father Pierz pulled his hands away. He went to his dresser, removed the rope cincture, tied it about his waste. "Do not do this to me, Thomas."

X followed the priest, took him by the robe and turned him around. "I am not Thomas," he said. "Look at me!"

Father Pierz tucked his rosary into his pocket but kept his hand within, fingering it. "You are a deacon in training of the one, holy, Catholic, and apostolic church. You are . . ." The priest's voice trembled.

"No!" X shouted. "I am a half-blood. A two-spirit. And I am in love with you." He fell at the priest's knees, embraced his legs, and buried his face in his robe.

Father Pierz stood still as a statue. He placed his hand on X's head, kept it there as the candle burned down on the bedside table behind them. "You are Thomas," Father Pierz said at last. "Named after Thomas Aquinas, priest of the Dominican order of the Catholic church, theologian and philosopher. You will use your learning to help others come to the faith."

"No," X whispered into the folds of the black robe. "I am not." He took the priest's hand. "This is how I know I exist," he said.

Father Pierz kept his hand there, and X let the warmth enter his body.

"I must go now, Thomas," the priest said. "I have to finish my sermon."

X moved once again into the corn shed behind the rectory. He no longer worked with Father Pierz. He spent his days wandering the woods, remembering the time after the Wah'petonwan when he studied plants and collected herbs. He dug up the bearberry root and bittersweet, smelled again its earthy aroma. He stripped the bark of the red willow and boiled it, mixing the water with other herbs, testing it to find ever better pain relievers. Anything that would numb his head. He still wore the cross about his neck, but found he pulled forth the Mide shell more and more, reciting prayers he'd learned from Sweet Grass. At first, they came in fragments, but the more he spoke them, the more he found the words. Father Pierz came knocking on the shed door early mornings in hopes of finding him, but if he was home, he would not answer. Evenings, Father Pierz returned again to invite him to dinner, but X stayed out into the dark, preferring to eat what he could scrounge. He stayed there through the spring.

Newobiik carries a candle from the fire. Steps over me and sets the candle on the ground beside her. Her face has the same shape as Flower's. I had not noticed that before. So, too, the almond cut of her eyes. But it is when she caresses his forehead that I am undone. How can a hand speak so much? I see the delicate curve of Flower's hand hovering before me in the morning as I wake. The soft green scent of her.

Newobiik removes her makizins, then her deerskin dress. Her wrinkled breasts softened by the warm glow of candle-light. What would it have been like to observe the changes in Flower's breasts day after day, the slow sag, the eventual withering? Newobiik blows out the candle and slips in beside her husband.

With each passing day, X found his walks through the forest took him closer and closer to his own cabin. From a distance, he watched Flower emerge in the morning to tend the garden he'd begun, and he was not unpleased to see her. Soon, he found himself passing whole mornings sitting on a stump or a rock, watching Flower work. One day she stopped her work, looked out to the horizon and gestured for him, as if she'd seen him there all along. He rose and went to her. Her arms felt like home.

For the rest of the spring and into early summer, X and Flower tended their garden. X made furniture, a bed, table and chairs for their cabin. Use to working only with his mind in the church, studying the liturgy, he took pride in the fact that he'd made something with his hands. And when Flower smiled at his work, he felt solid like the furniture.

They sat outside in the early hours of the evening before bed. Sometimes they'd sit in silence, listening to the occasional rapping of the woodpecker or the rustle of branches signaling a deer in the brush just beyond their house. They could stay like that for an hour or more until one of them broke the silence, usually Flower asking a question.

"Why did you choose to live here in Crow Wing instead of near your brother?" she asked one night as if spurred by the hoot of the grey owl in the distance.

"I don't know," he said at last. "I'd always thought it was my brother who moved away and not I who remained."

Flower laughed, then, a sound like tiny bells. "He's only a short distance up the road from here," she said. "You can still see him whenever you want."

"Yes," X replied, as if his mind were somewhere else.

"Let's see them tomorrow," Flower said. "You know how he likes to have tea."

"Yes."

The following afternoon, as they took tea on X's brother's front porch, Hole in the Day couldn't stop from grinning. His brother asked him what was so funny, but he would say nothing as they sipped their tea. It was only once they'd finished that Agida informed them she was with child. The moment she spoke the words, Hole in the Day sprang from his seat and gestured for them to follow him. He led them to a clearing at the edge of his property, a spot that overlooked the Great River.

"I cleared the ground myself," Hole in the Day said.

"For what purpose?" X asked.

"For a schoolhouse," Hole in the Day replied. "I want my children to be educated, as well as the children of all the Ojibwe."

Agida took her husband's arm in her own.

"But there are more Métis now than Ojibwe in Crow Wing," X said.

Hole in the Day turned to his brother, his broad grin strained only at the corners. "They will have a school someday, too," he said, gesturing the idea away with his hand. "I have already put in a request to the agency for a school teacher. They tell me I have to use a chimoo-komaan contractor to supervise the work on the school-house."

"Do they not trust you to supervise your own people?" Agida asked her husband.

"I don't care," he replied. "As long as we get the school."

"The school is a good thing," X said, but found he could say no more. He turned from his brother and walked to the edge of the clearing. The red stripe of a Kingfisher caught his eye as it flew over the river, then suddenly it dropped, disappearing beneath the surface.

Hole in the Day got his contractor, and then hired several Ojibwe from Crow Wing to work on the school. He spent his mornings hoisting beams into place, hammering supports. Afternoons, he worked on his own fields—or helped some of the other farmers who'd come to join him. The BIA agent, Walker, often came to visit, to see firsthand. And indeed, Walker's first report back to President Pierce spoke of how the chief was doing more to civilize the tribe than any white man had ever done. In those first months, Walker seemed to be a friend of the Ojibwe. He often walked with Hole in the Day to check on the progress of the school, the road to Crow Wing, and the ferry to the agency. Walker talked animatedly of the importance of bringing civilization to the Indian, how the worst that could happen now was for the people to fall back into savagery. Spit flew from the corners of his mouth as he talked, his eyes glazing over, as if with each word he spoke, he slipped into a place known only to him. Hole in the Day nodded along, as if he knew exactly how to handle the agent.

Beaulieu also joined them at times. He distrusted any man who might usurp his power, and Walker seemed like just such a man. So, he followed behind as the two talked of plans for the town, observing their manner, making mental notes in case he'd need them someday. Business for him had been good, especially since the start of the construction, and he wanted to keep it that way.

That autumn, when the last floorboard of the schoolhouse was in place, word came that Hole in the Day was made an official citizen of Minnesota and would be allowed to vote in the upcoming election at the end of the month, which he did, telling everyone how he signed the voter role as "H. Day, Esq." President Pierce had actually held true to his promise, even as he left office. Hole in the Day marched back through Crow Wing, triumphant, promising that by the next election all of his people would enjoy the same right he had to vote. The people listened and nodded their heads, much as Hole in the Day did with Walker. Their wariness proved correct. Hole in the Day was the only Indian to ever get the right to vote and still retain the rights granted to him by treaty. For that day, at least, it seemed he could live in both worlds.

The census taker arrived after the election. A tall man with a sloping brow and deep-set eyes that always looked tired as if he recited the names on his lists to get to sleep at night. But rather than attempt to spell the names or even to translate them, he and Walker often assigned new names to each person, Métis or full-blood. They made it into a game, laughing over the puns they created or the various rhyming names they could devise. The day they came to X's door and asked his name, he said nothing.

"I've heard the chief call you something," Walker said, rubbing his hand over his sweaty, bald head. "Ass something," I believe. He and the census taker burst out laughing. "Ass-once, maybe that was it," said the census taker.

X started to close the door, but Walker blocked it with his foot. "We need a name for the government rolls," he said. And X was about to give him the name of Thomas just to be rid of them when Walker smacked the census taker on the back. "Paulson," Walker said. "We'll call him Paul Paulson."

"That has a nice ring to it," the census taker agreed. The two laughed. And again, X tried to close the door.

"Your wife needs a name, too," Walker said, his skin looking almost translucent in the heat of the summer sun.

"How about Mary Paulson," the census taker offered, writing down the name even as he said it. "They're not really married, so let us give her the name of Mary Magdalene."

And so it went. Agida became Madeline Day just so they could call her "Mad Day" for short. Walker grew even more animated with the census taker than he did on his strolls with Hole in the Day. After they decided on a name, Walker would sing it out to himself over and over, changing it slightly each time until he was satisfied. He took particular pleasure in first bastardizing the names of the Métis, and then giving them new ones. Elzear Pierre he renamed Franklin after the outgoing pres-

133

ident and Ovide Tessier he renamed James after the new president.

Then one day the census taker didn't appear at the agency office for the day's rounds. Walker sent men to look for the man, as he was from the city, and they feared he could easily lose his way in the thick woods between the two towns. They didn't find the body for nearly a week, and when they did, Walker insisted upon seeing it for himself to determine the cause of death. He brought Father Pierz with him to the bottom of a steep bank at the edge of the Great River. The census taker's bloated body lay amongst weeds. It was crawling with maggots. The priest excused himself to vomit, but Walker donned his gloves and knelt beside the man, pushing at his body, searching for evidence of violence. He found nothing, though it didn't convince him. When he stood, he noticed some of the white worms crawling on his own ankles and pant leg. Calmly, he picked them off one by one. The official report said the census taker had slipped and fallen down into the ravine.

Walker was no longer the same man after that day. The change was slow. At first, no one noticed as he slapped at the air or at his legs, complaining of mosquitoes, deer flies and tics. On his morning walks with Hole in the Day, he began to question the possibility of civilization in a place so infested with insects. Over the following year, Walker's behavior got worse. Beaulieu took advantage of the situation and pointed out the odd antics to the Métis and full bloods living nearby, who would wait alongside the road just to watch Walker and laugh as the agent would begin slapping at himself with increasing speed until it reached such a point some evenings that he could be seen screaming and running for cover, shouting about bug infestations. The sight kept the townspeople entertained for quite some time. Then Walker stopped going out on the walks altogether and cloistered himself in his office. He sealed the crack beneath the door with a blanket and kept the windows shuttered until the agency felt like a sweat lodge. And there he sat fully clothed in his long wool pants and coat, actually tying cords around his ankles and wrists in an attempt to keep out the pesky insects. Those who wished to see him on business had to knock and even then it took urging with whiskey to get him to open the door, which is exactly what they had to do when Father Pierz' naked body was discovered hanging from the rafters of the rectory.

Beaulieu was the one who discovered the body, as he'd gone to see the priest in hopes of discussing his new daughter's baptism. He went straight to Walker. X would not have known anything until later had he not seen a group of men marching toward the agency, each with a bottle of whiskey. He followed, and when he heard what the commotion was about, he ran to the church.

The cry of dogs drowns all color. The afternoon sun blisters the day. Only shadows roam.

The red blanket shifts in the doorway. The wind blowing with numbed persistence.

"Don't leave me here alone in the darkness," I beg.

In reply, the soft breath of lovers entwined.

"Newobiik," I whisper. "Give me the sanctity of your marriage bed. Let me lie here awhile. If not, I fear I will take

root in this place." I close my eyes and pray for sleep. But it does not come.

"How would my life have been different had he lived?" I ask. "He did the act with his own rope cincture, the cloth of his office."

No matter how hard I try I cannot escape the other world. I climb the chair to cut the rope. I dress him, covering his body before the others arrive. I hold him even as they pound on the door I've locked. Beaulieu must break the window to get in.

"Sleep," I whisper to the air. "Give me sleep."

The church wasted little time in sending a replacement, despite Walker's failure to file the proper reports. When the new priest arrived in Crow Wing, no one saw him come; nobody even knew his name until he'd already moved into the rectory. His quiet, unassuming demeanor, however, belied his reputation as a man who would fight not only for the souls of the Ojibwe but for their rights as well.

Agida went into labor the week after the priest's arrival so that his first official duty was to baptize the baby. Hole in the Day insisted on the baptism, and insisted, too, that the baby be named John, after John the Baptist. He said his son would be a prophet in the new world.

X remained outside the church at Crow Wing. He knelt in the dirt, held his Mide shell and said his own prayer. He'd come thinking he would enter the church and saw the disappointment on his brother's face when he could not. The shadow of Father Pierz over the place was simply too strong for him.

After the ceremony, the congregation began filing out, mostly elders of the clan, but Curly Head and many members of his family had come down at Hole in the Day's urging. They were not in favor of the baptism and looked uncomfortable as the new priest approached them, trying to engage them in conversation.

The sun rose higher in the sky burning off the remaining traces of chill, promising to make this day the last warm one of the year. And so, the people lingered, taking turns holding the new baby, congratulating Agida, some even welcoming the new priest. X watched how Flower held the infant in her paler arms, touching its lips with her finger and cooing at it. He looked about him. Though the town now numbered nearly three hundred with over half of them Métis, there were no other half-bloods in attendance. He recalled the names of the Métis parishioners he'd come to know while working with Father Pierz: Alexis Pascal, Philippe, Elzear Pierre, but even as he said the names, the faces faded before him.

It was then he saw the ghostly black robe approach, and, for a moment, he swore it was Father Pierz. The robe floated closer, a blurred face appearing above it, and X realized the new priest stood before him. He was not what X expected. Where Father Pierz was thin, his look haunted, the new priest was filled out in a way that made him seem comfortable, even self-assured.

The priest reached out to touch X's shoulder but X shrunk away, clutching the Mide shell beneath his shirt.

"Are you the man I've heard about, the brother to the chief?" the priest asked. His eyes were soft.

"How do you know who I am?" X asked, not really caring what the priest said in return.

"I made it my business to know the situation here before I took on the job," the priest said. "Your brother is quite well known, and from what I can tell, quite misunderstood. No one seems to know what he'll do next."

X fought off the urge to touch the black robe, to run his hands over the material. "What do you want of me?" he asked.

"Only to meet you." The priest smiled then so that X could see the many lines that played about his eyes. He was older than he'd first appeared. "I'd heard you were in training to become a deacon of the church."

"I studied once," X replied. "But I no longer have the calling." X saw Father Pierz' haunted face in the flickering candlelight, felt the caress of his hand on his own. He grabbed the priest by the forearm.

The priest pulled back for a moment, unsure what was happening, and X let go. The priest nodded, as if he understood. "If you ever consider following the path of God again, I would be happy to guide you," he said. "There are those in the church who would frown on such a thing, but I would do it."

X stood silent before the priest, then turned and walked away.

"I am Father Tomazin," the priest said after him. "And you are, Paul Paulson, am I right?"

He didn't correct the priest.

It was nearly a year before X found any peace. In that time, he often wandered the woods as he'd done after the Wah'petonwan. He'd wake before dawn, walk down to the Great River and sit in the fog on its banks, hoping that the frost might fall like rain, washing him away.

Mornings, he gathered herbs, squeezing them until they weeped their juice in his hands. Afternoons, he hid away in a hovel he'd built, praying the Mide until he drifted off into sleep. His dreams warped and twisted themselves during this time. In the dream he had most often, he held his juice-stained hands out to a caterpillar that crept along the scattered pine needles on the forest floor. The caterpillar inched onto his hand, began nibbling at his fingers. When he'd looked again, the insect had eaten half of his hand. He'd felt no pain.

Flower kept a bowl of food out each night, even those nights when he didn't return until well after dark. And she kept his bed warm for him, so that he often drifted into sleep feeling as if he were cocooned. Then, one night he woke with a start. He understood. He hugged her tight, whispered his thanks in her ear as she woke to him.

The next few years X approached something close to happiness. He worked hard, helping his brother in the construction of the roads and the ferry. They taught the people how to cultivate their land. He only wished more of the Métis would join his brother's farming community. But still they stuck to their own, and his brother made no attempt to invite them in.

Each morning, Flower accompanied X to his brother's house where Hole in the Day and X would bid the women goodbye. Before leaving, Hole in the Day would take his child, John, in his arms, lift him high above his head, father and son laughing. When Hole in the Day talked of how he wanted nothing else than to transform the lives of his people, it was clear the reason why. His love for his son ran so deep he would change the world for him.

Caring for young John also brought Agida and Flower close. As she had with X, Flower gave of herself completely, taking the boy's soiled cloths to the river to wash without being asked or taking him from Agida even before she appeared tired. Occasionally, too, Agida's mother or sisters came down from Sandy Lake to live with them for a time and help, but inevitably they had to return, and Agida came to rely on Flower in those times when she had no one else.

When he wasn't working with his brother, X took baby John on walks through the forest, tapping the maple trees. He taught him how to extract the rich syrup, to boil it, and to make the candy cakes John loved. So, too, in the fall, he took John to the rice fields where he showed him how to seek out the flattest reeds then slice them off below the waterline with their knives. Hole in the Day complained that X was teaching his son women's work, but X countered that work was work.

And X was happy to cart the logs down the new road to his brother's home as they added a second story to the house. They worked side-by-side, cutting the logs and testing their fit while Hole in the Day talked of how many children he and Agida would have, how he wanted them to grow up living like the chimookomaanag, how he hoped they would soon forget the old ways.

"I don't understand," X said. "There is much worth remembering."

Hole in the Day pulled out his pipe and signaled to his brother that they should rest. X, too, pulled out a pipe, and they smoked quietly so that X thought his brother had dismissed his words.

"The fourth world is not ours," Hole in the Day said at last. "There are times when it is best to let go of the past." He puffed a great cloud of smoke and watched it rise.

X blew out a cloud of smoke as well, watched it mingle with his brother's, but all he could see were the decayed bodies of the Wah'peton girl, the three hanged Métis, and Father Pierz. "That is not possible," he whispered, his breath rising like the smoke. "The past lives with us whether we wish it to or not."

Beaulieu appeared on the road through the woods on his way to the agency office, waving to the two men, his red hair blowing about him like a fiery hat. Hole in the Day raised his pipe in return, but Beaulieu did not break his stride.

"I do not trust that man," X said. "He smiles and waves but beneath the skin he is all itches and nerves."

"A prosperous town only serves his best interest," Hole in the Day replied. "We can trust him yet." He tried to take a puff, but his pipe had gone out.

"Can you trust him once the town is built, once he has everything he needs?" X asked.

Hole in the Day knocked the burnt ashes out in frustration. He took the last pinch from his tobacco bag and filled his pipe. "We are the ones building this new world, brother," he said. "When it's done, it will be ours."

X puffed awhile on his pipe, waiting for the courage to say, "This isn't Rome. And you are not Aeneas."

Hole in the Day spilled some of his tobacco. He wiped it from his leg and tried to light what was left in his pipe. "Why do you not trust me?" he asked after his first failed attempt.

"I do not trust the time in which we live," X replied. "I can make no sense of it." He'd spoken truly, and was proud of it.

Hole in the Day tried again to light his pipe and again failed. He tossed the pipe aside. "Your problem is you're half-burnt," he said, rising as he spoke, brushing off the remainder of the tobacco. "You're split down the middle and cannot think clearly like the chimookomaanag or like the Ojibwe."

"It's not the first time you've insulted me in this way," X replied. He did not rise to meet his brother, did not even look up at him. The last remnant of smoke slowly dispersed before them.

"You say you are with me, but then you question," Hole in the Day said at last. "You tell me I don't love the half-burnts, when I give them a new town, a new life. What have they given to me?"

"*You* have given them?" X replied. "Should they feel grateful for your generosity?" X couldn't help the bitterness that crept into his voice. "Must they give something back, then? A tax perhaps?"

"That's not what I meant," Hole in the Day replied and that was all he said.

The two men stood facing the road, each working to translate the storm that moved between them.

The great gray owl stares down from above. Light bleeds from branches announcing summer's rank breath.

Niibiniishkang combs my hair, I'm almost sure of it. He works the pine needle bristles through my tangles as I lay beside them. I open my eyes, see the brush before me. Ne-wobiik's beadwork in red and blue. I reach for it, but as I do

*it vanishes. I hold instead the hem of Father Pierz' robe. I
bring it to my lips, but it, too, disappears. The room darkens
to pitch. I reach out again only to feel the rough bark of pine.
I stick both hands out. Trees surround me. I must still be
dreaming, I think and try to open my eyes, but they feel as if
they're already open. I bring my fingers to my face but find
only empty sockets where my eyes should be.*

The first night in their new cabin, Flower stood as if to
clear the dishes from their table, but instead hiked up her
calico skirt and straddled X. She didn't bother with the
buttons of his shirt, but rather nibbled on his neck and
ear as she worked his pants free. "I want a baby for us,"
she whispered. X did not move. She took his hands and
placed them on her breasts. She ground herself onto him.
A flutter of black robe. The rough tangle of beard against
his face. Flower took his hands, placed them on her slen-
der hips. The priest's smoky eyes, his mouth leaning in.
X's body woke to her. Moved with her. Followed the soft-
ness inside.

After, he lay still on the bed, listening to the rise and
fall of her breath. One question ate away at him. What
name would he give this child? He stayed awake through
the night but could not find an answer.

The next morning, X sat on the rock behind his hut,
as he had so many mornings, and gazed out at the gray
horizon, trying to call up the image of his parents.

What he saw instead was Father Tomazin, who was
passing by on his morning rounds. He'd picked up many
parishioners in Crow Wing and had high hopes of enlist-
ing X's help in the church. So, he sat on the ground beside X and talked to him about the lives of others, Métis

and Ojibwe alike, about their trials and their hopes for a better life. And he talked with such conviction that he pulled X out of himself.

"I want to believe," X said at last, taking his pipe from his pocket and filling it from the pouch about his waist. "But what good is that belief if I don't exist?"

Father Tomazin gave him a sidelong look. He grabbed X by the shoulder, shook him with his large hand. "You seem real to me," he said with a hearty laugh.

X couldn't help but smile. The priest's confidence was contagious. "The moment I begin to feel a sense of who I am, things change."

"Have you read Ovid?" Father Tomazin asked, knowing full well that X had, that both brothers were trained on the Roman poets. "He tells us over and over that change is both good and bad. We cannot separate one from the other."

X tamped down his pipe and lit it. The tobacco curled upon itself as it burned, glowing orange to gray. "I don't understand," he said between puffs.

Father Tomazin smiled, pleased to have engaged him. "In Daphne's plea to the river god, she begs him to change and destroy the body which would be used for delight."

"Why would she do that?" X decided he liked this priest. He was different from Father Pierz, but that difference was a good thing.

"She was chaste, had always scorned the love of men," Father Tomazin replied. "But driven by lust, Apollo hunted her through the wood. Hardly had she finished her prayer, when her limbs grew heavy, her soft breasts hardened to bark, and her hair turned to leaves. She stretched her arms to the sky as gnarled branches."

X nodded his head. "I think I understand." A loon called from the lake beyond the woods. Chickadees and finches twittered in the birch about them.

"Yes," Father Tomazin replied. "The change she asks for has a price. There is beauty but also great sadness in it."

"She denied her body," X said absently as he puffed. "She did not accept who she was."

"Who we are is never separate from how others view us," Father Tomazin added, and the two men sat in silence.

From that moment on, they talked often in the mornings. And afternoons, when Father Tomazin continued on his rounds, complaining that the deer flies ate him, X lunched and napped. In truth, he rarely slept but lay on the bed with half shut eyes, watching Flower as she worked, surprised at the feelings that overcame him during these moments. In her presence, he could stave off the thickening of blood that seemed to always be working within him. He thought it was the flight of her hands as she worked that kept him in this world, or perhaps the nest of desire in her eyes when she occasionally glanced at him. But in reality, it was his simple act of seeing that made him whole. The anxious shudder of her breath as she stirred the rice over the fire. Her outline as she stood in the doorway, holding the overflowing basket of chokecherries, the afternoon light warming her skin. The supple line of her neck as she sat to take her tea once her work was done. And the way she sipped it so quietly for fear of waking him.

Hole in the Day and Agida had another child, whom

they named Ignatius after Father Tomazin. A big, healthy baby, he was different from John in almost every way. Where John was cautious, Ignatius seemed to get into everything without consideration. And he grew quickly, so that soon Agida and Flower had their hands full in caring for the boys.

When X wasn't tending his garden, he worked as a hired hand for his brother's many projects. Hole in the Day wanted another road. This time to Fort Ripley, for he hoped to continue that road all the way down the Great River to St. Paul. They were going to negotiate deals with the furriers in the city, cutting out the shady middlemen whose pockets were always bigger than they first appeared. Beaulieu was in favor of the idea, of course, as he assumed he would be the sole middleman. He even obtained permission from Walker to have exclusive license. At first, X took part in the conversations about how to improve Crow Wing and the surrounding community his brother liked to call New Rome, but by dusk he tired of the endless bickering and would spend the last hour of the day playing with his nephews, John and Ignatius. Beaulieu and Hole in the Day would continue to argue about the direction of the town as they sat in the dark on Hole in the Day's porch. Beaulieu wanted to maintain Crow Wing as the commercial center of their ever-expanding enterprise, meaning he would maintain control over all business transactions. Hole in the Day, for his part, saw more value in finding ways for the roads and resources to support those who chose to farm the land in New Rome. In the end, they compromised on a mill for the farmers and a hotel to house important guests in their new trading venture. Once again, Walker sent back reports regularly praising Hole in the Day's plans, adding only: *We must keep a careful eye on him. He is proud and headstrong and liable to do anything in the name of his town.*

Their world could have continued like that, and X would have been more content than most, perhaps he and Flower would have even had a baby of their own, but Hole in the Day's eldest son, John, caught pneumonia and died that winter of 1861. All through that January, Hole in the Day and Agida sat beside the bed of their four-year-old son as X and Flower tended to Ignatius and the work of the house. At first, Hole in the Day asked for Father Tomazin, but the priest had left for Leech Lake on missionary work the week before. So, Hole in the Day called in Drinking Wood, the medicine man from Mille Lac, and he in turn called together his Mide healers. They purified themselves then built a healing lodge outside of Hole in the Day's cabin, where they took the boy and held secret ceremonies for seven days, dressed in bear robes and waving turtle shell rattles as the healers of old had done.

At the height of the ceremony, the medicine men allowed Hole in the Day, Agida, and X to see John, warning them that the evil spirits still held sway. X expected to see at least some improvement. And by his actions, Hole in the Day must have too, for after seeing John's pale and gaunt face, the way he fought to take even the smallest breath, Hole in the Day turned on the Mide healers, swearing to burn down the healing lodge and everyone in it if they didn't get out. He didn't care that they would likely freeze to death on their way home, as a heavy storm had settled over the area. Hole in the Day carried his son back to his house, laying him in the first floor bedroom. The next morning, he begged X to call Father Tomazin. They tried to send a messenger, but he could not make it through the three feet of snow that had already fallen.

Hole in the Day painted his face black as he'd done when his own father had died. X pulled out the rosary he'd kept beneath his calico shirt and sat, holding John's tiny hand, praying the Hail Mary over and over as he used to do with Father Pierz. Agida wailed over her son's body. Flower played with little Ignatius in another room, whispering to him that it was all right, that his mother's tears were her way of telling his brother John that she would care for him always and that they would be together again someday. The boy died before dawn.

Hole in the Day demanded a Christian burial for his son, but the ground was frozen and without Father Tomazin there was no one to perform the ceremony. X stared into the hole that was his brother's face and offered to perform the service. They would lay John in a casket and bury him in the cellar. Once spring thawed the earth, they could move him to a proper place and Father Tomazin could preside.

"I am the Resurrection and the Life," X chanted as Hole in the Day laid his son in the casket atop the cold cellar earth. He held onto his rosary in hopes of stilling his shaking hand and quelling his quivering voice

"Our Father who art in heaven, hallowed be thy name," he recited as Agida collapsed on the ground. X then sprinkled the holy water he'd stolen from the church in Crow Wing over the body. "Thy kingdom come. Thy will be done on earth as it is in heaven." He tried to continue with the ancient prayers, but stumbled over the lines: "Grant this mercy, O Lord, we beseech Thee." It was all he could remember. So, he kept repeating it, sprinkling the holy water until Flower was able to take Agida from the cellar.

Outside in the deep snow, X watched as Hole in the Day took the knife from his belt and cut off his hair in the traditional way, then walked barefoot into the thick wood, still singing his mourning song. He watched as his brother climbed the tallest hill and turned his black face to the heavens. A great rip in the sky.

In April, when war broke out among the states and Father Tomazin was able to return from Leech Lake, X packed his bags and went to him, begging to be trained in the ways of the priesthood.

Father Tomazin studied the young Métis, looking for a clue as to his change of heart. "Do you choose this path willingly?" he asked.

"Yes," he said, though he did not know what that meant. What had will to do with anything? He did only what he must.

"In doing this," Father Tomazin continued. "You will release the body that was Ojibwe, the body that was white, and you will create a new body in the image of Christ."

"That is what I wish," he whispered. "I want to change shape until I do not recognize who or what I am."

"I ask again. Do you take this path freely?"

"What do you mean?" X fought the urge to run. To forget everything. Father Tomazin. Flower. His brother.

"Sometimes we choose to change not because we see the benefit of the new life," Father Tomazin said. "But because we wish to destroy the old."

Yes. Yes. Destroy the old, he thought. "I understand," he said.

"Very well," Father Tomazin said. "You will live with me. I will make up a bed in the rectory closet. It will be close quarters, but it will do."

"People will talk."

"I've never cared about the chatter of others," Father Tomazin replied, giving a wry smile and putting his arm around X. "From this day forth you will be known as Deacon Paulson."

Flower never once visited X. She did not change her routine in any way, except to begin work on a new pair of makizins for her mate. Those makizins sat by the door for many years in the hope that someday he would return.

Starlings darken the trees. Shadows flitting across the heavens, falling into the great tear in the sky.

It is no use. My sleep is fitful, my dreams dark. Still, I lie there holding Niibiniishkang and his woman close, my own yellowed and withered hand curled to a question mark. Their blossoming hair reminds me of the petals of the flower I lost. I inhale them, draw their scent in deep. Over and over I breathe them in. It is almost enough.

I lie naked upon the damp earth, the chill air tonguing my skin. I shut my eyes and pray. Darkness. The sky opens to crooked wings.

You are still alive, brother, I can feel it. Your breath rises to the surface of the lake, drifts like steam only to wrap about me.

A phantom out of the corner of my eye, she hops, her wrinkled green skin older than the lake itself, older than this world. Mindimooyenh. Her ugliness frightens me. Her hair like the wet weeds we pull from the bottom of the lake in our nets. Babiigomakakii. I draw my knife. She leaps toward me, her mottled hand upon my face. I fall to the ground, unable to move, cool lake mud sliding down my forehead where her hand once was.

"Why did you not listen to Kingfisher?" she asks.

"He is not so easy to understand."

"That is because you do not know his song." Brackish water drips from her fingers, her hair.

"Are you a toad or a woman?"

"What matter is it to you?" she replies. "You called me. Your yearning carries you to this side. Only my breath can carry you back." And with these words, she leans her face in close. Her rasping breath bubbling through slime and peat.

"Teach me his song," I say.

"I will do better than that," she responds, mud gurgling up through her mouth, spilling upon me. "I will teach you the song of the toad, Babiigomakakii."

And with that she walks thrice about me, coughing up mud all the while. I spread it over the bare skin of my arms, my face, my neck.

"The toad's song is a haunting," she says, nodding her

head until her hair falls about my shoulders. She sways back and forth tracing tracks on the mud of my body. "And like any haunting, it can ensnare. Be wary."

I shut my eyes.

"Take in my breath," she says.

I inhale and gag on the stench of rotting fish, of stagnant loam and algae.

"All we are is breath," she says, and I repeat her words.

"And with breath we sing," she says.

"And with breath we sing."

"And with song we tell our stories."

"All my being is story," I say.

She opens her mouth to kiss me, and I receive her. Slime water and rancid mud running down my throat until I choke, cough it back up.

"Stories put us in contact with the other world," she croaks. "They tell us who we are."

"It is as necessary for me to tell the story as it is to breathe," I say.

My skin shades to green, my face cracking and splitting. Eyes bulging. I slip down into my toad haunches. I gather my strong tongue within me.

"Yes," she says. "Yes."

My slippery throat swells. I dig my webbed feet into the mud, fighting the desire to bury myself in the cool earth.

"Go," she croaks. "You know the song of Ogish-kimanissi now. Go down into the lake, swim deep until you can go no further. Wait for Piichoo Manidoo there." As she hops away, she dissolves back into the mud.

Deer flies buzz about me, and I eat them with great

pleasure before plunging into the brutal waters. A ripple across dark glass. Follow the dragonfly out of one nightmare and into the next.

DAY THREE

I wake to the blue hours and move in time with the groaning pine floor. The icy breath rises through the cracks, stinging my feet. I don the vestments of my office and notice the hem of one sleeve is coming loose. I pull the thread and watch it unravel.

The stove door is frozen shut, but I no longer care. What does heat matter, brother, when the spirit is forever rimed? I kiss my rosary. Once. Twice. Three times. Hang it from my neck where the Mide shell waits. An empty bowl sits on the table. No matter. Food no longer interests me. Time is running out.

I open the door to White Earth. The smell of woodsmoke and birch. A lone crow cawing as he sits on a barren pine. I want to follow him, brother. I have begun to doubt myself, and the crow may know the way. I go to him, but he flies off, and I remain, shrouded in the echo of his call.

I cross the crusted snow. Withered and knotted faces gaze out at me from cracked walls, shuttered windows. No one ventures out when the cloudless sky threatens to steal every bit of heat. I scan the treetops, but the great gray owl has abandoned me, too. Would I do the same if our roles were reversed? Leave a friend, lost in an unknown world. No. That is why I am here.

I work my way around Beaulieu's place, hoping to spy him inside, wondering what I will say to him. But he is nowhere to be seen. Instead, fresh tracks lead from his door to Niibiniishkang's sod hut. I follow, stepping in them, thinking he is not such a big man after all. As with so many things, his reputation is distorted, an illusion. The sweet smell of maple syrup hovers over the entryway to the old war chief's hut. Beaulieu's horse voice echoes within. I enter to find the old *trader sitting beside the dying chief who is eating Aninaatigo Ziigaigans. Newobiik squats by the fire, tending a pot of tea. Niibiniishkang's eyes are closed, so he does not notice me.*

"I told you it was good," Beaulieu's smile cracking through his gray-flecked beard.

"It will hurt his teeth," Newobiik says, shaking her head in disapproval.

In answer, Niibiniishkang bites off a large chunk of the maple syrup cake. His mouth merely goes through the motions of chewing. He is worse. My time is shorter than I thought.

Niibiniishkang stops chewing, swallows loudly. "I dreamt of Ase-anse," he says. "He came to me here, sat where you are sitting now Beaulieu." His hand quavers as he reaches to the empty air. "He told me a strange story."

"That is odd," Beaulieu says, scratching now at his full beard, then pulling on it as if he himself didn't believe it was real. "Because I came to tell you I received word this morning that Father Paulson died on his way here. They found him yesterday frozen to death, kneeling in the middle of Gull Lake, one hand clasping his wampum shells, the other his rosary." He scratches at the hair that runs out of the collar of his finely laundered shirt and up his neck.

Niibiniishkang opens his eyes, but cannot yet make me out in the shadows before him. His gaze is flat. The whites have yellowed. "What you say troubles me, Beaulieu." He works his mouth in the manner old people have, like a cow chewing cud, as if he would clean the last of the food from his teeth, or perhaps as if he wanted to say more, but had forgotten what it was. "He was a better friend than I thought," he says at last, and that is all.

I step forward from the shadows, kneel on the other side of Niibiniishkang. He turns to me, a flicker lighting the sockets.

"He was coming to give you last rites, old man." Beaulieu tries to hand Niibiniishkang more maple syrup cake, but the old war chief seems no longer interested in it. Not knowing what to do with the cake, Beaulieu stares at it until Newobiik rises to fetch it from him, then returns to her spot beside the fire. "Perhaps he has died in your place," Beaulieu adds with a chuckle. Maybe since he didn't make it you'll live a while longer."

Niibiniishkang grabs my hand, pulls it to his chest and holds it there. Strength remains in that grip. And something of the life, too, flows into me with the pulsing of his blood.

"Why do you grasp at the air, old man?" Beaulieu says, gesturing to Newobiik for the tea. She brings two steaming cups. "Your son will lead well when you are gone. He has proven himself. You need not fear for your people."

Niibiniishkang's face sets in place like a stone god, his grip tightening about my hand. Yes, he still has strength within him. Perhaps there is time. "Do not kill me off yet, trader," he whispers to Beaulieu. An accusation stirs in the sidelong look of his eyes. Does he believe in my story? I wonder. Does he know something I don't?

Beaulieu pulls back a bit, takes up his tea and waits for it to cool. "That was a long time ago, old friend," he replies, testing the tea with his lips. "You know I had nothing to do with it. He was killed by the Pillagers, or Father Paulson, or perhaps by his wife, jealous of her white rival. Or maybe it was you? There are those who've said as much." Now it's Beaulieu's turn to accuse. He sets his tea down, leans in close. "Why don't you tell me the truth before you move on to your next world?" he asks, his eyes closing to slits, his mouth the enigma it has always been. "It will do us all good to know what really happened to the Chief."

Niibiniishkang sits, his body now crumpling like an old melon, and still it is as if he looks down on Beaulieu as he speaks: "My time has not yet come," he says with the certainty of the old. "My part is reserved for the last act, and before I would speak, I would know your role."

Beaulieu reaches for his cup but stops short. He looks to the red curtain fluttering in the doorway, then back at Newobiik. "I never liked Walker," he says at last. He was a spy who double-crossed the government. He was only in it for himself. And in the end, he was crazy."

With that, Niibiniishkang smiles. "I have yet to meet a chimookomaan who was not," he says.

"I was not," Beaulieu replies. "I am not." And if you can judge the truth of a man by the certainty with which he speaks then it must have been true. Unfortunately, if life has taught me anything it's that our lives are built on lies. And the more certain we are of ourselves, the more lies we hide behind.

As if Niibiniishkang also understands, he replies, "It's easy to make such declarations, but much more difficult to explain our part." He reaches out for Beaulieu, something for which the trader is not prepared. The old war chief knows the story will come. It must come.

The great gray owl pulls at straw, catches the strands in his beak, then flies over the forest. He drops the strands one by one. They fall like lines on a map, and we follow. Take the lines as words. Draw them inside and make them real even as Beaulieu begins his tale:

I could see things didn't add up, the money from the Bureau of Indian Affairs wasn't going where it was supposed to go. The Chief was forced to halt the building of his town, waiting on the annuity checks. He told his people there would be no mill, no hotel. Worst of all, food was running out.

The Chief complained to Walker, but the agent swore there was nothing he could do. He said the War Between the States had tied up most of the funds so that all the government could manage for the Indians was a trickle. Something was foul. I knew it, and I knew it had to do with Walker. Once construction on the town stopped, Walker built himself a nice, big cellar. One with a thick, oak door, reinforced by steel struts. I asked him about it, and he mumbled something in that manner of his about preparing for end times. When I pressed him, he simply locked himself in the agency office, shouted at me through shuttered windows.

I'm a light sleeper. I wake several times a night. Sometimes I take short walks to get the itchiness out of my legs. It was on one of those walks I spied a wagon outside the agency house. Walker and two others were unloading boxes, taking them into his new cellar. I waited at the edge of the woods until they entered the agency, then crept to the window. I could make out enough through the crack in the shutter. Money was changing hands. Lots of it.

If I confronted him, he'd deny everything, then be on his guard against me. So I made an excuse to meet with the new traders in the north, but instead took a train to Washington. The capital's overwhelming at first, but it's easy enough to figure out the channels of power and how to manipulate those channels. Money. And I'd not come unprepared. I knew the right people to pay. Getting access to BIA files was easier than finding shit in a henhouse. I compared annuity roles, and it didn't take much intelligence to see that Walker and Thompson, the Bureau Chief, had arranged an elaborate system for stealing from the Chippewa. They'd faked their own census roles, changing the names of tribal members and adding new names, all so they could fund most of the money and supplies directly to themselves. I went straight to the President, but Lincoln would not or could not see me, for as his secretary said, he was, "deeply involved in the southern attempt at secession." So, I went to Vice President Hamlin. Not an easy man to see, either. But again, there are ways. I knew a few things about certain people. Hamlin was not pleased. They revoked my trader's license for my efforts. I should have known Hamlin and Thompson hunted together.

"That's not true!" I shout. "He didn't go to Washington to find out what happened to the money and supplies. He went to grease his own palm, to see if he could be cut into the deal." Niibiniishkang squints at me as if trying to hear through his eyes. I want to shake him, to make him listen, but Beaulieu goes on with his story, his voice capturing the old war chief's attention. A benefit of the living.

I tried other avenues, bribing official after official, but nothing worked. I stayed too long in Washington. By the time I returned, Walker had invited his own traders to set up shop in Crow Wing. He was making the Chief's people come to him, selling them their own annuity goods, the ones he'd been hording, at twice their normal price. Most of them couldn't afford the usual price much less this. But Walker didn't care. What wasn't sold, he stored in his cellar all for the judgment day he said was near.

The Chief saw all he'd worked for coming to an end. He questioned me about the reasons for my trip, said he'd trusted me and asked why I'd lied about where I was going. I tried to explain everything, but the Chief wasn't satisfied. He told me I'd failed him, that he should have gone to Washington and not me. I couldn't say anything. I'd nothing left myself. It didn't matter that I'd lost Hole in the Day's favor, too.

The Chief went straightaway to his old friend Deacon Paulson. I never knew what he saw in that man. Paulson had been living with Father Tomazin. People talked about what went on in that church at night between the two of them. Personally, I'd of run them both out of town if I had any power left. The Chief begged Paulson to get the church to intervene, to call for another round of donations from the churches in the city to get them through the winter. But Paulson ignored the Chief's request, saying he no longer answered to any man, Chippewa or white.

With his people starving and nowhere else to turn, Hole in the Day went directly to Walker. I followed at a distance, hoping to prove myself useful to the Chief once again, but also fearing he might do something rash and bring down the anger of the government on us all.

"My brother never called for me!" I say. "His pride kept him from asking for help. How was I to know?" I stand before Beaulieu, but he ignores me, as he's always done. I shout in his face. "You were nothing to him! I was his brother! I am the only one he could trust." He stares straight through me. I want to take his beard, rip it out hair by hair, so I can shut his traitorous mouth. I turn to Newobiik in hopes that she can stop this man from spilling his lies. But she is too engrossed in her knitting as Beaulieu chatters on.

Hole in the Day couldn't get past the front door of the agency office. Walker's new traders Morrison and Ruffee barred the way. "No one gets in without an appointment," Ruffee said, thrusting his finger at the Chief. Ruffee wore his hair up in a pompadour so tall it made him look as if he tilted his head too much to one side he'd fall over. I hated that man.

The Chief said nothing, didn't even acknowledge their presence. That's when Morrison put his big frame between the Chief and the door. I knew it would only lead to trouble, so I stepped up. "Tell Walker that we'll not stand for his petty thievery," I told them. "His thugs and his operation have no place here."

"I turned to the priesthood for him!" I say, and Niibini-ishkang's eyes open wider now. He hears me, I am sure of it. "I would not see him suffer the way he did when John died. I would be of use to him. To our people."

"Ase-anse," Niibiniishkang says at last. "Please. I cannot follow both your stories. It gives me a headache." He raises his hand as if to shoo me away.

"But this is not the way things happened."

"What am I to do?" Niibiniishkang asks. "How am I to judge?"

"To whom do you speak?" Beaulieu asks, then turns to Newobiik. "Your husband talks to the air," he says. "You must tend to him." Newobiik looks up from her work mending a shirt for her husband, but as if she knows better, she doesn't move.

"I'm just an old man raving," Niibiniishkang replies. "I talk with no one."

The words sting. There is more truth in them than the old man realizes.

I advised the Chief to send a complaint to Washington, to ask that Walker be removed. In response, Thompson brought countercharges against Hole in the Day, saying it was he who was skimming money off the top. That's when the Chief told me he wanted no more part of me. He blamed me for the mess we were in. He couldn't see I was trying to help. That didn't sit well with me I could tell you. I was all that sat between the Indians and ruin, and the Chief couldn't see it.

Spring came, and Crow Wing bustled with commerce. Not the Indian kind, mind you, but lumbermen checking out the lay of the land. The Chief grew more bitter with each passing day until I was worried he would lock himself in his house and end up crazy like Walker. I counseled him to meet with the other chiefs, to band together, to write to the President with one voice and explain the situation. But he wouldn't listen. Then Walker sent a group of his men from Crow Wing to recruit the young

Chippewa for the Union Army. Before anyone realized what was happening, Walker had signed a full platoon and shipped them off with a bottle of whiskey in each of their rations. I didn't know if it was Walker's own idea or if it had come from Washington. Either way, a fool could see it would lead to trouble.

I filled three pipes with my finest tobacco and sought you out, knowing if anyone could reach the Chief, it would be you. We found Hole in the Day sitting at his kitchen table, facing the door, holding his father's knife in his hand, looking as if he would attack the first person who entered. He'd already heard the news of the Chippewa platoon.

"Ogimaa," you said, setting the pipes on the table along with your tobacco bundle. "Your father was named when a great hole opened in the sky, swallowing the sun so that day turned to night. But you carry your father's name, and in your day the sun no longer needs to set for the sky to turn to pitch. Shadows gather. They rise up from the ground like trees and block the light until your face reflects the darkness of the world."

Hole in the Day sat and listened, then took the pipe before him and inhaled the pungent scent of its rich tobacco.

Niibiniishkang smiles at this recollection of his part. Though this is not what happened. Cannot be what happened. I creep forth through the sawdust spread over the frozen dirt in hope of hearing more. I circle Beaulieu like a powerful fish. Let him dangle a worm before me and see if I bite. "Go on," Niibiniishkang says. "Speak, Beaulieu. I would hear more of what you have to say."

Hole in the Day called the other chiefs to him: Buffalo and Flat Mouth from the Pillagers, Bad Boy and Curly Head from Sandy Lake, Eagle and First Seated Feather from Mille. Before them all, he made you his war chief, as you'd once been under the first Hole in the Day in the war with the Sioux. And you advised them to take up arms against the whites. But the others grumbled in fear. After so many lost battles, they were wary of taking on the whites again. As they argued over their course, the Chief sat and listened, all the while smoking the pipe you'd given him. Only when the tobacco had burnt itself out did he rise.

"The Great Father of the long knives denies us the money and supplies he promised. And now he dresses our men like soldiers and sends them away to fight in the south." He paused, turning one by one to each of the chiefs. "We must rise and fight the long knives. Take as many as we can prisoner. Take their horses and their food. Take their women and their children. Take all they have." And with that, he threw the pipe against the wall, breaking it in two. For my part, I didn't like the words spoken, but I wasn't about to stand in your way. The government had taken my license, taken my livelihood. How was I to feed my family? I had five children with another on the way.

Buffalo and Flat Mouth, nodded their heads, their grave faces understanding the seriousness of what Hole in the Day proposed. Eagle, First Seated Feather, Curly Head, and Bad Boy stood silent, and it was to them the Chief made his final appeal. "We cannot do this alone," he said. "We must forget past differences." The four chiefs gave no hint of their own minds. Then Curly Head's gaze shifted to me.

"What about him?" he asked.

"The trader?" the Chief replied, as if he'd not yet considered me.

"Former trader," I reminded him.

The Chief pulled his father's knife from his belt, held its point to the sky, traced his finger down the blade. "He is white," he said. "But to the government, he is invisible. He understands our situation well. Leave him."

"Ogimaa," you said, standing now before all the others. "You are right to say we must forget the past. Are you willing to forgive the Sioux and talk with Little Crow? If we have a chance of winning, we will need their help."

The Chief said nothing as all in attendance remembered it had been Little Crow who'd spit in his father's face, then burned his house to the ground. The Chief crossed the room and retrieved his green blanket from a hook by the door. He wrapped it about him in the same way he'd done when he met with President Pierce. "Though I don't like your words, Niibiniishkang, you give good counsel," he said. "You will meet with Little Crow, tell him we attack on the waning moon of the last month of niibin. Tell him to strike the agency in Redwood in the morning and we will do the same at Crow Wing. I go now to sound the hearts of the men at Gull Lake. Hurry, we have little time." And with that he was out the door. You followed, knowing that you, too, had a long ride. The remaining chiefs spoke not a word as, one by one, they walked slowly out into the gathering dusk.

News of the uprising got to Walker. Perhaps Bad Boy and Curly Head informed him in exchange for a bigger share of the always-promised annuity, or perhaps it was one of the discontented youths with whom the Chief spoke at Gull Lake. He already had more than a few enemies. But there are also those who say it was Deacon Paulson, that since he'd entered the priesthood, he'd turned his back on his burnt half, that he sought to stop his brother from initiating the hostilities that once before had nearly destroyed the Chippewa.

"What is this the liar Beaulieu speaks?" I whisper in Niibiniishkang's ear. The old war chief waves me away with his hand as if I were an annoying insect.

"Let him tell his story," he says.

"But he fills your head with falsehoods," I reply. "That is no way to leave this world."

Beaulieu begins chattering again. I claw at the frozen earth for something to throw. I find Newobiik's knitting and throw it at the trader's face, hoping the needles pierce deep.

"What devil's work is this?" Beaulieu shouts, fending away the needles with his hands.

Newobiik shakes her head. She knew something was different in her house. A woman always knows.

Good, I think. Let them fear. It's better that they fear and know the truth. And yet Beaulieu won't shut up.

Three days before the attack Deacon Paulson rode to Mille Lac and convinced Eagle and First Seated Feather to raise an army to defend Fort Ripley against the Chief's attack.

"No!" I shout, leaping for the old trader, taking his neck in my hands. "I would not betray him like that!" But the bastard ignores me.

Deacon Paulson then told Walker of the plan to hit his agency. And Walker in turn sent a messenger through the night to Fort Ripley for soldiers. They say Deacon Paulson himself led the soldiers to his adopted brother.

"You're a liar!" I shout. I hover over him, anchored only by my hands about his throat. Thrashing at him with my feet. "A fucking liar! It was you who betrayed him. Sold him out so that Walker would reinstate you. That's why you opened your store again after the uprising." But my mouth melts, dripping into his. My fingers on his throat dissolve, seeping into his skin.

"Ase-anse!" Niibiniishkang calls out. "You rain down into the trader. Stop, or you will lose yourself completely!"

I open my eyes, but it's as if I look out through cobwebbed panes. I try to speak with my new voice but only stutter.

"I've lost you," Niibiniishkang says. "Where have you gone? Are you inside the trader?"

I bang my head against the body until my world spins. And then it happens.

Beaulieu and I fly out over the oak, maple, elm, and birch. See the river otter playing in the current. The badger scouring for grub and the loon surfacing with a crayfish in its mouth. Yellow deepens to blue. We march with the soldiers. I hear his words ringing in my head and try to speak over them, to warn my brother.

We kept ahead of the twenty soldiers as they approached the Chief's house from behind. The area was thick with scrub oak, ivy lapping at our legs. We stopped and sounded the air, for we did not want to endanger the troops or the Chief. We must capture Hole in the Day by surprise, we told the soldiers. Shadows crept through the webs beneath our eyes. We smelled of gun-oil and slag. Our wild, red hair knotted and unkempt. The Chief sat smoking on a rock. But the men were too busy thinking of the battle to come. They didn't see the lean figure half hidden by the brush. Hole in the Day turned as if he'd been expecting an attack. We met our brother's eyes, then nodded in warning toward his home. They wait for you, we whispered. The Chief doused his pipe and stole away to gather his wife and child. By the time the soldiers arrived at Hole in the Day's home, he and his family were nearly across the Great River, paddling the canoe furiously. The soldiers ran to the bank and opened fire. We ran to the front line, shouted for them to stop. But they didn't listen. They kept shooting, round after round, until they'd nearly exhausted their ammunition. We knocked the rifle away from one soldier, then another. Someone shouted that the Chief had slumped in the canoe. He was hit. We fell to the ground, and the soldiers left us lying in the wet marsh of the riverbank.

The red curtain flutters. Niibiniishkang rises from his bed, gestures for Newobiik. They kneel beside us as we lie trembling upon the ground. "I cannot hear what the trader speaks," Niibiniishkang tells his wife. "It is as if two voices rise from inside him, each distorting the other."

"It is Ase-anse." It dawns on Newobiik. "He is here. He has been here since yesterday, hasn't he?"

"Brew your medicine thick and bring the pot so the steam may release him from this fevered dream," Niibiniishkang says, nodding his head.

"There is no release, my husband," Newobiik says. "You know that. At least none that we can give."

"I know nothing."

"Where is the warrior who was once so sure of himself?" Newobiik asks. She does not wait for an answer but gathers the herbs from the clay pots lining the back wall.

We focus only on the story, the words shifting before us like clouds burning in the sun's heat. Unformed faces haunt the shadows of our mind drawing out our darkest longing, while our body, the body of Beaulieu writhes and rages on the floor. We must see clearly to tell the story. We must hear the words, but they sound like the humming of grass in the wind. Still, we shout over the din.

We heard that our brother had been shot in the arm, and we immediately left the rectory in Crow Wing to aid him. We found him hiding in the woods near Otter Tail Lake, the wound a surface one. Agida remained by his side, nursing his wound as Hole in the Day dispatched messengers to the other bands. He told them there'd been a great battle, and he'd killed all the whites at Crow Wing. He ordered them to rouse themselves and exterminate all the long knives in the area then meet him at Fort Ripley in three days where they would make their stand.

"Hurry woman!" Niibiniishkang cries. "I fear for the old trader."

"Patience has never been your strength, my husband," Newobiik answers. "Why should I expect you to change in your final days?" She turns to her husband and smiles. "I cannot rush the pot."

We no longer recognized our brother, this man who lied to his people to salvage his wounded pride. We reminded him of our father's war with the Sioux, of the slaughter of the Wah'petonwan that night so long ago. We asked him if he would begin again the cycle of violence. Hole in the Day replied that it was not his fault, that it was inevitable.

"What an interesting choice of words," we said, but our brother paid no attention to us. Still, we went on: "Do you mean we have no choice? There is always a choice."

"I don't have time for this," Hole in the Day said, walking away.

"Men say it's inevitable when they don't want to face the void in their own heart," we said to his back as he disappeared in the thick brush along the lake's bank.

At night, we sat together on that same bank waiting for word from the messengers. Hole in the Day pointed out the one red light in the heavens, saying it was the spirit of Mars, the god of war. He went on, talking of the defeat of the Achaeans at Troy, how the loss of that battle did not stop them, but through the courage of one man, the Roman civilization was born anew. We knew this. We'd read the book, too. But we no longer believed in the story, at least not in the way he believed.

"You speak of nothing but warriors and heroes," we said at last. "It is wiser to fear people who need heroes."

"What do you call your Jesus, then?" Hole in the Day said, turning to us. "Is he not simply another hero?"

It was then Agida arrived, carrying salve to treat her husband's wounds.

Long after our brother returned to his summer wigwam with Agida, we remained lying against a pine on the banks of the lake, listening to the chorus of crickets and frogs, unable to clear the vision of the Wah'peton girl's agate eyes from our mind. We closed our eyes, but as soon as her face came into focus, it blurred again, shifting in the darkness until we saw our mother's face, shimmering for a brief moment, a kind face, a face that would refuse nothing to her son. A face with the same agate eyes.

The next morning a messenger arrived with news that the Pillagers had attacked a family of whites near Leech Lake and taken them prisoner, Norwegians who'd only recently arrived in the area. Hole in the Day was ecstatic until he heard that Flat Mouth and Buffalo were in disagreement about what to do with the white prisoners. In short, Flat Mouth didn't believe Hole in the Day's claim that he'd slaughtered so many whites. Worse still, Bad Boy had joined the Mille Lac chiefs Eagle and First Seated Feather and taken their warriors to defend Fort Ripley. The remaining chiefs marched south with their warriors to see for themselves the truth of Hole in the Day's claim.

Upon hearing the news, Hole in the Day spent the morning walking along the circumference of the lake, alone. With each step, he seemed more uncertain, stopping often, staring up into the birch and pine. We knew we should go to our brother, but we did not, staying instead near Agida and Little Ignatius on the farther shore of the lake. They would not win the war, not even if the Sioux came to their aid.

"Maybe I've already passed into the next world," Niibiniishkang says. *"And that is why I hear these voices inside my head."*

"If you are dead, then I have died with you, my husband, and I can assure you I am still very much alive." Newobiik *adds another herb to the pot.*

"That is good to know, my wife," Niibinishkang *replies.* *"I am not ready to leave this world, though if these voices continue one atop the other, I may yet take my own life. Hurry!"*

Two days later, Buffalo arrived with one hundred Pillagers armed with rifles and shotguns. Niibiniishkang rode in hours after followed by another hundred of the Red Lake and Pembina bands. And fifty more came along with Curly Head. The Pillagers in particular were incensed to find out that Hole in the Day had lied about slaughtering the whites at Crow Wing because they had taken the Norwegian family prisoner and knew they would bear the brunt of the white thirst for justice.

"You've doomed us," Buffalo said. "And for what? Your petty pride."

Hole in the Day stood facing the lake, his back to the chiefs. He picked up a pebble and tossed it into the water, stared at the ever-widening circles.

"Your people need the Hole in the Day who saved them at Sandy Lake, the same Hole in the Day who kept face with the Great Father in Washington," Niibiniishkang spoke to his chief's back. "But who is this figure who stands in his place? How can we trust you now?"

We watched from the edge of the clearing, as our brother stumbled looking for an answer.

"We will march to Fort Ripley," Hole in the Day said at last. "Make a show of force as has not been seen in this country for a long time. But we will not use that force for war.

"I do not understand," Niibinishkang replied.

"We will use it to force a negotiation, to win more for our people."

The chiefs stood in silence.

Our brother's face shone like the sky, and we bathed in its light.

"Good can come of this yet," Buffalo added. "We can use the prisoners as leverage and press our claims to get what we've been promised."

"And what of the Sioux?" Niibiniishkang asked. "Do we betray them? Leave them to the chimookomaanag justice? I do not like it."

"I don't like this plan," Curly Head exclaimed. "It will split us. And what about Bad Boy, Eagle, and First Seated Feather? Where does it put them?"

"We are already split," our brother replied. "As to Bad Boy and the Mille Lac clan, let them stew inside the fort with the rest of the long knives while we show them what it means to be Anishinabe." With that, he signaled Niibiniishkang to prepare their people to ride to Fort Ripley.

"I see the wisdom behind this plan, but I am not yet sure I approve of it." Niibiniishkang said, then left without another word.

Newobiik carries the steaming pot and sets it beside our prostrate body. Together, she and her husband raise us to a sitting position.

"The Free Soul of Ase-anse has entered him," Newobiik says. "Am I right?"

Niibiniishkang nods his head in answer, but says nothing as if he fears we will enter him next.

They tip us forward so that our face hangs over the pot. Newobiik fans the steam toward us. Our eyes flutter. Spittle dribbles from the corner of our mouth and onto our red beard.

Beaulieu tries to speak but I drown the words in his own saliva before they come out. He tries to rise, but I shove him to the ground. I am no longer of his body, and he cannot take this story from me.

A delegation of whites led by Beaulieu and a man named George Sweet arrived in Crow Wing the next day under a flag of truce. Sweet claimed he spoke for Commissioner Dole who was staying in St. Paul until they could discern the situation. He asked if Hole in the Day meant to lead his people to war, and Hole in the Day answered that he did not wish for war, only that the chimookomaanag keep their word and pay his people the money owed them. Hole in the Day demanded they remove Walker, complaining that there could be no peace while that man remained among them. And he argued for the return of the Ojibwe platoon. In the end, they agreed to a four-day truce, setting a meeting with Commissioner Dole in Beaulieu's house on the morning of the fifth day. As a gesture of good faith, the Commissioner would allow Hole in the Day to bring an escort of thirty warriors, no more. Hole in the Day agreed to the terms, though he saw nothing to trust in the words that came from Sweet's crooked mouth.

That night, X watched from across the fire as Niibini-ishkang and Hole in the Day shared a pipe by the lake, smoking late into the night. He listened as the two chiefs talked of their distrust of the meeting at Fort Ripley and planned a response that would show the chimoo-komaanag they would not be fooled. Hole in the Day was thirty-four and already the lines of the map drawn around the Ojibwe had worked to fold the features of his face, to crease the soft curve of his mouth, to bend the once strong angle of his neck.

Hole in the Day and X marched with thirty warriors all through the night of the fourth day and waited for sunrise sitting on the dew drenched ground in front of Beaulieu's two-story, Greek-revival house, a house strategically set on a promontory overlooking the town of Crow Wing. It was easily the biggest house in the region. A fitting residence for one so concerned with money. As the morning light broke, the house shone with an unearthly radiance. It was then Dole, Beaulieu, and Sweet stepped out on the porch. Dole raised his hand as if in greeting, when suddenly over a hundred long knife soldiers emerged from the woods behind the house, rifles aimed at the delegation, bayonets locked in place.

Hole in the Day sat for a long moment as if tallying the soldiers, measuring his odds, and then he stood. The lower half of his face was painted black. A touch of white like two moons beneath each eye. His long hair plaited and wound like a turban about his head, with three eagle feathers fastened there. He was dressed in a gray striped shirt and frockcoat, his trademark green blanket wrapped about him, pulled back along his right hip to reveal the Colt revolver given to him by President Pierce.

"You tell me to come in peace," he said. "Then threaten war. But you do not know who you are dealing with." It was then he let out a loud cry. Niibiniishkang emerged from the woods beside the house. He stood alone for a moment, then, slowly, warrior upon warrior emerged from the woods. All told, there were over two hundred and fifty warriors, weapons at the ready, surrounding Dole's men.

Beaulieu jolts forward, choking uncontrollably. Niibiniishkang grabs him, hits him on the back. Newobiik presses her kettle closer, wafts the steam to his nose. At last, he breaths deeply, eyes rolling into his head. "Paulson does not speak for me," he says. "I was there."

Niibiniishkang covers Beaulieu's mouth with his hand. "I was there, too," he tells the trader. "Do not ruin my moment of glory. We had so few of them against the chimookomaanag."

"But I was the one who came to him, advised him in his time of need," Beaulieu goes on, mumbling beneath Niibiniishkang's bony hand. "I arranged the meeting with Dole, a meeting that averted the war." As if going into a convulsion,

his body shakes uncontrollably. He thrashes about, knocking the kettle to the ground. Newobiik's medicine seeps into the frozen earth, steam rising. Still, Niibiniishkang keeps his hand about the trader's mouth. Beaulieu bites down hard, draws blood, and Niibiniishkang releases his grip. The trader speaks, even as I wrestle his tongue. But he is stronger now. I will strike again when he least expects. Let him begin his story, but see if he continues for long.

The Chief entered my house along with you and Buffalo. Deacon Paulson was not with them, having hidden in the rectory with Father Tomazin. I interpreted during the negotiations and assisted where I could. The three chiefs sat on the ground facing Commissioner Dole, George Sweet and Captain Hall, the leader of the soldiers outside. Dole was clearly unnerved by the morning's events. Before anyone could speak, he started yelling, spittle flying from his mouth. He demanded the release of the white family and that the road be cleared of all Chippewa. He said he would not negotiate until he was guaranteed a safe route home. I raised my hands to calm the Commissioner, tell him all would be worked out. Captain Hall stepped forward, hand on his holstered pistol. He said nothing, but kept a wary eye as Dole continued to speak. No one could follow what the Commissioner said. I shouted for him to stop screaming, for Captain Hall to step back. In the brief silence that followed, the Chief stood and pointed a finger at the Commissioner. Dole shut up.

"Are you the smartest man that the Great Father can send?" the Chief asked. "Because if that is the case, then I pity the Great Father. You talk as if I am a child. I am not a child. Look. Here on my head." The Chief parted his plaited hair, bent his head before the Commissioner. "I have gray hairs like you. To me your talk sounds like that of a baby, an infant unable yet to give voice to the spirit within. You want me to leave. You want my people to disappear. We will not disappear. And because we don't turn into trees you can sell to your lumbermen, you play games with us, to see if we are real. I tell you we are real!"

Dole stood stunned. Captain Hall kept his hand on his pistol as he studied the situation. Sweet looked from one to the other unsure what to do. I gestured for Dole and Sweet to trust in me to negotiate a deal. I told them the Chief needed ten thousand dollars to clothe and feed his people and begin construction of the mill.

"Tell your Great Father," the Chief continued. "That we would be Americans. But how can we when he sends us such poor models? How can we act with dignity when the people he sends to work with us, to ensure our well-being, betray us time and time again?" And now he turned his gaze from Dole, staring into the air beyond him as if the Commissioner did not exist. "I have no stomach for these kinds of Americans. Send me real ones, and I will talk." And with that he pulled his blanket about him and gestured for you and Buffalo to follow him out.

"Shoot him!" Dole shouted. "Shoot the son-of-a-bitch!" he raved.

The Chief turned and walked to the door.

"Shoot him, damn it!" Dole shouted again.

Captain Hall watched the Chief leave the house, then looked back to guage Dole and Sweet's astonished faces.

"What are you waiting for?" Dole asked.

Hall released the strap locking his pistol in the holster and followed them. I moved in close behind, ready to intervene. Once outside, he pulled his pistol from the holster, but still did not raise it. I counted the seconds as the three chiefs marched first through the parting soldiers and then into the cheering crowd of their own people. One of Hall's men, raised his weapon, took aim at the Chief. That's when the Captain aimed his pistol to the heavens and fired. The Chief did not turn or slow his gait. "Let them go," Captain Hall shouted. "I don't shoot men in the back." It was a tribute to the esteem in which his men held him that they did not move a hair.

The chiefs retired with their warriors to their camp at Otter Tail Lake waiting for word of what might come next. And the next morning I rode out to meet them with news that the Sioux had attacked the agency at Redwood as they'd promised they would. You spoke forcefully in favor of joining the Sioux, as you'd given your word that the two ancient enemies would unite to make the whites remember the price for betrayal. But Buffalo and Flat Mouth feared what another loss might do to their people. They'd heard about First Seated Feather and Bad Boy taking their warriors to join forces with the whites at Ft. Ripley. There were now almost as many Ojibwe fighting against them as with them. They could not help the Sioux.

"Long past is the time when we could rise up against any enemy," Buffalo argued.

The Chief turned to Curly Head, knowing the Sandy Lake chief had never supported him. And Curly Head savored the moment, looking from one leader to the next, reminding each of the times in his long life he had advised them. At last, he counseled surrender, suggesting they stick to the reservation land already ceded them and put their faith in the Great Father to send his aid when he saw how the Chippewa submitted to his will.

The Chief did not grow angry, nor did he call forth another great speech to persuade Curly Head and the others. I advised him to wait, to give Dole time to reconsider his words. I told him the Great Father would be angry with Dole for the way in which he conducted himself, and that the whites would move to make amends. "I hear your concerns, Beaulieu," the Chief said at last. "I understand that war may mean the end. But I ask you, have the Anishinabe not already met their end?"

You gripped your war club, but the others were not as easy to read. Flat Mouth moved his lips as if he would spit. Buffalo shut his eyes. Curly Head pulled his weather beaten derby low over his head. The whites had given that hat to him at a time when he looked to become the leader of all the Chippewa. I did not want more hostilities to break out. War was in no one's interest. I still had hopes of regaining my shop. My children were hungry. My wife, Elizabeth, tired of hearing my excuses. But it was too late.

"We ride to war in the morning," the Chief said. "We will attack the agency at Crow Wing first and from there move to Ft. Ripley. I for one do not care to meet my end rooted in place." You and the Chief walked toward the lake, leaving the others to decide their course.

The next morning, when the Chief called his warriors

to him, all except Curly Head showed up. He and his men had left during the night, going back to their ceded land along Sandy Lake. Despite his absence, the Chief looked pleased as they rode south two hundred strong. I grew despondent then. I knew what lay in store for them. I rode at the back, thinking now only of how to keep my family safe.

The war party reached the agency an hour before noon, but Captain Hall had learned from the previous encounter. The Chief marched into the trap. From behind the five saloons that dotted Main Street, three hundred soldiers emerged. The Gatling gun poked through the window of the agency just as Captain Hall stepped through the door, his hand on his pistol.

"You are a brave man and a skillful orator, Hole in the Day," Captain Hall began. "Do not force me to cut short a life that seems so promising. Do not send your men needlessly to their deaths."

The Chief said nothing.

"I am authorized by Commissioner Dole," Hall went on, "to escort you safely back to your lands and to ensure that if you go peacefully, you will receive the needed supplies before the coming winter." With that, Captain Hall removed his hand from his pistol, took out a match, then pulled a rolled cigarette from his breast pocket, struck the match against the porch railing and lit his cigarette.

The Chief sat atop his horse, you beside him. Still, he said nothing, waiting for the whites to fire the first shot so he could ride to his death. But Captain Hall would not give him death so easily.

Buffalo and Flat Mouth spoke hushed words with

each other, Flat Mouth's gaze flitting to the Gatling gun in the window, then back to the gritty faces of the soldiers all about them. At last, Buffalo spoke. "For our part, the Pillagers will surrender," he shouted. "We will walk away from here."

The Chief watched as one by one the Pillagers laid down their weapons. He watched, too, when many of your own clan also laid down their arms and followed the Pillagers. But I remember well how you did not leave the Chief, but sniffed at the air as if you'd scented something foul and sat erect by his side, waiting for the signal to attack.

Captain Hall took a long puff from his cigarette, then another. He waved at the smoke before him. "You have but fifty warriors left," he said. "Go home, unless you would add your name to the long list of those slaughtered for no reason in this endless war." This time, it was he who turned his back on the Chief and walked inside the agency to finish his cigarette.

I saw my chance. I broke the line of warriors, riding up to the Chief. I told him there was no point in dying such a meaningless death. I told him there were still things that could be done to save his people, that if we played this right there would still be a chance to start fresh. He could go to the President once again. I told him I would accompany him if he wished. That I would use what little influence I had in Washington to make things right. I told him to think of his child, Ignatius. To think of all our children.

The Chief sat atop his horse for half an hour staring at the agency door, as if waiting for Hall to appear again.

But the captain did not appear, and finally the Chief turned his horse toward home. You followed him out of town, then turned north toward your own home. For my part, I walked to Fletcher's saloon, spending the afternoon alone in the corner drinking whiskey after whiskey and watching the soldiers tell stories of how the Indians had fled at the mere sight of their power.

The Chief returned to find his house burned to the ground, Agida and the child, Ignatius, barely escaped into the woods. Some said it had been the Pillagers who torched his house on their retreat, still angry at him for lying about starting the war and endangering their position when they took the Norwegian family prisoner. Others said it was a battalion of white soldiers sent to further humiliate the chief. Either way, it didn't matter.

Walker went mad with word of the Sioux and Chippewa uprising. Though it was nearly fall, the cicadas had been particularly horrible that summer. While Captain Hall had been facing off with the Chief, Walker had put on several layers of clothes and tied them tight to his ankles and wrists for fear the bugs would get in. Worse still, he'd tied a potato sack around his head, cutting only a hole to breathe through. When Hall came back inside smoking his cigarette and saw Walker like that sitting on top of his desk, Hall almost shot the agent on the spot.

I reach for Niibiniishkang's bleeding finger, take it to my mouth. My shadow darts before me, and I jump toward it. Pull it over me until I am free.

"Ase-anse, you have returned," Niibiniishkang exclaims, his drizzly eyes looking as if soon he will follow me.

For a moment, Newobiik glances in my direction. "Be gone!" she shouts. She reaches into her pocket and begins throwing a powder about the hut. It smells of turned earth, rotting leaf, and pepper. "Be gone!" she says again. "You have done enough harm here. My husband hangs by a thread." She goes to her husband, kisses his forehead. "I must get word to Bishop Whipple," she says, then leaves through the red curtain. She must know the Bishop cannot possibly make it in time.

Beaulieu sits upright, staring past us into the fire. Shadows of flame contort his face.

It's so cold I can barely work my fingers. My mouth no longer feels like it's my own. I crawl toward the fire.

The old trader gibbers on and on, though I've shut him out of my mind. Perhaps he, too, will need to confess before my time here is over.

Niibiniishkang glances back and forth between us. He looks tired. Death almost has hold of him. I wonder if he cares who tells the story, or if he cares to hear the story any more at all. The webbed lines of his face paint a picture of indifference. I lie as near to the fire as I dare. I must not let Beaulieu go on. My mouth crackles in the warmth. I try to speak, but my tongue catches on the words. I force them out. My frozen jaw nearly shatters. Still, they will both hear me before all is over.

Hole in the Day and his family disappeared from Crow Wing and the settlement at New Rome. Word spread that he'd died, taken his own life in shame after the failed uprising. And in his death, his fame among both white and Ojibwe grew. Soon the story went that Hole in the Day had won the battle that day, then given himself up to the whites in exchange for peace. Every few months the story changed until eventually people stopped talking about him.

He'd moved his family deep in the north shore of Otter Tail Lake where he remained silent for a year and a half until the birth of his first daughter, Isabelle. Only then did he send word to his brother that he was needed. X brought many books from the church library, including *The Aeneid,* hoping the books would remind his brother of his once great vision and of the time they'd shared. At his brother's request, he baptized the girl, though he was not yet certified to do so. X left after a few days, promising to return when his studies permitted. Hole in the Day spent mornings hunting for his family, then passed the afternoon teaching his children to read and write with the books his brother had brought.

For his part, X dove deep into his studies. The fact that he once again could not do what his brother asked ate at him. And so, he worked side by side with Father Tomazin, walking with him on his rounds, studying beside him late into the evening. X began giving short sermons every Sunday and took pride in seeing more and more faces in the church with each passing week. Once he became a priest, he would ask for his own church.

"You are a natural speaker," Father Tomazin told him one evening over dinner. "The congregation grows with each passing day. The Métis flock to hear you speak." He smiled then and took X's hand.

It was not the first time the priest had done so. At first, X was sure the priest had feelings for him. But then he noticed how Father Tomazin touched everyone as he spoke with them. He was comfortable with himself physically, and with others. X grew confused and often withdrew from the priest to avoid the feeling.

"You're ready to be deacon," Father Tomazin said, finishing the last of his soup.

"What?"

"I'm filling out the paperwork now," the priest replied. "You are officially a deacon of this church." He rose, smiling now, opening his arms.

"I can't believe it," X said. He rose, hugged the priest in return. They held each other a long moment, the priest patting X's back.

"You must give me your secret," he said. "How do you hook these new parishioners?" He moved to the other side of the table, pretended as if he was looking for a pen and paper.

X thought of asking the priest directly if he cared for him. But he feared the answer. He feared he'd misread this man, that he'd seen the desires of Father Pierz in this other priest. "I simply tell them they cannot continue to hide, to live as they have always done," X said at last.

"Yes, more and more, our congregation is neither white nor Chippewa," Father Tomazin said. Not finding pen and paper, he spooned himself another ladle of soup.

"But I do not want to call them Métis, either," X replied, sitting again, pushing his own bowl away.

"What would you call them?" Father Tomazin sat, spooned the soup into his mouth.

"The day will come," X replied, "when we don't need to call them anything. We won't need to make such distinctions."

"I had no idea you were such an idealist," Father Tomazin replied, picking up the bowl and drinking from it.

"What is the point of such distinctions?" X asked, realizing he hadn't thought about it before but that it mattered to him.

"I don't know," Father Tomazin answered. "I suppose so we can tell one group from another. So we can know who is who."

"Or so we can label one group, erase them from the stories we tell," X went on. As he talked, he grew angry, though he knew not why. "It's easier to determine who exists and who doesn't."

"I take back what I said before," Father Tomazin said, laughing. "You are no idealist!" He rose, patted X on the shoulder. "Your thoughtfulness will serve you well as deacon."

X didn't respond, still trying to sound his heart.

"Now, if you'll excuse me, I've got my own sermon to write," the priest said. "If I'm going to keep up with you that is." He gave a last smile and left for the study.

X remained seated at the table as night fell. He did not light a candle, but remained in the dark.

The next morning he asked Father Tomazin if he could do the rounds alone, his first official duty as the new deacon.

"Of course," Tomazin replied. "With my blessing."

After checking in with his parishioners, seeing who was in need of food or medicine, he found himself heading towards his old home, the one he'd kept with Flower. Only when he came near the door did he stop and stare as if unsure of the way. His hut was much improved since he'd left. A vegetable garden surrounded the south and east sides, dotted by rocks piled into the shapes of bears, rabbit and deer.

Beaulieu tears off his beaver skin coat, rips at the flesh of his left arm as if he would rend it from the bone leaving only a wiindigoo made of snow and ice. The poor man must still think I inhabit his skin. His mouth chatters on, and I move to shut it. He will not take over my story again. But Niibini-ishkang stops me with a look of stone.

"I will not have the insanity of before," he says. "Each will have his turn to speak."

I stay where I am, warm by the fire, waiting for my time as the fiery haired trader speaks more lies.

The spring after the Chippewa surrender, Walker ran off into the woods never to be seen alive again. He took his rifle with him, saying he was going to hunt some Indians, then sealed his arms and legs against the insects and donned his potato sack mask as he'd grown accustomed to doing. He loped along the riverbank like a scarecrow escaped from his field. I sent word immediately to the Chief, for I'd heard of his hiding place above Otter Tail Lake. I was one of the few who knew he still lived. And I warned him of Walker's intent. He sent no reply. So, I sought out Captain Hall, advising him to dispatch soldiers to save Walker before more bloodshed ignited the tribes to war.

Two days later, the soldiers found Walker dead by the side of the road, his body stripped and covered with mud, a bullet in his brain. Hall's report called it a suicide, though the location and angle of entry would have been impossible coming from Walker's own rifle, not to mention the fact that they found no shells near the body. The report also failed to mention his face had been painted, the lower half black with two full moons beneath his eyes. The half-breeds at Crow Wing didn't give a damn for Hall's report. They swore the ghost of the Chief had killed Walker. And they feared he would come for all those who failed him in his war. Word was that the Chief had promised a large reward to anyone who brought him the scalps of Bad Boy, First Seated Feather, and even his adopted brother, Deacon Paulson. He'd never forgiven them for their betrayal. I have to admit I feared for anyone who crossed the Chief. I even gave thought to moving my own family out, just in case the Chief began to think I'd double-crossed him. But then one Sunday after service, Deacon Paulson came to me and changed everything.

I will not stand for this. I will not listen to that flayed head. I will not let him take my face in his hands and scratch me a new one. I will tear my own face into his skin and see how he likes it. But Niibinishkang raises his hand, and I am made silent. Let the memory scraper talk on.

"I hear you're thinking of leaving," Deacon Paulson said, slipping his arm around me the way he liked to do. It gave me the creeps, as if he was trying to make me one of his kind, if you know what I mean. "It would be a shame to lose someone who is a friend to both Chippewa and the whites."

"I've done what I can here," I told Paulson. "And now it's time to think of my family."

"Of course a man should always think of his family," Deacon Paulson replied. "I've got to think of their future. What chance do they have here?"

"Well that's just it." Deacon Paulson pressed his hands to his lips as if in prayer and looked out at the ramshackle town before him. "You've got a chance here to make a name for yourself, and for your children," he said at last. "A better chance to be somebody than you'd ever have in the city."

"I'm not sure what you mean."

"Hole in the Day is no more. But his people still exist, and more importantly the half-breeds still exist. They outnumber everyone else in this town, and they need a leader. Someone to bring them through, to take them into the new world."

"You know as well as I do the Chief's not dead," I told him.

"I didn't say he was dead."

"What can I do?"

"You can make this town what it needs to be," Deacon Paulson replied. "You can do what Hole in the Day was not able to do."

The red curtain hangs before me solid as any cage. I cannot leave Niibiniishkang's hut, not yet. And still this madman babbles in the dark. He knows nothing, and yet his words cluster in my head forming mountains that threaten to block out the sun. I can be silent no more. Let the memories rise from my blood, let them bubble forth so that Niibiniishkang may hear the truth!

One morning after completing his rounds, X did not pass by his old hut as he was accustomed to do but walked through the front door as if he'd only been gone a few hours instead of years. Inside, herbs and dried flowers hung from the ceiling; shelves lined the walls topped with jars filled with wild rice and maple sugar. And furniture filled the hut: benches, a worktable, even a soft bed of poplar in the corner. But what impressed him most was the new pair of makizins sitting under the bed. They'd been made with such care, the seams sewn tight, the beadwork fine and in the shape of a white mi-igis shell.

Flower had been sitting on the bed, sewing, when X entered. She smiled and nodded as he noticed the shoes. He bent down, took them in his hands, admiring the smooth skin. Sitting next to her on the bed, he tried to explain why he'd left, why there were times when he could not bear her love, and why the church seemed to him the only place to go, the only place he felt whole. She shook her head and placed a finger to his lips, signaling him to be quiet. He went on, alternating between Anishinabe and English, hoping that if he talked long enough he might find the words. But Flower would not hear him. She cared only that he had returned to her. Knot by knot, she unloosened the ties of her robe, then lifted his shirt from him, removed his pants and straddled him on the bed. X lay still as she rocked above him, letting the motion settle him in place. Her dark hair tickled his chest as she swung it back and forth. Her hands pinned his shoulders against the cot. And as her hips slowly ground into him, he finally understood why he'd committed himself to the church. There, he could feel nothing at all.

Beaulieu murmurs and prattles, his breath a cloud steaming forth into the chill air. I want to tell him he is free of me. But I know better. We are possessed by many spirits. Not all of them so easy to toss off.

He starts his story, and to my surprise I let him.

Bad Boy and Curly Head took advantage of the Chief's supposed death and arranged for their own visit to Washington, hoping to solidify their position with the whites and with their own people. I did not accompany them this time. I had all I could do getting my trading post in working order once again. And I was searching for partners willing to invest in Crow Wing. I wouldn't have made a difference anyway. The whites were deep in their own pockets as a result of the Civil War and in no mood to give anything away. It was a mistake for them to go. No one wanted to talk to Indians. The two chiefs ended up ceding half the Minnesota territory in exchange for the marsh east of Lake Winnibigoshish. A very bad deal. When Bad Boy and Curly Head returned, they tried to put a good face on the negotiations, saying they would receive a bigger annuity as a result, that the new land was indeed better for farming. But the people knew the lies for what they were. They killed Bad Boy before he could return to the protection of Fort Ripley. Shot him in the back, his wife and children fleeing into the wilderness. Curly Head made it back to Sandy Lake and his own people, but was banished the day he arrived. They say the chicots in Canada found his skeleton wandering the vast wastes looking for food.

And still, the Chief did not make his presence known, choosing to hide on the shores of Otter Tail Lake where he passed his days reading to his children and tending to his garden. In the meantime, I was traveling, making contacts with lumbermen and furriers. I was now determined to make Crow Wing the center of trade in the newly formed state. We had the advantage over many other towns, as the Métis couriers had to come our way to avoid the Sioux. And Crow Wing had swelled to over six hundred as a result. We were on the map. My kids went to a private school in St. Cloud. My wife had everything she desired. Soon I would be the wealthiest man in the county.

And then it happened. It was the winter of 1866, and I was returning from a survey of the land north of Crow Wing when I spied the Chief wrapped in his thick green blanket, walking along the Pine River. He looked like an old beggar. No trace of his haughty bearing left. It was too much. I thought of taking another path, avoiding him altogether. But something compelled me to stay and watch in the waning dusk. I think I wanted to see what manner of man he'd become. But the Chief simply climbed atop a boulder that looked out over the river, lit his pipe and sat smoking as if he had no thought of ever returning. His people already thought of him as dead. They spoke little of him and what he'd done for them. It made me sick. And I vowed the same would never happen to me. I'd make a name for myself so that my children would not forget me. The darkening light cast an eerie glow over the ice. I approached, but he remained still as a dying deer.

"It's time you rose from the ashes, my friend," I told

him, pulling out my own pipe, gesturing for a pinch of tobacco as if we'd not been apart all these years.

The Chief smiled, reached into his tobacco pouch and handed me a generous portion, but he didn't speak a word.

"Your people need you," I continued. "Bad Boy and Curly Head betrayed them."

"I heard as much," he said at last.

"Then you know how your people suffer," I said, puffing now on the rich tobacco. "It is not yet another Sandy Lake, but soon it will be."

The Chief looked askance. "Why do you come to me now?" he asked. "I know you, Beaulieu. You do not ask for things unless there is something in it for you."

Now it was my turn to smile. "You know me well," I replied. "Then you should also know a prosperous town only means more business for me. The town is booming, but the Métis are unreliable. I wouldn't mind the consistency of a government contract."

Again, the Chief eyed me. He puffed on his pipe, considering my words. "Somewhere in what you say there is truth. Though I think you have other motives."

"Motives that will only benefit the Chippewa," I replied, leaning now against the rock, listening to the gurgling of the water as it churned beneath the ice.

"What do you suggest?"

"Ride once again to Washington," I told him. "Meet with the new President. And get the land back that was lost in Curly Head's treaty. Your people will never forget you then."

"I am dead, haven't you heard?"

"All the more reason to go to Washington," I replied. "They won't be expecting a dead man."

The Chief's smile was like the new moon. He pulled his blanket about him and stepped down from the rock.

I stayed with the Chief and Agida that first night after our talk on Pine River. The next day, when I awoke, the Chief was ready, dressed in his finest shirt and frockcoat with an otterskin trimmed in red and wrapped around his neck like a muffler. He'd braided his hair the way he liked to do, wrapping it about his head like a turban, with several eagle feathers sticking from it. And of course, he had his green blanket over his shoulders. I sent word to my connections in St. Paul to arrange for two tickets to Washington.

Though President Johnson came to office under the cloud of Lincoln's assassination, he was riding the euphoria sweeping the nation after the end of the civil war the month before. That was before he ran afoul of the Republicans at a time when he could do no wrong, and he was of a generous spirit. Word of the Chief's "resurrection" made it easy to gain entrance to the White House. Everyone wanted to be seen with the Indian who rose from the dead. The Chief presented his case eloquently as he'd done so often in the past. He demanded that the President annul the previous treaty giving back the good timberland, and he argued once again that the annuity system would only lead his people to ruin. I was not sure if it was because he didn't want his people to get used to government money, or if it was because he knew that money would dry up within months after it was promised. Either way, he knew the answer was to get what he could then and return to his people, playing the part of the hero.

We'd agreed to ask for ten thousand for the short term to build infrastructure, farms and schools to train the people in agriculture. When he first demanded this money, President Johnson blanched and left the room. He returned with a tall, grim faced man named Senator Wade. I knew the man only by his reputation as a tough negotiator. Nothing got past him in the senate without his approval.

"I have made mistakes," Hole in the Day told the President and Senator. "I am a human being. I am not a god as some have made me out to be." Wade poured himself a scotch, though he never turned his back on the Chief. "But I have learned from my mistakes," the Chief went on. "I wonder if it's possible to learn anything here when the Great Father must step down so quickly."

President Johnson smiled and nodded his head. "I like your honesty. It's refreshing to hear someone admit he made mistakes. If only we had more of that in Washington." The President laughed and gestured the Chief to sit with him on the sofa as if he were an equal. Wade downed his whiskey in one gulp and poured us each a new glass. I noted how he filled the Chief's glass to the top.

The Chief talked on, the President listening, or at least pretending to listen, warming him with his southern charm. After a few minutes, Wade thought he'd found the right time to make his move. He thought wrong. He offered the Chief five thousand extra, saying it would go a long way toward making life easier for his wife and children. The Chief unwrapped his green blanket and set it beside him on the sofa, then politely refused the money.

Wade almost choked on his whiskey. But he didn't rise to control of the senate for nothing. He would not give up so easily.

"If you're not going to take my money, at least accept my whiskey," Wade said, pouring a new glass for the Chief.

"When they destroyed my home," Hole in the Day said, taking the glass without thinking. "I lost the picture President Pierce gave me and the tea set they honored me with on my last visit."

Wade saw his opening. "Of course, we can replace those things," he said, now pulling up a chair to sit between the Chief and the President. "We will replace all the gifts you lost." He placed his hand on the Chief's shoulder as if they were old friends.

The Chief took his whiskey, and Wade pressed his advantage. "I understand your concern," he said. "You want to show your people the way. But think with the extra money we offer, you can rebuild your house that was burned. You can show your people what it means to live a civilized life."

The Chief took another sip of whiskey and another as he considered the words. Soon, he began asking for everything, not simply the five thousand dollars offered but the finest silverware and china, a case of the President's own whiskey, beds and furniture for his house. I tried to break in, but he had the politicians' full attention. The Chief went on, asking for more land to cultivate, for a dozen horses and three dozen cattle, crystal decanters like he'd seen in the White House, a picture of Johnson to go with the one of Pierce, money for private schooling for his children, Ignatius and Isabelle, the list ran on and on. With each item the Chief listed, Wade's smile grew bigger and bigger.

"What do you think, Wade?" the President asked when the Chief had finished his speech and his whiskey. "Can we grant this man's requests?"

"I don't see why not," the senator replied. "I know I can push it through congress if the Chief is willing to grant a few small concessions of our own."

"I'm not finished." The Chief stood and walked toward the door where he knew the reporters waited. "The treaty the impostors Bad Boy and Curly Head negotiated was not acceptable. Our people will not abide by it."

Wade set down his whiskey. The President stepped toward the door as if only now he understood the Chief's intent.

"We want the land back." The Chief reached for the doorknob. "All of it. Or else I cannot promise what my people will do. The Sioux uprising is still strong in their minds. And there are many more of us than Sioux in Minnesota."

"Are you threatening violence against the United States of America?" President Johnson met the Chief before the door. Wade followed his lead.

"I'm merely stating that my people won't abide by the terms of a false treaty." The Chief turned the handle on the door, pushed it open an inch. I could hear the rustle of the reporters beyond. "Shall we see what the American public thinks of the possibility of another uprising?"

Wade placed his hand on the Chief's arm, held the door back for a moment. "That won't be necessary," President Johnson said. "I believe we have our deal."

Without wasting another moment, Senator Wade opened the door. Photographers and reporters streamed in, all wanting to get an exclusive on the deal between the President and the "dead" Indian. The meeting had already been designated an historic one. It was clear as the Chief and the politicians smiled for the camera, their arms around each other, that both sides wanted to capitalize on it.

"We will do for the Indians what the past administration did for our Negro brothers," President Johnson told the press. All in the room smiled and nodded their heads.

A few months later Johnson would face impeachment. No one would ever know if he meant what he said or not. Within two years, the Chief would be dead, murdered in his carriage as he rode again to Washington in an attempt to win back more land.

Back in Crow Wing, the Chief celebrated his good fortune in Fletcher's bar before returning home. He drank one whiskey after another, boasting to the two full-bloods at the bar and the handful of half-breeds sitting around one of the tables of how he sat together as an equal with the Great Father and made him give in to each and every one of his demands. How he would be the greatest of the Chippewa chiefs. That the Chippewa would rise again just as he had and would not disappear from the earth as so many had foretold.

I took my whiskey and slipped to the back. The town would grow, but the Chief's ego had grown as well. He went on, bragging of his victory over Commissioner Dole and Captain Hall's men. How in the end, he got what he wanted, how his children would go to private schools in St. Paul and learn alongside the whites. That last comment turned the whiskey sour in my gut.

"What about my kids?" I asked. The Chief went on talking, ignoring me. "It's a small thing," I said. The least that should be done for one who has done so much to help the Chippewa. Or does a good education only go to those with pure blood, white or Ojibwe?"

The Chief turned slowly, his face shifting in the dim light of the bar. "Who speaks?" he asked.

"Beaulieu," I said, setting my empty glass upon the table.

"And who are you?" the Chief asked, stepping forward, his hand reaching into his green blanket.

The red curtain flutters as if waking to this world. The call of the gray owl sounds in the distance, and I know the third day has passed. Niibiniishkang sleeps. Beaulieu chatters. With each word he speaks, the flames licking my feet grow more distant until their warmth is a fading memory. I see Fletcher's bar as it stood so many years ago. I feel the pine boards beneath my feet, the shuffling sawdust that keeps the cold away. The years contract, and I am there.

I watch from the shadows in the back as my brother brags of his exploits, of the ease in which he won the people's hearts and minds. I watch as he turns to me. I listen as my brother asks who I am, but his voice no longer makes sense to me. He slurs his words. So I ask him what he is saying, tell him his words have no meaning. He asks a question, and I answer. "I am your brother."

"You are not my brother," the Chief said.

"I didn't say I was," I responded.

"You are Beaulieu," the Chief said. "You are nobody," he continued, his glazed eyes panning the shadows.

"You've had too much to drink." I pushed back from the table, raised my hand to shake him off. "Your success of late has gone to your head."

The Chief pulled his Colt from beneath his blanket. "Take off your shirt," he said.

"What?"

"Take off your shirt." The Chief aimed the wavering gun at me. "I want to see if your chest is as hairy and red as that beard."

I didn't think he could hit a damn thing in his condition, but I wasn't going to take any chances.

Slowly, I remove my cassock, then loosen the ties of my shirt. The two full bloods at the bar turn to each other and walk out without a word, leaving their nearly full drinks. The Métis shift forward in their seats, curious to see what will unfold. I lie my clothes upon the table. Sweat glistens upon my scorched skin, though the air outside is below freezing. "Enough, brother," I say.

The Chief jerked his hand above his head. "I am Hole in the Day," he yelled. "Like my father. And I have once again saved our people."

"Are we not all your people?" I ask, realizing then the Mide shell and rosary still hang about my neck. I will not give them up so easily.

"Who are you?" the Chief asked again, waving the Colt in the darkness.

I had no answer to his question.

"You are wissakode. Half-burnt," the Chief stumbled forward. "I knew it all along. Look at your skin. Beneath the red hair, I see it."

"What does it matter?" I reply. "Are we not all half breeds? Is it not the only way, my brother?"

"I am the son of Bagone-giizhig, the first Hole in the Day!" he replies, pushing the gun close to my face. "You are not! My blood is the blood of the original people!" I see the dirt grimed under his nails and want to tell him he is no different, but instead I kiss his hand, run the Mide shell over it.

He pulls it away; the shell falls to the floor. "Who are you?" he asks again, as if he is no longer sure.

"I am your brother."

"You are Beaulieu," he replies, his hand shaking now.

"Whatever you say," I told the Chief. "You earned all this. Look around you."

The Chief blinked and stared at the remaining half-breeds clutching their bottles and glasses. "Are you mocking me, Beaulieu?" he demanded. "Do you think I won't make the Chippewa great again?"

"I think nothing."

"You think nothing because you are nothing."

"Yes," I whisper. "You are right, my brother." With each word, I fade until my own voice echoes from the rafters.

Fletcher, the barkeep stepped back into the storeroom doorway, going for the shotgun he kept there, his bald pate dull beneath the shadow of the door.

"Put down the gun," I told the Chief. "Before this ends badly for all of us." I signaled with my hand for him to stop.

The Chief continued waving his gun in the air. He stepped forward, leaned in close until I could smell his sour breath, could taste it on my beard.

I cannot see him or smell him. Yet I know he is there before me. My brother.

"You're a half breed," the Chief whispered. "You are nothing until I say so. Until I make you something. Watch, as I create you." He breathed out long and slow upon my face. "Watch, now, as I destroy what I create," the Chief went on. He faltered then, swaying for a moment, raised the gun high into the air.

I brought down his hand, knocked him to the ground. The half-breeds from the table rose in unison, upturned bottles in hand and jumped the Chief, beating him as he lay in the dust on the hard floor.

"Let's kill him, Beaulieu," one of the half-breeds said, kicking the Chief in the stomach.

"No!" I replied. The sight made me sick. I couldn't bear to stay, and so I gave him into the care of the half-breeds. I left him there, but I did not kill him.

I watch from the rafters above. See my brother lying in the sawdust, looking as he did when he held that girl in the tepee of the Wah'petonwan on that night so long ago. They kick him, blood streaming from cuts beneath his eyes, a gash running from his lip to his chin. I wait, looking for my chance, but I can do nothing. The moment is a string of words I can't find.

"It's as if Bagone-giizhig slipped out of this world," Niibiniishkang says.

"Yes," I answer.

"I wonder where the real Bagone-giizhig went to," Niibiniishkang says.

"Perhaps he fled through the hole in his name to the other side," I reply. "Leaving this fake in his place," Niibiniishkang says. "He was rightfully named then."

"Without story it is difficult to find your way back," I say. "He could have gotten lost."

"Maybe it is for that reason you tell the story now, Ase-anse."

"That is my hope." I shake the old war chief, but he will not open his eyes. I try to force them open, but he gestures for me to stop.

"I must rest," Niibiniishkang says. "This labyrinth you weave may lead you from the circle, but it ensnares me." With that, he pushes me away.

Beaulieu dons his cap, pulls his coat tight about him, without worrying about refastening it. "You talk at nothing, Niibiniishkang," he says. "You are passing from this world, and I fear to be near you now. I don't like this place. There is evil here." He crosses himself and makes for the door, but before he leaves, he turns once again. "I will not pray for you," he says. "But I will find the priest so that you may pass quietly into the next world." And then the old trader is gone, *the smile playing on Niibiniishkang's face the only hint that he has been there at all.*

"He should pray for himself," he says, folding his arms over his chest. "Leave me, Ase-anse. My time is short, but I think I will still be here tomorrow." His breath grows heavy.

I rise to go, but stop before reaching the door, as if the wings of the great gray owl block my path. I retreat to the shadows, tuck my feet up under me, wrap my arms about my knees and watch over Niibiniishkang, the same way I watched over you, my brother.

While Hole in the Day lay half dead in the hospital in St. Paul, Beaulieu plotted how to finish him off for good. He called his business associates to his house: John and George Morrison and Charles Ruffee. He offered a thousand dollars to each of them for the deed, told them that if Hole in the Day was not killed, he would be like a great log lying across the road of progress.

Ruffee later said he refused, said he was a businessman not a hired killer, said his only goal was to make money selling whiskey and wares. The others said his problem was that he wanted to be paid in advance, and Beaulieu was nothing if not cheap. Whatever happened that night, the Judases named the Morrison brothers would not reveal their part, never telling of the gold coin that passed across the table into George's sweaty palm, nor the fact that John kept his gaze on the flickering candle for fear of looking the others in the face.

As soon as X heard the news that Hole in the Day had been badly beaten, he went to his brother's side at the hospital in St. Paul. Flower did not stop him, though she knew that this time he would not return to her. She gathered her belongings and walked home over the frozen earth to her own people. They say she married a German named Baumgartner and bore him many children. That she still lives outside the reservation border watching over her grandchildren.

For three weeks Hole in the Day lay comatose in the St. Paul hospital. And for three weeks X sat beside him, reading to him from the Bible as Father Pierz had once done to both of them, but also reading from Ovid. He'd found Dryden's translation of *The Metamorphoses* in the hospital library. Each night he read to him a different story: "Apollo and Daphne," "The Story of Actaeon," "The Fighting of Perseus," and "Jason and Medea." But it was not until he read how Orpheus ventured to the underworld as Aeneas had once done that his brother's eyes shifted beneath the bandages:

I come not curious to explore your Hell
Nor come to boast (by vain ambition fir'd)
How Cerberus at my approach retir'd.
My wife alone I seek; for her lov'd sake
These terrors I support, this journey take.

"He lies," Hole in the Day mumbled. They were the first words he'd spoken since entering the coma.

"What did you say, brother?"

"Ambition is all," Hole in the Day replied.

Barely able to hear him, X leaned in close, his ear just above his brother's mouth. Faint as a moth's wing, his brother's breath graced his cheek. "Ambition or love?" X asked, fearing the answer even as he spoke the question. His brother did not reply. "Why did you build your community?" X continued. "Why try to follow the path of the whites?"

"Why have you come here?" Hole in the Day answered with a question of his own.

X wrapped his arms around his brother. "Ambition or love?" he whispered this time.

"To exist and to be remembered," Hole in the Day answered. "That is why I built the town. That is why you are here." And with that he kissed his brother's head.

X walked to the window overlooking the alley below. A lone dog tracked slantwise through the snow, sniffing for food. "Do you remember, brother, the days we played along the river, the days before the Wah'petonwan?"

"Geget." Hole in the Day closed his eyes. "Of course. It was a different world then."

"I would have done anything to help you that night."

"We have been through much." Hole in the Day tried to sit up. "Too much for one life."

"Now you were nearly beaten to death, and where was I?"

"Time changes all of us," Hole in the Day replied. "Until we can barely recognize ourselves."

I lie in wait on the bottom, settling my great haunches in the black loam. My tongue swells, filling my mouth. I am the fixed point about which the world spins. A shape takes form in the distance. The crow caws at me from within the hollow of his chest. Seaweed swirls about his head, drifting on the current. It is Piichoo Manidoo.

"Can you help me, brother?" he asks as he gets closer.

I dig my haunches further into the dark mud to cover my body.

"Can you pull this arrow from my shoulder?" he asks. "It causes me much pain."

When I speak, mud falls from my mouth. My great haunches twitch. The water grows murky. I close my heavy lids, then open them again. It is Piichoo Manidoo, I am sure.

I spring on him, my back haunches pinning him to the ground as my forelegs drive the arrow in further. I push the arrow in until the feathers are lost in the blood pouring from his shoulder. I shove my hand deep in his mouth, searching for you, brother. I try to pull you free, yanking out heart, liver and lungs, long, curving lines of intestines.

My breath runs out, and I struggle to the surface. The moonlight shines on my green skin. I run my hands over my naked body, flinging away seaweed and shells. The great gray owl watches from the branches above.

"I have killed Piichoo Manidoo," I tell him. "I have saved my brother."

The owl stares back at me, and I fear the consequences of what I've done. Behind me the wind kicks up waves along the rime-covered shore. No disguise can fool the coming manidoog or save me from the end of this world.

DAY FOUR

I rise like a fish thrashing upon the frozen earth. Niibiniish-kang sits cross-legged facing me, a caricature of the war chief he once was. Pale blue light peels through the curtained door, signaling the approaching dawn.

"Do you yet live?" I ask him.

A smile cracks his stone face. "I think so," he replies. "Though I am talking with you, and that gives me doubt."

"We are near the end, old man," I say. "But I am not sure that we are any closer to the truth."

"That is because you haven't let me talk," Niibiniishkang replies. "You are like the chimookomaanag, always talking, never listening. It is fitting you became a priest. Now it is my turn to tell the tale, and I would do it before I pass from this world. I want my spirit to be clear when I walk the path of souls."

"If you must continue," I reply. "Heed the words of Toad Woman. I am weary and lack the strength to fight my way out any more."

"I am old, Ase-anse. But I am not stupid," he says. And with that, he begins. The sound of his voice like a low murmur, like the grinding of stone on stone.

It was niibin, 1867, and the timber companies came with a writ from the government ceding our land to them once again. Bagone-giizhig had just finished rebuilding his house. His children Ignatius and Isabelle were in boarding school. And he had again begun work on building his community of New Rome, this time hiring out farmers from Ohio to train his people in working the land. But now the government proclaimed he would have to remove himself and his people to a reservation called White Earth west of Leech Lake.

He sent word that he would make yet another trip to Washington to speak once again with his friend, President Johnson. And he asked that I accompany him, as Green Feather was now too old to make the journey. Had our ogimaa not been drunk so much of the time, I might have believed he would succeed as he'd done so long ago. I was not young either, but I was the leader of my clan, my children, and so I did what I had to do. We met at Crow Wing, where the new agent Bassett made it known that Ruffee and John Morrison would "escort" us all the way to the White House. Ruffee's hair sat stacked on his head as if he thought to trap his spirit there. He looked fatter than before. I named Morrison the Cowboy because of the handlebar mustache he never tired of grooming. They were useless men, and I wondered why they'd been sent to accompany us. But then I realized their only duty was to report back to Beaulieu, who'd become quite a power, using Crow Wing as a base to sell liquor throughout the area. We rode south to St. Paul, Beaulieu watching closely from his storefront as we went.

I don't know if it's true that President Johnson welcomed Bagone-giizhig the first time they met two years earlier, but if it was, the President was a changed man. Battles with the republicans and impending impeachment had made him paranoid. I don't know why he'd agreed to see us, for as soon as Bagone-giizhig began to speak, demanding the President make good on his previous promises and explaining once again why his community of New Rome was essential to counter the pernicious influence of Crow Wing, the President cut him off, saying there would be no farming community, there would be no concessions, and if Bagone-giizhig didn't remove himself from the designated land, he would be forcefully removed. Then he walked out, saying we could meet with his secretary the next day if we wished to discuss the details of the removal. I wished then I would not have come. Not because we'd failed, but because I knew Bagone-giizhig did not want me to see him this way. I understood his humiliation. I had many failures to count my own. But Bagone-giizhig never understood that leading your people often means failure. Our greatness is judged by how we respond to those failures. He could not look within to examine his mistakes, but instead threw his anger out at me and the world.

"I am tired of the chimookomaanag," he said, as he stormed from the President's office, Ruffee and Morrison trying to keep up. "We will draw our warriors together and fight them once again."

I grabbed him by the arm. "No one will join you," I told him. "The Sioux have not forgotten your betrayal of them five years ago, when they rode alone during the uprising. They paid dearly for the blood they shed. Nearly all have been hanged or imprisoned."

"It was not I who betrayed the Sioux," Bagone-giizhig replied, yanking his arm free. "My people betrayed me."

"No matter," I said. "No one will follow you into another war. Negotiation is our only hope."

Bagone-giizhig tried to move past me, but I stepped before him, blocking his path. Ruffee and Morrison signaled the guards and moved in.

"Do you doubt me?" Bagone-giizhig asked. "Do you doubt my ability to lead?"

I stared deep into my chief's eyes for the answer but

could find none. "I'm tired," I said at last. "My part is done. My oldest, Medwe-ganoonind, has already taken over for me at home. He says he is for the reservation if you can secure a guarantee of supplies. That is all I know. I doubt everything else." Then the guards pulled us apart.

They escorted us back to the hotel where Ruffee and Morrison took turns standing watch outside our door. Bagone-giizhig said nothing more, and I retired, deciding it was best to leave him alone.

We woke the next morning to a knock at the door. I opened it, thinking it was Ruffee or Morrison coming to bring us to the President's secretary, but instead found several reporters, hoping to get a scoop on the famed Hole in the Day. I told them there would be no interviews. I asked them to go, when one of the reporters, a young, blonde woman with a thin face and sharp, blue eyes broke from the crowd and entered the room. She asked to see Hole in the Day, said she'd studied everything about him and thought that he was one of the greatest of all Indian chiefs. She said she wanted to know why he thought so few knew his name, while the name of the Sioux chief, Little Crow, was spoken far and wide and more and more heard of Red Cloud and Crazy Horse with each passing day. I asked her to leave, insisting we had nothing to say, but then Bagone-giizhig emerged from his quarters dressed in the finery for which he was justly famous. The otter skin scarf about his neck, his hair tied in the turban, the long black frockcoat.

"Little Crow is dead," Bagone-giizhig said, standing proud as the line of reporters streamed into the room.

"The whites prefer us that way. We fit better into their stories dead."

The reporters began asking questions, shouting one over the other. The young woman tried again to break free of them.

Bagone-giizhig silenced them with a wave of his hand. "A dead Indian allows the whites to talk of how noble we once were," he continued. "To say how sad they are that we are no more."

"But you are alive," the young woman stepped forward. She wore a green calico dress with a low neckline. Her skin so white it was nearly translucent.

"Yes," Bagone-giizhig replied. "And because I'm alive the whites do not want to talk about me."

"But Red Cloud and Crazy Horse are alive," the young woman continued. "And new stories are told of them every day."

"Red Cloud and Crazy Horse fit into another story."

"What story is that?"

"They are warriors," he replied. "Whites like to enshrine those who fight against them and lose. It makes them feel bigger than they are. But I choose a different path, a path no one dares to talk about." He reached out, offering his hand to the young woman.

"What path is that?" she asked, before taking his hand.

Bagone-giizhig took her hand, leaned in close. "The path of assimilation." He said. "The path that scares them most. It's bad enough to deal with a living Indian, but a living Indian who lives as you do, that doesn't fit any story they want to hear."

Ruffee and Morrison arrived then, asking the reporters to leave. The reporters tried to get a picture of Bagone-giizhig and the young woman, but the two men grabbed their cameras and ushered them out. Still, Bagone-giizhig held onto the young woman's hand, as each studied the other.

"The lady will have to leave now," Ruffee said, putting his hand on her back.

"For which paper do you write?" Bagone-giizhig said at last.

"The Milwaukee Sentinel," she replied. "Wisconsin's the prettiest country I've come across yet. The forests stretch on and on until you think they'll never end." She laughed then, a hearty, farm-girl laugh.

"We need you to go now," Ruffee said, pulling her from Bagone-giizhig.

"I was hoping to get an interview with this greatest of chiefs," she said, holding her ground.

"I'm sorry, that won't be possible," Ruffee said. "The chief has a busy schedule this morning." Morrison went to his aid, and both escorted the young woman to the door.

"If the young woman will tell me her name," Bagone-giizhig said. "I will grant her an interview this evening over dinner."

The woman elbowed her way out of the arms of the two men and walked of her own accord to the doorway. "Ellen," she said. "Ellen McCarty." She looked quite beautiful, almost disarmingly so.

"The secretary is waiting," Ruffee said.

Bagone-giizhig nodded, giving the faintest hint of a

smile. Ruffee and Morrison escorted the lady out, then returned a moment later, clearly upset.

"You certainly can't expect to meet this woman for dinner in public in our nation's capital," Ruffee said.

I tried to step between them, saying that we were late. It was better to talk of these things later, but neither of the men moved.

"Again, we are treated like children," Bagone-giizhig said. "As if we cannot know what is best for us."

"It's not that," Ruffee tried to say, but Bagone-giizhig interrupted him.

"Is it that they do not want us to know what's best for us because that might mean we live with them, we live like them?" Bagone-giizhig appeared then as I'd not seen him look in many years, perhaps not since the victory of his first negotiation with President Pierce. He was a man who knew what he must do regardless of the consequences.

"Take up your problems with the secretary," Ruffee said, then he and Morrison demanded we follow.

"You are wissakode, aren't you?" Bagone-giizhig asked. "Half-burnt."

"Yes," Ruffee replied.

"I thought so. Why do you try so hard to hide who you are?" Bagone-giizhig adjusted the turban that held his own hair

Rufee said nothing.

The meeting with the secretary was brief. Our ogima started by listing his visits to the various presidents, citing all he'd accomplished for his people. And yet his people still suffered. I didn't understand what he was doing or where he was going until he announced he would agree to the treaty only if it stipulated that no half-burnts would receive reservation land or annuity payments. That White Earth would be only for pure bloods.

My first thought was of Ase-anse. Then of all the wissakode living quietly on their own in huts and cabins about the lakes. They would be required to leave Crow Wing and New Rome as well, but would have no home to which to move. "How many pure bloods are left in the tribe?" I asked. "Certainly the wissakode outnumber them."

The secretary stiffened, picked up the feather pen on his desk and dipped it in the ink. "I suppose we could add an article stipulating such a thing," he said. "The half-breeds are of no importance to the government. They have no claim to the land."

Bagone-giizhig glanced toward the grandfather clock by the door, as if he were late to an appointment. His face betrayed nothing.

"You are making a mistake," I told him. "What good will it do to alienate so many of our people?"

"They are not my people," Bagone-giizhig replied, "Nor are they yours. Let them find their own path."

"Whatever point you're trying to make, my friend, it is misguided," I told him. "We need everyone on our side if we are going to survive."

The secretary put down the pen and watched with an amused look. I did not want to give him what he hoped for.

Bagone-giizhig's smile darkened his face. "Are we sure survival is a good thing?" he asked, stepping before me.

"I do not know you," I replied. At that moment, it was

as if the weight of all my sixty-seven winters fell down upon me. "I've seen too many changes for one life."

"I am your ogimaa, chief of all the Ojibwe," Bagone-giizhig said. "That is all you need to know."

"That title is beginning to mean less and less," I said, then walked out on my friend for the second time in two days. I did not know then that there would be one more time to come, and it would be the worst of all.

I hold Niibiniishkang's head in my lap. "It was not the beating in the saloon," I say, "but his father's old blood, his pride that turned our brother."

"Again you talk, Ase-anse," Niibiniishkang replies, opening his eyes enough to peer through a squint. "But if you are so wise, tell me what sins has your father left you?"

The question hovers in the air between us. How would it have been had Niibiniishkang been my father? His own boys have grown to be fine men with families of their own. Medwe-ganoonind still leads his people and has proven a fair chief. But why are they not here with him now? Why in his last days is he accompanied only by a half-burnt priest who knew him mostly by reputation? "My father is a ghost to me."

"You are proof that we cannot escape our ghosts," Niibiniishkang replies.

"Why do you think he did it?"

"I think as always he wanted the last word," Niibiniishkang replies. "If the chimookomaanag denied him assimilation, what power did he have left except to deny others their own path?"

"White, Métis, or Ojibwe, the human heart makes no sense."

He silences me with a wave of his hand. He grows impatient to finish the tale.

I left Bagone-giizhig in Washington and headed home to counsel my sons on what I'd feared would come to pass. The next time I saw my chief would be the last time.

Bagone-giizhig remained in Washington, living with Ellen, the young woman reporter, and creating quite a scandal. Finally, the hotel kicked them out, the manager pounding on their door himself in the middle of one of their raucous lovemaking sessions. They say Bagone-giizhig answered the door in the nude and invited him in. The manager entered, took one look at the state of the room, then began gathering up their clothes and throwing them out the door. Still naked, Bagone-giizhig grabbed his wooden war club from off the divan and threatened the man's life. He and the reporter left together, taking the train across the country, leaving gossip and ruined hotel rooms in their wake. I don't know where he got money for the trip. There had been talk of the gold he'd kept hidden beneath his house, his savings from extra allotments, or the money he skimmed off the top of Walker's whiskey sales. Or maybe Ellen had money of her own. But for a brief time they lived the life of the rich and famous.

"Agida and I waited each night for his return," I say. "Sitting together on the porch at dusk and not leaving until the Snipe began their singing."

"Would you like to tell this story?" Niibiniishkang asks. "For I am growing tired of your interruptions." He stretches his legs out, massaging his knees.

"Each day we received another report of how Hole in the Day narrowly escaped arrest or hanging for miscegenation," I say. "Agida asked me what she should do, if she should leave her husband."

"What did you advise her?"

I stare at the flickering candlelight that grows faint with dawn's approach. Maybe the story should end here. Maybe it should never have been told at all. "I told her that marriage was a sacred bond made before God, and that her husband had broken that bond. I spoke the words of my office."

"It does not seem like a bad thing." Niibiniishkang reaches toward the candle, snuffs out the weak flame between his fingers.

"I suggested that she was a proud woman, the daughter of an important chief and that she should not put up with such a situation." I want to tell him to get back to the story, to leave me out of it.

"You spoke your mind, Ase-anse," Niibiniishkang says, peering at the smoke rising from the dead flame. "That in itself is not bad."

"That all depends on one's motives," I reply. "And I was haunted."

"By what?"

"I think I'm here to find that out."

Niibiniishkang takes a deep breath and lets it out slowly, knowing he may need all his strength for what is to come. He lies down once again and gestures for me to come closer. "You may as well tell the tale," he says. "It seems to be yours."

And so I begin once again.

Hole in the Day and Ellen McCarty were married in St. Paul, in the same church where X and his brother appeared seeking aid all those years ago. X held Agida's hand when he told her she could not live in a house of sin, that she must leave her husband to face the consequences of his actions. He told himself it had nothing to do with his own anger, that he was doing what he should do as deacon of the church. Agida said nothing, her face hard as a grinding stone as she rocked back and forth on the porch. X squeezed her hand in his own, telling her she was not the only one hurt by her husband's actions. She tried to stand, to walk away from the words, but X wouldn't let go.

As deacon, he threw himself into his work. Attendance at the church was decreasing rapidly as word spread of the impending removal of the Ojibwe and dismantling of Crow Wing. The Métis had been left out before. They knew they would have to move on quickly, find new homes, a new place to live. And so they quietly made their preparations, talking again of slipping deep into the woods. X made his morning rounds, telling them not to give up hope, that something would be done, but few would listen.

X now lived on his own in a small hut behind the rectory. And except for the nights when he visited Agida he kept no company. Occasionally, Father Tomazin came by with a book, hoping they could read together and talk, but X almost always stood in the doorway in such a way as to make it clear he didn't want to be disturbed. He would then curl into his lone chair with the well-worn copy of Ovid he'd kept from the hospital library.

Three months later, word came that Commissioner Dole was calling for all full-blood Ojibwe males over the age of eighteen to meet in Crow Wing to ratify the new treaty before the end of the year. Hole in the Day returned from his cross-country jaunt that very evening, marching straight up to his old house with his new wife following close behind. X and Agida sat on the porch of the two-story house, watching the leaves turn, saying little to each other as they'd grown accustomed to do. They waited like that night after night, staring out at the bruised dusk, not sure what they were waiting for, unless it was this moment.

As the newlyweds approached, X noted how Ellen waddled slightly like a porcupine, how her belly already showed signs of the child she carried.

Agida nodded to her husband, rose from her chair and went inside as if to fetch him dinner after a long day of working in the field. Hole in the Day smiled broadly, nodding assurance to his new wife that they would be welcome. But X was not so sure. He'd seen the way Agida's eyes went flat when Hole in the Day walked up the porch steps and the way her trembling hands slipped inside her sleeves for fear they would betray her.

When she returned, she carried only a birch bark basket, but instead of the maple sugar she normally gathered in it, the basket held the few belongings she held dear: the paisley dress he bought her on his second trip to Washington, the comb and brush her own mother had given her and the blankets she'd made for their two children, now sent away to boarding school.

She walked right up to Hole in the Day and kissed him lightly on the lips. "We are no longer husband and wife," she said. "We were married according to our traditions, so I can leave you according to those same traditions. I hope you enjoy the sacred bond you share with your new wife. May you never be able to break it."

"You will not leave me, wife," Hole in the Day said. It was not an order but a plea from a man unused to others making decisions for him.

"You do not command me anymore, Gwiiwizens," Agida replied, using his old name of Boy. "Your father was right in his naming. You still have not outgrown it."

Hole in the Day's face flashed. Before anyone could think, he had his father's old knife out from within his frockcoat and sliced at Agida's face, cutting her along the line of the cheek. Agida dropped the basket upon the porch steps, spilling the contents. "You are no longer my wife," Hole in the Day said, looking past her. "So, when you go, it is not me you are leaving."

Agida used one of the children's blankets to wipe the line of blood from her face, but said nothing more. X picked up the contents of the basket, never once looking at his brother or his brother's new wife. He handed the basket back to Agida, wanting to say something, to tell her he knew what she felt, that his brother's betrayal burned inside him as well, but found no words with which to speak. He nodded to Agida, and she disappeared into the night.

Months passed, and it was as if Hole in the Day had died once again, for he and his young wife never left their house. Occasionally, the people of Crow Wing and New Rome found excuses to meander by Hole in the Day's house, encouraged by the rumors of their riotous sex, but also to catch a glimpse of the young white girl's full belly through the window. Each time, they returned saying the same thing: Does he not understand that he damns his own child with his treaty?

Word came through Bishop Whipple that when the treaty was signed, X would be transferred to Fairibault. He swore he would not go. After his morning rounds, he often wandered far along the banks of the Great River searching for a spot for his own church, one that would service the Métis living in the woods. He thought often of this new church, planning exactly where it would sit, what it would look like, how the parishioners would flock to him, how his brother might one day walk through the door and down the aisle, praising him for finding a path to the fourth world.

By November, word came that Dole was frustrated over the lack of action among the Ojibwe. The timber companies needed the land, and they would not wait longer. He asked specifically what Hole in the Day was doing that he would not abide by the terms of his own treaty. And he did not like the word he received in return. On the advice of Bassett and Beaulieu, Dole set a date for the signing, stating that the treaty would go forward whether Hole in the Day signed it or not.

Only then did Hole in the Day emerge from his house, once again dressed in his calico shirt, frockcoat and green blanket. He strode down Main so that all could see he was still their chief. He stopped in each of the five saloons in Crow Wing, promising bottles of whiskey to all those full-blooded Ojibwe over eighteen who would show up the following week and sign. It seemed he would do anything to hold onto the appearance of power. The Métis cursed the chief beneath their breath. Fights broke out. And twice Hole in the Day was nearly stabbed, saved at the last moment by those who remained loyal to him. Still, he continued. He would not let Dole give the orders.

X watched from the church steps, remembering how his brother cried nights at his own father's drunkenness. He remembered, too, how they held each other the day they learned of Strong Ground's death by the bottle. And now he watched his brother drinking alongside the other young men, noting the false bravado that came with the whiskey, remembering the same bravado in his adopted father weeks before he died, drunk, his head crushed by his own wagon wheel. It was then he decided what he must do.

He asked permission from Father Tomazin to go north to speak with Niibiniishkang and his people, telling the Father it was part of his mission as deacon of the church to spread the word of the Lord. It would not be the last lie he told the priest.

X met Niibiniishkang just north of Leech Lake where he'd been talking with the Pillagers. They'd wanted Hole in the Day dead for some time, and they made no attempt to hide their feelings. Until now, Niibiniishkang had counseled peace and the older Pillagers had agreed, but the younger Pillagers had gained a voice. After all, many of their generation were Métis, and they saw themselves losing everything: their homes, their culture, and their people.

"You come at a grave time, Ase-anse," Niibiniishkang told him. "The people are divided, and I fear we are heading for our own civil war." The lines that etched his face looked deeper now, and worn. His once proud head sat atop a back that was beginning to curve.

"Pray with me," X said, putting his arm around the old leader.

"What good is prayer?" Niibiniishkang asked. "Your kind or the prayers of the Midewiwin. We are beyond them both."

"Maybe we haven't yet reached the point where those prayers will be heard." X pointed the way to the lake. He waited for Niibiniishkang to move first, then fell in beside him. "The world has turned upside down and no path seems clear," X said as he walked. "I do not understand my brother's actions, and am unsure what he might do next."

The pine and birch about him creaked and groaned in the slight breeze. Niibiniishkang stopped, as if he would listen. And so X stopped as well, closing his eyes, knowing the answer to his prayers could come in any form. When the breeze died and the forest stilled, he spoke: "It seems to me there are three paths. Three choices."

"What do you mean?"

"The Ojibwe are no more," X replied, surprising himself. "They can follow the path of assimilation as Hole in the Day has done. Live like the whites. And you have seen where that leads."

"And what other paths are there?"

"Or they can follow the path of war as you have counseled in the past. But you have seen the results of the Sioux uprising. They are no more. That path vanished long ago if it ever existed at all."

"You said there were three paths, Ase-anse. I do not see the possibility of a third."

"That's because your eyes have already taken root," X said. "You think of the world in terms of Ojibwe and Sioux, Anishinabeg and chimookomaanag. But those words no longer have meaning." Again X stopped, mostly because he was not sure of what he was saying or where it was coming from. The breeze picked up again, and the trees bent over them, as if to be sure no one else heard what they discussed.

There was a knotted hammering in the distance before him. A rustling of leaves. A large, red headed bird burst forth, flying low before them. The woodpecker lighted on a branch further down the trail toward the lake. X followed it, gesturing for Niibiniishkang to join him.

It flew into a bower of birch and maple near the northern shore. The two men stopped and kneeled together there beneath a canopy of leaves, as the woodpecker began hammering again.

"What is this third path of which you speak?" Niibiniishkang asked. "I must confess, I have lost my way."

"Look around you," X replied. A baby hare emerged from the brush. The hare stood on its hind legs just outside the honeysuckle and sweetfern, as if guarding the entrance. It waited, staring out through the wood to the lake, and, like the woodpecker, occasionally glancing at them. Then, just as quickly, it disappeared back into the brush.

"All about this lake are hovels and huts, cabins and wigwams in which our people live hidden away in the forest. They are wissakode, Métis, half-bloods, and they want nothing to do with white or Ojibwe. They only want to live in peace. To follow their own way."

"What are you saying, Ase-anse?"

"Only that a handful of people will decide their fate. That the whites use blood quantum to refuse us our rights and now the Ojibwe would do the same. In another generation, how many of those Ojibwe will have to turn on their own children?"

Niibiniishkang walked to where the hare had been and stared through the woods to the lake. "I must smoke on this," he said at last, fingering the tobacco pouch around his waist.

"May I teach you something first?"

"You may have already," Niibiniishkang replied. "But one thing more won't hurt."

X recited the Lord's Prayer, straight through at first and then working over each line with the old chief, having him repeat it over and over. But Niibiniishkang did not last long for he had too many questions: "Why does the chimookomaan God live so far away from the world? What is this heaven, and can we return from there as Geezhig does from the Land of the Souls when he goes to look for his love, Wabun-anung?"

"I know that story well," X replied. "And I know, too, that the Greeks, the grandfathers of the whites, have a similar story about a man named Orpheus who goes to the land of the dead in search of his wife."

"Does he find her?" Niibiniishkang asked. "Is he able to take her back with him?"

"He finds her, but fails to bring her back."

"Then the religion of the chimookomaanag is no more powerful than that of the Ojibwe, for Geezhig fails as well. Why do you study it?"

"There is another who made a journey to the land of the dead and succeeded," X replied, knowing that this man who'd witnessed so much change deserved more if he were to guide his people. "The gospel says that after our Lord, Jesus Christ, was killed on the cross, he went to the land of the dead and released all of the souls there, leading them to heaven."

Niibiniishkang listened and thought about the words before speaking again. "To release everyone is an impressive act, Ase-anse," he said. "But still your god cheated. He was already dead when he made the trip!" A wry smile played upon the war chief's lips, and X knew that he had not lost all hope, or humor.

"Promise me you will pray tonight," he said.

Niibiniishkang squinted for a moment, looking out to where the woodpecker had flown. But it was no longer there. "I will pray both the Lord's Prayer and the Mide," he said at last. "Perhaps combined they will work a more powerful magic, create a new path that may lead our people home. Métis and Ojibwe.

"Your people are lucky to have you. We are all lucky to have you."

After their meeting, X set out for home, and that night Niibiniishkang kneeled inside his birch bark hut as he'd seen the deacon do and recited the prayer. The words tripped up his tongue. So he began inserting bits and pieces of the Mide into his prayer. Mixing words and phrases of both until he created his own language, one he didn't yet understand, but one that sounded good to his ears. One that didn't stop his tongue. He repeated the mish mash of prayers again and again, until his mind was soothed and his vision stretched across the lake and to all the lands around it.

Niibiniishkang's head twitches in my lap. His eyes flutter beneath closed lids, and I know he sees the dream once again.

"Tell me what you see," I whisper in his ear. "By chance it will help you now as it did then."

Niibiniishkang's lips part, and he exhales, as if releasing his Free Spirit. He mumbles words with no meaning, the sound of which works like an incantation working him deeper into the dream. "The woods are on fire," he says at last. "I stand before them, watching as angry Animkee throws his lightening arrows one after another into the forest until every tree burns. I run to the forest's edge, carrying my pipe, my tobacco, before me as an offering to Animkee. Please stop! I tell him. How will the Anishinabeg live? But his anger continues unabated until at last he runs out of arrows and must return to the sky. The forest glows orange as if a thousand fires rage there. The heat from the burning wood is so intense I fight the urge to turn and run. What can I do? Nanabozho! I shout. Your people need you now. Call forth the water manidoog! Make the monster Misshepeshu rise up and flood these woods! And he must hear me for the water begins to boil, and great waves pitch forth from the very center of the lake, rolling out over the surface only to crash upon the shore. More, Nanabozho! More! I shout, until at last the waters of the lake are drawn down toward the center, swirling and roiling. Then a lone wave bursts forth, a wave taller than the great White House of the chimookomaanag. As it moves across the lake, I fear for my life.

I have nowhere else to go. There is no path left open to me. I close my eyes and wait for death. The wave hits like a great slap against my body, but still I stand. The water moves over me, freezing the tips of my hair, numbing my ears and nose with pain. A sound like thunder rolls across the land, and I fear to open my eyes. I am sure I have died and now have to cross the Great River.

At last I summon the courage to look and before me stands a forest of blackened trees, their leafless limbs stretched to the heavens. Is all lost? I ask myself. Has the world been burnt beyond recognition? Is there no life left worth saving? And then the baby hare appears again from behind a half-burnt tree. I know it is Nanabozho, and offer him my tobacco though it is soaked. This time he stares at me just as he stared out at the lake before. There is life here, yet, he says. Though I do not hear his voice or see how he speaks, for his mouth does not move. Perhaps the words sound only in my mind. This life has changed, he says. It is not the one you knew, but it is no less precious. The hare returns to its hovel beneath a scorched and fallen log. And I know what I must do."

The red curtain flutters. A cold wind slaps my back, and I turn to see Beaulieu and Newobiik standing in the doorway. Icicles hang from Beaulieu's beard; his frosty breath fills the air. Newobiik kneels beside her husband who remains in his trance, unaware of their presence.

"I tried to make it to Red Lake," she says. "To bring Father Tomazin, but I could not get through." The name Tomazin jabs its way into my ribcage. I cannot breathe. Though he must be very old, he yet lives. When he holds the hands of the people to which he ministers, he feels their warmth.

When he wraps his arms around each member of his congregation after the ceremony, he feels the weight of their being against him. "I should go now," Beaulieu says, his hands fidgeting about him. Does he sense my presence? Does he understand what is to come?

"No," Newobiik tells him, gesturing for him to sit. "Stay until you warm yourself. I will make bread to fill your stomach and tea to warm you."

Beaulieu reluctantly nods his head and sits in the far corner away from us, keeping his fur cap and beaver skin coat pulled tightly about him, as if to ward off any spirits.

"Go on with the story," Niibiniishkang whispers so low I'm not sure he speaks at all. "I feign sleep because I must hear what comes next. And I do not want any further interruptions. Newobiik means well, but she dotes on me."

I laugh at this old man who is so full of surprises, and the laughter lightens me, making me think it is possible to go on.

Three feet of snow covered the ground the day of the treaty signing. Commissioner Dole never made it in from the city but gave his authority to the new agent. Bassett was a middle-aged sloth of a man from the east, probably sent by the government to slow the proceedings down to such a crawl that all would give up and sign out of boredom. All he hoped for on this day was that nothing out of the ordinary would occur. To that end, he stationed Beaulieu, John and George Morrison and Charles Ruffee about the agency office. For his part, Beaulieu kept his men at a distance, placing them at the edge of the woods to watch for any surprises. He had an uneasy feeling and wanted his men far enough away to decide their own actions instead of letting circumstances force their hand.

X took the long route from the church, coming to the agency by way of the eastern woods. He'd gone earlier to Hole in the Day's house, hoping perhaps to talk with him, to change his mind before the signing, though he hadn't spoken with him in months. Not since his brother had returned with the white woman, not since he'd sworn to cut the half-bloods out of the reservation. He'd approached the house, but stopped short of the door. Had his brother walked past a window, he would have seen a figure standing silent, the falling snow slowly piling on his shoulders and head. He might have mistaken the figure for a tree. But Hole in the Day did not pass by the window, and X stood alone in the cold.

All waited as the sun crept above the treetops, the only sound the cawing of crows having just discovered the remains of a squirrel left half eaten by the dogs. In the distance, Hole in the Day came walking down the very road he'd built from the agency to his house. He was wrapped in his green blanket, his hair plaited under his turban, as if he were once again on his way to Washington. And fifty or so young men followed behind him, drinking and shouting. Bassett watched from the window until he was sure of their intent, then stepped onto the agency porch visibly relieved, greeting Hole in the Day with much ceremony, then shaking hands with the men one by one as they entered to sign the treaty. Later, as each man emerged from the cabin, Bassett patted him on the back and stuffed a bottle of whiskey in his pocket, small price for the thousands of acres of prime timberland the government would receive.

After the signing, Hole in the Day lingered with Bassett on the porch, laughing and toasting to the new deal. What extra allotments or annuity had been thrown in to make his brother so jovial? He hated the way he stood so close to the man, practically falling against Bassett's potbelly when he laughed. The way they looked out toward the west, making plans for building a sawmill and gristmill, and homes for every Ojibwe on the White Earth reservation. X could practically hear the talk, his brother's hopes for a new beginning, his boasting of how his town would rival any in the area, perhaps some day surpass the twin cities in the south, and the way the agency man played on those hopes, promising everything.

The first thing they heard was the muffled sound of feet crunching snow, then chanting and singing, as from a great many voices. Either the crisp air worked to amplify the sound or an army approached. Beaulieu signaled his men to move from the woods and draw their guns, though they still kept their distance. Hole in the Day's men stopped their celebrating and whispered to each other, panic in their eyes. Was it a trap? Had the chimookomaanag finally decided to eliminate them for good?

Hole in the Day walked to the center of the clearing in front of the agency and waited, head high, arms folded within his green blanket, determined to save face no matter who emerged from the woods. A few of the young men with him that morning followed, placing themselves behind him, but most others backed away either behind the agency or into the woods.

Niibiniishkang emerged dressed in a long deerskin robe with Mide shells hanging over the entire surface. In one hand he carried the cross X had left him, and in the other a walking stick from which hung a Mide shell. His eldest son, Medwe-ganoonind, stood at his side, his other two boys behind him. Niibiniishkang stood for a moment, surveying the area. When he spotted Hole in the Day, he raised his staff high above his head. Row upon row of Ojibwe and Métis suddenly emerged from the forest behind him. All told there were over five hundred, mostly half breeds gathered from the woods that circled the lakes in the area: Leech and Gull, Sandy, White Fish, Red and Otter Tail, among others. Many of these people had never been seen or known before.

Bassett ran inside and barred the door. No one saw any more of him that day. He applied for a transfer east the following year. Beaulieu moved his men to the agency porch, figuring that if a standoff occurred the office would provide the best cover, or at the very least it would seem as if they were protecting the office from Indian attack and even in failure they might hope to gain commendation from the government, perhaps a trading license renewed at a better rate.

Niibiniishkang walked ahead of the long line of warriors, farmers, trappers, women, and children. As the old war chief headed straight for Hole in the Day, X backed slowly into the dark wood, all the while keeping his eyes fixed on his brother's uncomprehending face, the same face he'd worn that night in the tepee of the Wah'peton-wan as he held the young girl, the face of a boy whose world has spun beyond his control.

Birds fly screaming into the trees as dogs crack marrow. The sky is empty, a great hole, through which nothing more can fall.

"I did not walk toward Hole in the Day," Niibiniishkang *says from the floor, eyes still closed. "My vision was not that good. I was simply leading my people across the clearing."*

"Open your eyes," I tell him. *"What do you see?"*

"A field of snow before me, a lone figure standing there, wrapped in a green blanket. Others in the distance behind."

"Bring your tea, Newobiik," Beaulieu shouts. *"Your husband is talking once again to the air."* He backs further into the shadows as if they might offer protection. I know better. It is in the shadows we know ourselves best.

"I see my brother as well," I say. And I do see him. I am sure if I reach out my hand, I will once again be able to touch him.

"I am close, Ase-anse. I see him clearly now," Niibiniishkang *goes on. "I stand but a few feet from him and feel once again the hope of reconciliation."*

Hole in the Day dropped his green blanket to the snow and pulled the Colt from his belt, aiming it at Niibiniishkang. Medwe-ganoonind moved between the two men, but his father gestured him back. The two chiefs stood face to face as Niibiniishkang pulled a great bowie knife from his own belt and ripped open his deerskin robes exposing his breast. He stepped forward until the cold barrel of Hole in the Day's gun pressed against his skin.

I take the gun in my hands, try to force my brother's finger on the trigger. Better to die. Better to not exist than to stand before him like this. I am a liar. My life a house of lies. Blow them away, and I am no more.

Hole in the Day shoved the gun hard against the old war chief's chest, shouting that he would shoot anyone who attempted to go to White Earth without his permission. He ordered Niibiniishkang to return to the north, to send the half-burnts back to their homes.

"What homes do they have?" I reply. I hold the cross in my hand out to my brother. "This is my only home," I tell him. "And even it is a lie." I pull the Mide shell from beneath my robe. "Another lie."

"I can no longer see clearly, Ase-anse," Niibiniishkang says, opening his eyes. I want to take his head in my hands again, but I cannot, for I hold the gun to my chest, the cross out to my brother. Only now the cross is a Bowie knife. My hand does not look like my own. It is bigger, darker. A warrior's hand. "You offer nothing," I say to my brother. "Like the wiindigoo, your breath freezes the world. When you turn your hungry gaze on your people, they are devoured."

"These are not my people," he says, keeping the gun planted on my chest. "And you are not my brother. You will not set foot in White Earth."

I take the Bowie, set the razor tip to his breast, just beneath his otter skin scarf. I do not want to do it, but I cannot stop myself. "I see salvation for my children in White Earth," I tell him, though my voice doesn't sound like my own. "And all of the people here with me now are my children. And all those others who still hide in the woods, wanting to be left alone. They, too, are my children and will have a home at White Earth. I will bury this knife deep in your breast if you try and stop me. And if you shoot me, my son, Medwe-ganoonind, He Who Is Spoken To, will take up the knife and bury it in your breast, and if you stop him, his brother will in turn take up the knife."

"It is not fair, Ase-anse," Niibiniishkang tells me. "You say my words. You use my knife. But these are my actions. You must let me accept responsibility for them."

Newobiik brings more of her tea, a concoction of Burdock Root, Slippery Elm, and Turkey Rhubarb. Her most powerful medicine; the smell overwhelms. She forces her husband's head up, places the cup to his lips and makes him sip. Beaulieu also helps himself to a cup, then returns to the corner. "Drink, husband," she says. "And do not talk more with these spirits. You know what you have done and why."

But Niibiniishkang shakes her off. They have been married for so long there is no need for words.

I sheathe my knife and signal for the caravan to continue. Hole in the Day drops his gun and doesn't bother to pick it up. He stands alone as a sea of Ojibwe and Métis move past him, and in his face there is the haughty look of his father as the Sioux burned down his home.

The great gray owl flutters in the distance, creating such a noise I can no longer think. I step toward my brother but with each step I fall further back into the woods. I shout to him, but cannot even hear myself above the roar. I reach out my arms, stretching them to my brother, but they reach only shadow. I retreat back into the woods and lose myself there for the second time in my life. The cyclonic flapping of the great gray owl encloses me like the dark caul of winter.

Full of sleep, I come upon a narrow path leading through a forest. A thick mist enshrouds the trees, the wetness sinking to my marrow. Leaves drip upon my face, my hands. The great gray owl calls in the distance. I think I hear my name. Thomas. Paul Paulson. Ase-anse. X. I follow, entering a blanket of fog. The white mist murmurs its way into my pores. It is no fog. I swing wildly about, following the call of the gray owl until I climb a ridge rising above this land of lost souls.

I peer through the window of my brother's house, watching, as he picks up the newborn boy from his crib. He holds the boy close, gazing into his eyes with a love I'd not seen before with his other children. Does he not recognize what it is? Though others have left for White Earth, he refuses to move until he can renegotiate a treaty that will keep the half-bloods out. They say President Johnson narrowly escaped impeachment and Hole in the Day is once again hopeful. He will go to Washington at the end of June.

Ellen enters the room, smiles to see the love her husband bestows on their new baby. She says something, laughs, then takes the baby from him and suckles it. He is so small. I wonder how he will survive. Hole in the Day grows quiet, his mouth agape, eyes glazed, staring at an unseen ghost, as if only contact with the baby kept him in this world at all.

It is time.

I knock on the door and wait dressed in the robes of my office. I come here on official business. They do not answer. I expect this, as reports about town say that they keep to themselves, except in the middle of the night when Hole in the Day sneaks off to Fletcher's bar. Even then, they say he drinks alone. And so I knock again, more forcefully this time. The door opens a crack. My brother peers out with tired eyes.

"What do you want, Ase-anse?" he asks. He does not look at my face.

"On this visit, you can call me Deacon Paulson," I say. The distance of the name helps me, allows me to fulfill the duties of my office. "I am here in the hopes you will allow me to baptize your new baby." I wait as my brother stares past me to the birch and maple beyond. "It would be an honor for me," I add. He holds the door tight, ready to close it.

"Bishop Whipple will be passing through next week, and he has promised to baptize the baby," my brother tells me.

"Bishop Whipple is an important man. It is an honor that he comes to visit you. Your child will be blessed for it."

"Yes, I know."

Then Ellen is at his side, the baby back in the crib. A crib ordered from New York with fine silk sheets. Something his other children certainly never had. He opens the door further so that she can see who is at the door.

"The child is beautiful," I tell her. "Have you thought of a name?"

"Joseph," she says. "But please come in." She opens the door wide, playing the gracious hostess, the smile on her face seeming genuine. "Family is always welcome."

"I have many things to do. My rounds as deacon, you understand."

They both nod. I can't help but feel my brother looks relieved. As I turn and walk down the road away from the house, the Mourning Doves call one to another. And above them trill the chickadees, buntings, and finches. Spring has arrived, though at the moment it makes no difference to me.

An old woman in a deerskin frock covered in Mide shells stands atop the ridge. Her face is so lined and worn I wonder why it doesn't crumple in upon itself, crack into dust. She raises her hand, points her finger at me. The long fingernails twist in circles about her hand. "I have been expecting you," she says.

"Why is that, grandmother," I reply, afraid to get too close. Her breath smells like rotting leaves.

"I know your sorrow," she says. "But this place is not for you. You must go back."

"I do not want to return," I say. I try to move past her, but she is quick, and before I know it, she stands before me again, her finger pressing against my cheek, scratching it, drawing blood.

"You don't even know your name," she says with a cackle. "Go back!"

Once again, the fog that is colder than the sea enshrouds me. I run, searching for the way out.

I sit in the darkness of the cabin, the faces of Ruffee and the Morrisons lit by the wavering light of a lone candle on the oak table. A long, serrated Bowie lies beside it. We pour another round of whiskey as if we need it to stir our courage to talk about what we must do. It burns my throat, souring my stomach. Still, I take another shot and another.

"You brought us here, Beaulieu," Ruffee begins, never the patient one. "We know what you want done, so out with it." John and George Morrison look one to another, as if to assure themselves they are in this together.

My face itches, and I scratch at it like a dog. I'm not accustomed to this red beard, to the hair that runs up the back of my neck. And my hands are blocks, thick and unwieldy. I try to speak, but my tongue is too big for my mouth. I stumble over the words, hating the sound of my new voice. "If Hole in the Day is not killed soon, he will be like a great log, and none of us will be able to step over him."

"What do you suggest?" The Morrisons ask together, as if they didn't already know.

The croaking of toads punctures the night. I sit back, let it work over the men before answering. "Bassett's leaving, going back east come summer and Dole has promised Ruffee the job, provided we can get rid of certain obstacles."

"Why would he want a job like that?" George Morrison asks, his hands hidden beneath the table.

"Because he's going to do it right," I say, pouring myself one more whiskey. "He's going to make sure we get all the business from White Earth, first rights to set up shop, and extra rifles thrown in for good measure."

"So why is the Chief a problem?" John Morrison asks, braving more than I thought he dared. "He no longer leads the Chippewa." He taps his fingers upon the table, one after the other like a piano player, or like a man who is considering bluffing. Perhaps he's going to back out, or worse, betray our meeting.

"Because he's hell bent on keeping the half-breeds out of White Earth, and the half-breeds represent most of our business. Besides, as long as he's in power, he'll keep skimming off the top. How do you think he can afford to keep a white woman in the manner in which she's been accustomed?" We all laugh at that point because we know that woman never saw money until she met the Chief.

The candle burns down to a nub before anyone says anything more. We know the words that follow will not simply be words but will connect us to the deed. Set it in motion.

"He leaves for Washington next week," Ruffee says at last, his face only half visible in the dimming light. "We should hit him the morning he sets out. Stop him on the road. Use guns. Maybe a knife. Make it look like random thieves." When he stops speaking, he shakes, as if a tremor ran through him. None of us is meant for this work. But the words have been spoken.

We sit about the table until the candle burns out completely, each man lost in his own thoughts. In the end, John Morrison makes a joke about Ruffee's hair. The mood lightens, and they depart. I reach for the bottle, but it is empty. I rise, search about for another. Behind the silver service set, the china decorating the hutch. Nothing. I see the trappings from so many years in business: the silk sheets and embroidered quilt for the bed, paintings bought in St. Paul and Chicago, the porcelain vase and knick knacks on the mantle. And I wish more than ever that I had not sent Elizabeth and the children away.

The tunnel is dark, winding deep into the earth. The dank air lies heavy upon me, making it difficult to breathe. Ahead, four figures stand in sepulchral light. There is no other way out of this place. I step warily, as the figures emerge, withered men, each looking older than the next. Their long, wiry gray hair and bushy eyebrows hide their hollow eyes.

"I want to go to the Land of the Dead," I tell them. But they say nothing. Their clothes are a mismatch of traditional Ojibwe dress and white clothing. And all are in tatters.

"You cannot go," the eldest says at last.

"Then kill me!" I say, pulling a knife from my belt and handing it to him. He does not take it.

"That is not the problem." He has no teeth, his mouth like a dark hole. He reaches out to me, takes my head in his skeletal hands. "You think like the chimookomaanag," he tells me. "That one thing leads to another, one cause leads to one effect. You think you can undo what has been done, but there are too many strands and you are tangled in them all. Best to find your way out and start again."

"I don't understand," I reply, but already the four men are fading into darkness,

"Go back." His rimy breath falls upon my face. "Go back and find your name. Then you may begin."

The muddy earth cannot absorb more rain, and the water runs deep in ditches along the side of the road. The leaden sky hangs over the land, until everyone at Crow Wing moves as if under a heavy burden. I make my morning rounds but find my heart is not in it. Many have gone on to White Earth with hope that the government promises will prove true, and those who remain seem sullen, as if they've resigned themselves to haunting the abandoned huts, stores and saloons. They no longer look to me for salvation.

Fletcher's bar still remains, the last outpost, and it's outside of that place I find my brother lying in a ditch, the rain matting his dark hair against the brown of his craggy face.

I kneel before him, the muddy water running over my cassock. Though his eyes are open, he doesn't seem to notice me.

"Tomorrow," he says, "I go to meet with the President. He wishes to see me." The words pass through my ears and into my body, making me solid once again.

"That is good, my brother," I tell him, though I know the purpose of his visit.

He gestures for me to bend closer, and I take his hand. He does not resist as I pull him from the muddy water. "Let me take you home," I tell him.

We walk, my arm about him, as the rain falls. It couldn't possibly soak us further. I say nothing, though in my heart I work through a thousand speeches.

"I've been thinking," Hole in the Day says as we draw near to his home. The downpour shadows the woods around us, making them look ancient, as if they'd always been there and always would be. "I'm going to ask for a separate reservation for the half-burnts," he says. "Let those who want to stay in White Earth, but I'm going to create a new home for them in Long Prairie. What do you think, my brother?"

It is the words "my brother" that undo me. I have not heard them from his mouth in so long. I almost wonder if I have ever heard them. "I think it is good that you reconsider," I say. "But a separate reservation will do little to heal the wounds of our people."

He pushes himself from me like a hurt child, then stumbles to the ground. Picking himself up again, he walks toward his house without turning back. I return to my rounds as if I'd never seen him at all.

I emerge from the tunnel only to face a raging river, a thick mist rising from its roiling surface. Impossible to cross, I think. And just as I think it, a log appears spanning the wild water. I set foot upon it. The log writhes and rises up, a great yellow snake with dark splotches and rings upon its tail. It strikes at me, but I roll out of the way and hide in the bushes along the bank. The mist rises like smoke. I know what I must do. I step forward, carrying my tobacco pouch before me. The snake hisses at my approach, his head darting. He scents the tobacco and bows his head, flicking his tongue at my outstretched hands. He takes it in his mouth, and when he does, he turns back into a log and falls across the river. I run across and into the mist.

I squat in my deerskin robe, Mide shells sewn over the surface. Around my neck, I wear a cross. In my hand, I hold a staff, which helps me sit now that I have grown old. I know these hands, I tell myself. The calloused surface. The strong grip, the sure way in which I hold the staff. I feel the thick dark hair, now streaked with gray, fall about my shoulders. I breathe deep and my chest expands as if it could take in the world. I reach out with my hand, feel the rolling muscles in my arm, and I can't help but smile, for I have often wondered what it would be like to be this man.

My sons sit in a row across from me in the dark hut, the oldest, Medwe-ganoonind, in the center. "He will kill you if we don't do something, father," he says. "There was a time when you dealt harshly with your enemies." "And then I grew up," I say. Again my voice sounds strange. I know it is that of the old war chief, but I cannot help but hear the echo of my own voice buried within. "When we are young, we think that killing is an answer, but it is not."

Medwe-ganoonind shakes his head. "He has threatened your life in front of everyone." His brothers nod their heads in agreement. "Even now, he plans to take back all you have worked for. He would destroy White Earth. He would destroy us."

A Red Crested Woodpecker hammers at a tree beside the hut. The burning sun sets over the lake. I fight the urge to go and wander the woods, to feel the world's breath about me. I want to tell my boys that the orange fire rippling over the lake is more important than the talk of a warrior, but I know they will not hear me. "If you think I will give you my blessing to kill Bagone-giizhig, you are wrong," I say at last, drawing a line in the dirt with my staff. It has come to this. "And if you think you can return to this place after committing such an act, you are also wrong." I try to hold my eldest's gaze, to let him know I am serious, but he will not look at me.

"You were aptly named, Medwe-ganoonind, He Who Is Spoken To," I tell him, trying a different tact. "For a person must repeat themselves many times before you will listen." I smile and wait, but he is sullen, afraid now to show weakness in front of his brothers.

My eldest takes a handful of dirt from the ground, lets it sift through his fingers, then tosses the remainder aside. "There comes a time," he says. "When a son must do what he thinks is right, even when it goes against the will of the father." He raises his gaze to me now, and the eyes of his brothers follow. It is not a challenge, rather, an act of contrition before the deed.

"What you say is true," I tell him, and the younger sons look wide eyed, not expecting me to agree. "But this is not that time. And if you make it so, you will cease to be my son." The words are spoken. Once said they cannot be taken back, no matter how often wished.

I journey on through the darkness until I no longer know where I am. Too tired to continue, I slump to the earth. My sleep is fitful, as if deep inside winter's belly. I dream of the strange mist; it enshrouds me once again, but this time lifting me into the sky, forming itself into the great gray owl, who carries me on his back. He signals for me to look below, and there I see another river, this one even wilder than the first. He leaves me there on the bank, nods his head and is gone, his call floating back to me on the breeze. I feel stronger somehow, as if the flight has infused me with vision, or as if, perhaps, I now see through the eyes of my childhood. The world shimmers in all its varied colors. The frothy blue of the water. The verdant green of the woods beyond, and the dark, rich reds and browns of the river's bank. I look with my new sight for a way to cross and spy a canoe buried in the bush. As I set the canoe in amongst the reeds on the water's shore, the river grows placid, and I paddle across freely. All the while, the gaze of the gray owl sits upon me. But when I turn my attention to the sky, I find nothing.

The dress rides stiff against my skin. I had imagined it more airy, moving with me. But it confines me about the breasts, the hips. I want to tear it off and feel the air on my breasts. I want to sway my hips, walk naked through the house and take pleasure in my new body. It is not what I expected. This being a woman. No matter what they say, just because I desire men does not mean I understand a woman. The house is bigger than anything I've ever seen. I've been here three months, and still I cannot get used to its size. Perhaps that's because when you must clean it, your work is never done. But I wasn't thinking that when I came to Little Falls, only that I needed to get away, to change my life and my world. And the chimookomaan who hired me seems a good woman. She lets me sleep in the attic and even, sometimes, asks me to drink tea with her. I wonder what she would say if she knew I once had a tea set nicer than hers. The constant dusting keeps me occupied, and, mostly, I don't think of my husband, except at night when I remember his sturdy arms about me. Then it's as if the long knives have ripped me open, exposed my insides. But I know it is not them; it is my husband who has done so when he took up with the white woman. No. Even before. That is what I think one day when I stop in front of the full-length mirror in the entry hall. I see myself there. The first thing I notice are my hands. Strong hands, a man's hands, good for grinding corn all day or for gathering rice in the fields. Then I see how I have grown old. My eyes are still those of the child bride he fell in love with. My mouth, too, is still supple, the lips full. But my cheeks sag a little, and my head bows, as if it were too big for my body to carry. "I would kill you, if I could," I say to the mirror one day. And at first I'm not sure if I'm talking about killing my husband or myself. But then I imagine the knife in my hand, the great release it gives me as I plunge it in his chest and rip him open the way he has done to me. My breath grows light as I imagine the deed until I feel dizzy and must sit in the chair the master of the house uses to change his shoes before he takes his walks. It is then I loosen the top buttons choking my neck. And with each one I unfasten, I feel a tingle as the air hits my breasts, long chafed by the tight dress. I have been bound for so long. I unbutton more until I'm exposed. Then I return to the mirror. Though they sag a little, their shape is still beautiful, I think. My breathing grows excited as I realize I could do anything I wanted, anything I dared. And I say the words once again, "I could kill you," not knowing that once those words are breathed, they gain life only to crawl back into your ears, worm their way into your head until you go mad.

My canoe leaks. The icy water rises slowly. My feet ache by the time the water hits my thighs, my hips. Still, I row. The white mist thick as pale hands about me. I wade into the black water, testing the depth with my oar. Dead fish float about me, bumping against my belly. Their eyes pecked away. I push on through the starving water. Weeds tangle their long fingers about my legs. I clear the sludge of leaves and carp with my oar and know I'm near the shore. I rise from the dead water and toss the slime on the ground, globs as dark as my insides. The great, gray owl calls, and again I follow.

The agency office seems smaller than I remember, perhaps because my bloated body seems to take up so much space. I run the palm of my hand along the oak desk, studying my thick fingers. When did I become so fat?

Night. Silence hovers about us. An oil lamp burns in the center of the table. Two faces stare back at me from the shadows, one bearded gray, the other clean-shaven but smoking a cigarette. "How do you suggest we do it, Bassett?" the cigarette smoker asks. I've heard the voice before.

I wait for the other man to reply. Instead, he leans forward into the light. It is Commissioner Dole. I'd recognize his narrow gaze no matter how much he tried to hide the rest of his face with his finely trimmed beard. He studies me as the other face finally comes into focus. Captain Hall. I understand my situation and ask for a cigarette myself to give me time to think. Hall pulls a pouch of tobacco and paper from his shirt pocket and rolls it himself.

"I will not be humiliated by that so called chief again," Dole says, ever the impatient one. "I wanted him dead before. Why should it change now?" He stands and paces just beyond the meager light of the lamp. I steal a glance at the window but there is only the dark of a new moon. "He thinks he can change the treaty he negotiated!" Dole says, flecks of spit showering the table.

"The land has already been promised to the lumber companies," Hall adds, handing me the cigarette. "What can he do?"

"He can do plenty!" Dole shouts. "He might just get the separate reservation for the half-breeds. Then where does that leave us?" Dole slams his fist on the table. "I'm already hearing complaints from my constituents about the amount of land rewarded."

I lean into the lamp to light my cigarette.

"What do you say, Bassett?" Dole asks again, sitting down, fixing his gaze upon me. "Can we count on you?"

The cigarette feels too small in my fingers. The smoke burns the back of my mouth. I don't like the taste at all.

"It sounds as if you've made up your mind," I reply.

"Can we count on your silence, then?" Dole asks, his eyes reflecting back the light of the lamp.

I say nothing.

Hall pulls his pistol from his holster and lays it on the table. "It's decided," he says, then spins the pistol.

I watch the barrel turning round and round, knowing where it must stop.

I enter a meadow filled with wildflowers. Their once-white petals stained red. A hill rises above the valley, and I climb it. A lone pine stands atop the hill, and a man steps out from behind it. At least I think it's a man. It is more a shade of a man, as I cannot see his face or even the type of clothes he wears or the color of his hair. Whenever I try to look at him, it's as if his surface shifts and blurs to shadow, until it makes me dizzy. He pulls a bow and two arrows from behind his back; these I see clearly. One arrow is dark, the other light. He asks me to choose between the two. I don't understand, and he doesn't explain. "Choose," he says, his voice shifting, making it difficult to hear, as if it were a wind blowing through a deep cave. I tell him that I refuse his choice. And so he takes both arrows in hand, notches them to his bowstring and shoots them over the hill. I run to follow, though I do not know why.

It is raining. Long ruts cut through the muddy road like wounds. The roots of the trees along the edge of the road grasp the ground, searching for a hold. Trunks thicken until they choke upon themselves. I think I see the arrows lying upon the road, but then they're gone. I stand at the edge of the forest, trying to see, the rain lashing at me like tiny whips.

The wet neighing of horses through the mist signals my brother's approach. Wagon wheels churning. The squish and suck of hooves in the mud. When he saw the rain wasn't going to let up for his trip to Washington, he hired the carriage and driver out of Little Falls. Nothing fancy, but it keeps him dry. The hot breath of horses rises in the chill morning air. Low in the sky, the pale sun looks defeated against the gray horizon, its meager light trancing the day, as if dreaming was the only route through. The carriage draws closer. For the first time, I want to become invisible, to hide from the relentless approach. But I cannot. Like a suicide, I am rooted to this place.

Four figures emerge from the woods, shadows from a darker world. Try as I might, I cannot see their faces, though I'm sure the tallest wears a halo of fire. He walks in front of the carriage, carrying a shotgun. He makes no attempt to hide himself as he draws near the carriage door. And then it is as if I'm standing next to this figure, as if I am him, for I can see my brother sitting erect in the carriage. He is calm, and I wonder if he has been drinking. He squints in my direction as if he cannot quite see me. His eyes open wide in surprise. His first impulse is to turn away, to hide his head, but it's as if he's discovered his own reflection and is caught there. He cannot move. Then his gaze goes flat, his face devoid of any emotion. And I know that this is how he has chosen to face his end. "You have caught me in a bad moment," he says. "I am unarmed."

The first shotgun blast tears away the left side of his neck. The second goes through his face. He slumps forward into the carriage door, and it swings open, his body falling into the mud. I do not kneel beside him. I don't say a prayer over his body. I watch as the figures take from him his gold watch and his green blanket. "Where was your Colt revolver?" I want to ask, but I know he stopped wearing it after the face off with Niibiniishkang outside the agency, saying it was no longer of use to him.

I'm back on the side of the road, standing in the lashing rain, watching the steamy breath of the horses rise as the carriage approaches. The squish and suck. Three sons step from the woods. Try as I might, I cannot see their faces. But the oldest walks in front of the carriage, carrying a revolver. He makes no attempt to hide himself, as he draws near the carriage door. And then it's as if I'm standing next to this figure, as if I am he, for I can see my brother sitting erect in the carriage. He is calm, and I wonder if he has been drinking. I close my eyes for I know what comes next, but I cannot drown out his voice: "You have caught me in a bad moment," he says. "I am unarmed." And then the report of the revolver once, twice, three times. He falls through the carriage door face down into the mud.

Standing on the side of the road in the rain. The breath of the horses rising like steam as the carriage approaches. A lone woman steps from the woods and walks in front of the carriage, carrying a long, serrated kitchen knife. And then it's as if I'm standing next to her, for I can see my brother in the carriage. He is calm. I close my eyes and cover my ears. Still his voice finds its way through. "You have caught me." The dull splatter of his body in the mud. I wretch in a vain attempt to be rid of it.

On the side of the road. Rain. The carriage. Two figures approach, one bearded, the other not. A fat man watches from the distance. The clean-shaven shouts for the carriage to halt. He raises his pistol, points it through the window. "I am unarmed." I reach out to stop it, but the pistol goes off. My brother falls to the mud. The bearded man grabs the gun and presses it to my brother's head until the mud rises over it. He shoots again, and again.

The rain lashes steamy breath. Mide shell and cross. The squish and suck. Creaking wheels turn in the mud. "Unarmed," he says, then stops. He squints through the rain. His eyes go wide. "You," he says under his breath. My brother's eyes like gold.

A small cabin stands on the edge of the stream. I run down the hill for I recognize this place, though I don't know how. It exists only in a dream. As I approach the cabin and see the care with which the wood has been piled in the back, the attention given to the dark, churned earth in the garden, I'm suddenly afraid. The door opens. My mother stands in her apron, her hair tied up in a red scarf. I know her name, Biidaaban. I recognize her face, the soft glow of her skin, the arched eyebrows poised always to question.

"You're late!" she says, holding a dead chicken upside down by the legs. She hands it to me as if I should know what to do with it. I hesitate. "Xenopha Grumbo," she whispers, a wry smile playing across her lips. I reach for the chicken as mist enshrouds me. My world begins to spin.

Swollen toads emerge after rain to cross the muddy road. A crow hops stealthily after. He pecks one. Two. But the third escapes in the grass. And so I must finish my story.

After Hole in the Day's murder, Agida returned with two other Ojibwe women to clean out her husband's house. They took the blankets and clothes, the dishes and the various tea sets, one for each of his trips to Washington. The Pillager men came for his guns, his horses and saddles and collection of farm equipment. One of the Pillagers grabbed Ellen McCarty, who'd been shielding baby Joseph in the upstairs bedroom. He threw her on the bed, looked as if he would do with her what he wished, but Agida told him if he touched her she would curse him and his prick would fall off, and then the long knives would know who had raped one of their own and would come to hang what was left of him. He took what he could from the bedroom in his arms—a night table and picture frame, a small vase—and left, as if these objects were enough to sate his desire.

Ellen followed the Ojibwe women out of her house, holding Joseph to her breast. When the women shooed her away, she kept walking into the forest, fading like a ghost among the trees. Two months later, she was reported in Minneapolis working as a domestic. And some months after that it was said she married a white man named Sullivan who forced her to put Joseph up for adoption.

Hole in the Day was buried just outside the perimeter of the Catholic cemetery in Crow Wing. Father Tomazin presided over the service, and I assisted with the sacrament. Father Tomazin had asked me to deliver a brief eulogy, but I refused. He did not ask why.

I kept my distance during the burial, focusing not on the service but on the line of birch and maple beyond. Beaulieu and his family were there along with the Morrisons, though Ruffee didn't bother to show up. Agida also stood apart from the crowd. Before they began to cover the grave, she asked Father Tomazin for permission to place something within. She knelt beside the hole and from under her skirt pulled the Colt revolver my brother had cherished and laid it upon the casket. When the service was over, Ruffee appeared flanked by two government men and dressed in a suit for his new role as Indian agent. Under orders from President Johnson, the men quickly raised the flag of the United States on a small flagpole above the grave. The only marker it would receive.

On hearing of his father's death, fourteen-year-old Ignatius threw a rock at his teacher at the private school he was attending. He nearly killed the man, though he was not expelled for he'd been an exemplary student until that time. A few years later he would graduate from St. John's College only to return to White Earth as hereditary chief, calling himself Hole in the Day like his father and his father's father before him. He visited President Grant, fighting for a percentage of the profit from the timber cut on Ojibwe land, but, getting nowhere, soon grew sullen. He joined the Haley and Bigelow Medicine Show, traveling the country, acting the role of "Indian Chief." They found him drowned in the north branch of the Chicago River.

"I am confused," Niibiniishkang says. "How do you know things that have not yet come to pass? Ignatius still lives as far as I know." His eyes are open now, and he sits up of his own accord.

"You forget that time works differently in the shadow land," I tell him. "I know, too, for example, that Ignatius' only son, William, went on to become a great warrior, fighting in both the Spanish American War and World War I."

"That is good." Niibiniishkang says, visibly relieved. "That one of the line survived."

"What does it mean to survive?" I ask him. "There is

death, and there is change." I do not mean it to sound so strong, but there it is. "William was gassed by the Germans on the fields of France."

"At least it was a warrior's death."

"Death is death," I say. "Let those who live call it what they must."

"You still have not told me what you came for, Ase-anse," Niibiniishkang says. "Who killed Bagone-giizhig? Who killed our Chief? You must tell me before I part this world."

Beaulieu rises, backs toward the door. "I want no more of this," he says. "I am sorry." It is then I notice how much he has changed. His frail body curves upon itself as if to hide from the ghosts that haunt it.

Newobiik's eyes never stray from her husband. "Do you still talk with the spirit?" she asks.

"Yes," he replies. "Our business is almost finished."

"Good," she says. "Tell him I want you back for a little while yet before you must leave me." Her face breaks into a smile like dawn.

"Well, Ase-anse?" he asks.

"The story is the only answer I have," I tell him. "I can't say more."

"Can't or won't?" he asks.

"Does it matter?"

And now it is his turn to smile, though it is a sad one. "This story you tell does not bring me peace."

"It was not meant to." I take his hand in my own, for I know our time is waning.

"Then what was the point?" he asks. "Why have you spent these last four days here by my bedside, if not so that you could return to the land of the dead in peace?"

"My name is Xenopha Grumbo," I tell him.

Niibiniishkang blinks many times, as if his eyes have dried out, or as if he is having trouble seeing me. "I do not think you will become another tree, Xenopha," he says. "I think you will find the next life." Newobiik comes near now, wraps her arms around her husband for support, or to keep him from going with me. Don't let me disappear, I want to tell him. Don't let me fly to the next world. But I am already fading. I can see it in the way the light shimmers like the surface of a lake. I can feel it in the dark pulsing of my blood that lifts me skyward. My words already move beyond this life, and I race to catch up with them.

ACKNOWLEDGEMENTS

Though this story is a work of fiction, it is indebted to the following books for opening up the history on which this book is based: *Chiefs Hole in the Day of the Mississippi Chippewa* by Mark Diedrich, *Indian Heroes and Great Chieftains* by Charles Eastman, *The Manitous, Ojibway Heritage,* and *Ojibway Ceremonies* by Basil Johnston, *A Concise Dictionary of Minnesota Ojibwe* ed. by John D. Nichols and Earl Nyholm, and *The Assassination of Hole in the Day* by Anton Treuer.

PETER GRANDBOIS is the author of nine previous books, the most recent of which is *Kissing the Lobster* (Spuyten Duyvil, 2018). His poems, stories, and essays have appeared in over one hundred journals. His plays have been performed in St. Louis, Columbus, Los Angeles, and New York. He is a senior editor at *Boulevard* magazine and teaches at Denison University in Ohio. You can find him at www.petergrandbois.com.